THE

INGHAM PAPERS:

SOME MEMORIALS OF THE LIFE OF

CAPT. FREDERIC INGHAM, U.S.N.,

SOMETIME

PASTOR OF THE FIRST SANDEMANIAN CHURCH IN NAGUADAVICK, AND MAJOR-GENERAL BY BREVET IN THE PATRIOT SERVICE IN ITALY.

By EDWARD E. HALE,

AUTHOR OF "IF, YES, AND PERHAPS."

BOSTON:
FIELDS, OSGOOD, & CO.,
SUCCESSORS TO TICKNOR AND FIELDS.
1869.

UNIVERSITY PRESS: WELCH, BIGELOW, & CO.,
CAMBRIDGE.

CONTENTS.

MEMOIR

OF

CAPTAIN FREDERIC INGHAM.

It is always difficult to write the biography of the living. It is more difficult to write the biography of a friend. In attempting to put on paper a few memoranda of Captain Frederic Ingham's life, I am hampered by both difficulties. We have lived on the most intimate terms. I have shared his thoughts, his purse, his confidence. I have slept under the same blanket with him; have bivouacked on the same mountain-top with him; have shared in the same adventure. Yet he never told me in set form the order of his life; nor do I know, from any memoranda of his, what he would wish me to put down, and what he would wish to have omitted.

He is now absent in Siberia, in connection with the telegraph enterprise, which is alluded to in this volume. His wife is visiting in Bohemia, on some estates of a friend of theirs. I am sometimes led to think that there is Bohemian blood in both of them. Meanwhile, I am left with a general direction to prepare these papers for the press, and a general permission to state what is necessary in the way of biography, with a hint that Colonel Ingham has himself on the stocks an "autobiography," which, if it is ever finished, and the public ever want it, the public will probably have.

The intimate relations of Mr. and Mrs. Ingham with Mr. George Hackmatack and Mrs. Julia Hackmatack, with Mr. George Haliburton and Mrs. Anna Haliburton, with Mr. Felix Carter and Mrs. Fausta Carter, — relations which are alluded to in all parts of his papers, — have not so often relieved the difficulties of his biographer as might have been hoped. It is true that, when in Boston, these amiable persons spend much time together. It is also true that most of the gentlemen are great talkers, fond of recalling the incidents of their lives, which they narrate at very considerable length, not careful whether the listeners have or have not heard them mentioned before. It is also true that the ladies are quite good listeners, and but seldom cut short their historical or biographical narrations. But, almost always, when I recur to the gentlemen of this little coterie for detail as to Ingham's life, I find they have paid but little attention to his narratives, except as they opened the way to their own; and the ladies, if I recur to them, show an indifference to dates, to synchronisms, and to succession of event, which, to the historian, is appalling. They have a habit, when they commit to writing any of these memoirs, of using Towndrow's first system of shorthand, — a stenography easily written and read. But, unfortunately, they all learned it of each other in their boyhood; so that, of a given memoir of any past time, it is impossible to tell from the handwriting which of the four jotted it down, and even the facts stated in the first person cannot be verified without repeated reference to personal authorities.

Yet another source of confusion arises from the fact that there are two Frederic Inghams, so closely connected with each other at one time, and indeed so strongly resembling each other personally, that they are often mistaken for each other, even by intimate friends. An inadvertence on the part of one of these gentlemen, at a public meeting in Naguadavick, threw the other, the Rev. Mr. Ingham (whom I have already spoken of as the Captain and the Colonel) out of the station which he then filled in the ministry in that town. You are never certain, therefore, whether a given narration of Mr. Frederic Ingham's goings and comings belongs to the clergyman, or to the fellow-citizen who acted as his double, unless you can get the testimony of one of them or the other.

Subject to the drawbacks at which I have thus hinted, the following sketch of Mr. Ingham's life is offered, as a skeleton, on which may be hung the disjoined members found in these pages, and in a similar volume published last year by Messrs. Fields, Osgood, and Company, under the title "If, Yes, and Perhaps."

Frederic Ingham, first spoken of above, from whose voluminous papers the sketches in this volume are taken, is the seventh son of Benoni and Blanche Ingham, of South Warwick, Connecticut, being born, if I understand rightly, in the district known as the "New Society" in that town. He descended on the father's side, as he himself at one period supposed, from Samuel Ingham, of Saybrook, probably the son of John or Joseph Ingham of the same town, who was admitted freeman, or who was free, in 1669. But, among the Ingham papers which I have not published, I find a careful genealogical tree in Colonel Ingham's own handwriting, in which his descent or ascent is carried out, apparently with some questioning, to Thomas Ingham, born in Scituate, Mass., in 1654. It is clear that, although every man has four great-grandfathers, both these theories cannot be true, and I am not able to decide between them. I leave them to the study of the curious, in particular to those who share the curiosity of the late Dr. Moses Harris, on transmitted qualities. For, if our Colonel, as I may call him, be descended from the Inghams of Scituate, he is descended from the only woman who was ever tried as a witch in the colony of Plymouth. The trial is interesting, because her husband was suspected of being a witch or wizard also. But, happily for posterity, they were both acquitted. The Inghams of Scituate, as I learn from Mr. Savage, came perhaps from Norfolk, in England, where Thomas Ingham the younger was buried, in the church of St. Somebody, in the year 1451, as was Sir Oliver Ingham, in 1292, which was in the reign of Edward the First. If, on the other hand, the Rev. Mr. Ingham were descended from Samuel of Saybrook, who was probably the son of John or Joseph, of the same town, it is to be observed that, in the earlier generations, the name was spelt beginning with the letter H. This fact indicates a geographical proximity to the Scituate family. I ought to mention, in this connection, that Ingham, in England, is a parish on the east coast of Norfolk, in the hundred of Happing.

Colonel Ingham's mother was the daughter of Capt. Heddart and Octavia Goad, of the "Farms," in Paterson, Connecticut. She was a reticent person, seldom speaking unless she was spoken to; and I have ascribed to her influence, or to the inherited graces derived from her, the taciturnity so apparent in the memoirs and in the personal demeanor of our friend.

He was himself the seventh of fourteen children, all, but the youngest, boys. They grew up together on a large grazing farm, with the admirable opportunities for the best self-culture which such an institution gives, — themselves, indeed, turned out to grass. And a certain indifference which Colonel Ingham shows from day to day, as to the particular duty to which he shall put his hand, is perhaps the result of the somewhat miscellaneous or jack-at-all-trades life, which a boy on a large farm like that almost of necessity pursues. He was fond of books, and had the opportunity in boyhood to improve his mind by the careful study of Mackenzie's Receipts, of Marshall's Life of Washington, of the Virginia Housewife, and of the few volumes then published of the reprint of Rees's Cyclopædia. He is used to say that he is much better able to sustain conversation on such subjects as the Amazon, on Botany, or on Cryptography, than he is on the Zendavesta, on Yucatan, or on Xerxes; his early winter studies having given him a proficiency and accuracy regarding the beginning of the alphabet, which no subsequent opportunities have made good as to the end.

I see, however, that I am somewhat in advance of my subject. Captain Ingham, as his friends, perhaps, prefer to call him, was born on the 1st of April, a day which has been marked quite curiously in the course of his after life, in the year 1812. He spent the first eleven years of his life in the miscellaneous training which I have described, which to this hour he regards as the best foundation for any man's education; an opinion in which I have been led to agree, so far as I have been taught by my own observation. This boy, at all events, developed a physical constitution wellnigh perfect, — very quick habits of observation and memory, very simple personal tastes, and the capacity of enjoyment of simple pleasures, together with the warmest affections, which have bound him in the closest ties to his brothers and his sister, and given him his life-long attachment to his home. Thirteen weeks' schooling in winter and eight in summer, with the miscellaneous reading which I have described, seem to have advanced the boy in the first eleven years of his life, as far as I now observe those model pupils of his age have come, who have attended the model grammar schools, and whose faces are pictured and whose biographies are related in the pictorial journals of the day. It was at the age of eleven or twelve that he was sent to the family school kept by the Rev. Mr. Whipple, whom he affectionately calls Parson Whipple in the first of the papers published in this volume. He remained at this school, with the intention of entering Yale College, for three or four years, when his plans in life were wholly changed by his unexpectedly receiving, one morning, from his mother's uncle, the honorable Eli Goad, who then represented the Eleventh Congressional District of Connecticut in Congress, an appointment as midshipman in the service of the United States. It subsequently proved that the friends of Mr. Goad had been making such interest as they could, with the administration, to secure that gentleman's appointment to the bench of the Supreme Court. These overtures were not successful, but they were courteously notified that the government, though not able to confer this honor upon him, would gladly name any person as midshipman whom he would recommend. Mr. Goad accordingly named young Ingham, and to his surprise, therefore, he was informed that he was appointed midshipman, and that he was to report immediately on board the Razee President, then fitting out in New York for the Mediterranean station. As I have already intimated, it is a peculiarity, perhaps a weakness, of Mr. Ingham's character that he had as lief do one thing as another, if each require positive effort and a good hardy bending of every faculty to the result to be obtained. I have heard him say that he was never more staggered than he was by Mr. Emerson's direction that men should buy books in the line of their genius. Poor Ingham was painfully conscious that he had no peculiar genius for one duty rather than another. If it were his duty to write verses, he wrote verses; to lay telegraph, he laid telegraph; to fight slavers, he fought slavers; to preach sermons, he preached sermons. And he did one of these things with just as much alacrity as the other; the moral purpose entirely controlling such mental aptness or physical habits as he could bring to bear. This catholicity of disposition took him into the navy at a day's warning. His maternal grandfather had served in the navy of England.

His naval experiences, both as a midshipman and afterwards as a lieutenant acting as captain, are constantly alluded to in the sketches which have passed under the eye of the public. But after several years of varied service, when he was, at last, a past midshipman waiting promotion, he was satisfied that advance was so slow in the navy, in those days of peace, that he resigned his commission and resumed his plan of entering college.

I do not think Colonel Ingham ever regretted this determination. It was, however, made in face of the general opinion of practical men, and has resulted in a certain duality of his life, which sometimes makes him seem like a man riding two horses. I have found that readers of his papers are sometimes confused by finding the clergyman, who is addressing a congregation, illustrating his sermon from experiences he has gained in laying telegraph wire in Nebraska, or in cruising to and fro in the South Atlantic. For my own part, I think the sermons are better for such illustrations. I know, however, that the mere difference of age made Ingham's school and college life very different from that of the boys who were around him. According to his dates, he must have been in the Boston Latin School and in Harvard College at the same time that I was. I find it difficult, however, to recall his personal appearance then. I remember very well several of the big boys, as we called them, or the really manly men who attacked study in a way quite different from ours; but at that time I had not any acquaintance with him, and I do not associate any of them with his name. He says he was chosen into the Phi Beta Kappa in 1837, but I do not find his name on the catalogue of that society. He never took his Bachelor's degree, and he is not, therefore, entered on the Triennial Catalogue of the college.

I think that he was induced by pecuniary consideration to re-enter the navy, but I do not know; and I am sure he has never told me by what means his second commission was given him. The Exploring Expedition was fitted out about that time, but I never heard that he ever accepted a place in it. Nor do I know whether he intended at this time to make the navy his career, or whether the predilections which afterwards drew him into the Sandemanian ministry were not already substantially formed.

Many allusions will be found in his papers to his second career in the navy. All the officers whom I have ever known, who were acquainted with him, speak of him affectionately, and agree in testifying to his willingness to carry out any duty that was assigned to him, to a certain warm-heartedness which made him a general favorite among them, and to the curious indifference, to which I have already alluded, as to the nature or field of the particular duty to which he was assigned. But, after several years spent in such service, he satisfied himself that the Christian ministry opened to him a wider field for energy and activity, and he again withdrew from active service in the navy, that he might enter the ministry of the Sandemanian Church.

I have been somewhat surprised, and indeed annoyed to find how many intelligent persons, who, probably, share themselves in the principles of Robert Sandeman, are, nevertheless, ignorant of the very existence of the Sandemanian communion. This is no place for the discussion of those principles. It is enough to say here that John Glass, the founder of this body, was expelled from the Established Church of Scotland "for maintaining that the kingdom of Christ was not of this world," — a declaration for which he certainly had the highest authority. His followers, the Glassites, were subsequently called Sandemanians, from Robert Sandeman, his son-in-law. In the last century, this distinguished preacher was charged with giving intellect too high a place in the operations of faith, — a charge which, to the present generation, does not seem as heinous as it seemed then.

Mr. Ingham was soon settled in the ministry, having received a unanimous call from one of the Sandemanian churches in Naguadavick. His ministry was one of great usefulness in this flourishing town. By a misunderstanding, one evening, which has been already alluded to, of the relations between him and his namesake, Mr. Frederic Ingham, who at that time hewed his wood and pumped his water, our friend was compelled to shake the dust from his feet the next morning, and took the parsonage lot of No. 9, in the 3d range, with his wife and his daughter Paulina. He occupied himself there in literary pursuits. He also eventually succeeded in developing the immense water-power of that region for the trial of the great experiment of the Brick Moon, and, long after his permanent residence there was broken up, he used to return there for the purpose of watching the great enterprise thus undertaken. While this was the residence of his family, he made many excursions westward in the employment of government or of the different telegraph companies, as he had indeed done previously, in different intervals of his naval and his ministerial experience.

It was in one of his absences from Maine that he took the temporary charge of a chapel in this city. He subsequently removed his family hither. He volunteered into Garibaldi's service in the course of a short vacation in Europe. He has himself explained the circumstances of his curious cruise in the Florida. His interest in the development of the telegraphic system led to his various employments in Siberia, on one of which he is now absent. It is this absence which compels me to substitute this inadequate, and, I fear, incorrect memoir, for the careful autobiography which he would himself have furnished so gladly for this volume. I had intended to add to it some study of his character; but if, as I have said, it be difficult to write the biography of a friend, how much more difficult is it to present to him your view of his faults and virtues in print, without giving him an opportunity to correct the proof-sheets.

In the hope of obtaining some illustrative detail on the subject, I addressed a line to the other Mr. Ingham, who once lived in Rev. F. Ingham's family at Naguadavick. He is now in Boston, fitting himself, under the auspices of the Provident Association, to compete for the office of talesman, by a course of instruction conducted at the theatre meetings, the free concerts, and the Lowell Institute.

I received the following reply : —

BOSTON, Friday evening, 1869.

DEAR SIR : —

I was born, myself, in Kilbarron, near Ballyshannon, County Donegal, at Easter, now fifty-five or sixty years gone by, I am not certain which; and I think his reverence, who never told me, was born about the same time, though not the same place. We crossed to this country, — I do not mean his reverence, but myself and family, — when I was nine years old, in the good ship Harkaway, from Liverpool for New York; you understand I was not then married, nor had I yet met his reverence, who had never visited Ireland, then nor since. Nor do I know where he was at that time. My father was not living, and I went to work myself on my own account, though not of age. My wife, whom I afterwards married, had no voice and did not hear well, — indeed she did not hear at all, but she was a silent partner. We got a position in the government institution at Monson; and I resided there till I entered his reverence's service at Naguadavick, having first changed my name, which was before that time, as I see I have not said, Dennis Shea. I was myself chosen to the legislature, and was at one time a director of the Enlightenment

Society. His reverence, I think, was still about my age, which must then have been between thirty and forty.

You have known him better since he went into the woods than I; so no more at present, from

Yours to command,

F. INGHAM.

There is an account of life at Naguadavick, and another of the city of Sybaris, by Mr. Ingham, which will be published with some other studies of city life by him, in another volume.

E. E. H.

BOSTON, March 27, 1869.

THE GOOD-NATURED PENDULUM.

[The oldest memorials of Mr. Ingham's life, which I have found, are his copy-books, — and the "compositions," which he wrote at Rev. Mr. Whipple's "Family Boarding School." "On the Fear of appearing Singular," "On the Passion of Emulation," "On the Bridge described by Cæsar," — such are the subjects of three of these papers. I find also a poetical translation of Ovid's Palace of the Gods, and another of Deucalion's Flood, for which Master Frederic received premiums. I do not print any of these, for fear of too much enlarging the volume. The copy-books, indeed, are somewhat monotonous. In the following narrative some little account is given of the manner of life at the school, about the year 1826, if I calculate rightly.]

An old clock which stood in the corner of Parson Whipple's school-room suddenly began to tick twice as fast as usual. It did so for two or four hours, according as you counted time by its beat or by an hour-glass. Then it ticked for the remainder of its life at apparently the same rate as usual. This was never a discontented pendulum; and on that day, Singleton and I, who were the only boys in its counsels, thought it was very good-natured.

But I do not pretend it was right. Have I said it was right for the pendulum to tick so? I have not said it. I have only said that it was good-natured in the pendulum to tick twice as fast as usual, when it simply knew that I wished it to do so. I am not holding up the pendulum as an example for other pendulums, or for readers of the Atlantic. I wish people would not be so eager in their lookout for morals. I have not even said that the pendulum is the hero of this story. I have only said that it was good-natured, and that, as before, it ticked as I then said. Having simply said that, and hardly said even that, I am attacked with this question, whether my story is moral or not, whether the pendulum did right or not; and you tell me coolly that you do not know whether you will take the magazine another year, if the conduct of such pendulums is approved in it. Once and again, then, although I was then responsible for what the pendulum did, I assert that I am not now responsible for it. I was then fourteen, and am now hard on fifty-six, so I must have changed atomically six times since then. I reject responsibility for all my acts at Parson Whipple's. I do not justify the pendulum, I do not justify myself, far less do I justify Singleton. I only say it was a good-natured pendulum.

It happened thus: —

We were all to go after chestnuts, and we had made immense preparation, the old dominie not unwilling.

We had sewed up into many bags some old bed-tick dear, kind Miss Tryphosa had given us; we had coaxed Clapp's cousin Perkins, — son of Matthew Perkins third, of the old black Perkins blood, — we had coaxed him into getting the black mare for us from his father. Clapp was to harness her, and we were to have the school wagon to bring our spoils home. We had laid in with the Varnum boys to meet us at the cross-roads in the Hollow; and, in short, we were to give the trees such a belaboring as chestnut-trees had not known in many years. For all this we had the grant of a half-holiday; we had by great luck a capital sharp frost on Tuesday, we had everything but — time.

Red Jacket would have told us we had all the time there was, and, if Mr. Emerson had come along, he might have enforced the lesson. But he was elsewhere just then, and the trouble with us was, that, having all the time there was, we wanted more. And no hard bestead conductor on a single-track road, eager to "make the time," which he must have to reach the predestined switch in season, ever questioned and entreated his engineer more volubly than we assailed each other as to how we could make the short afternoon answer for the gigantic purposes of this expedition. You see there is a compensation in all things. If you have ever gone after chestnuts, you have found out that the sun sets mighty near five o'clock when you come to the 20th of October; and if you don't get through school till one, and then must all have dinner, I tell you it is very hard to start fourteen boys after dinner, and drive the wagon, and walk the boys down to the Hollow, and then meet the Varnums and drive up that rough road to Clapp's grandmother's, and then take down the bars and lead the horse in through the pasture to where we meant to tie him in the edge of the hemlock second-growth, and then to carry the bags across the stream, and so work up on the hill where the best trees are; — I say it is very hard to do all that and come out on the road again and on the way home before dark. And if you think it is easy to do it in three hours and a half, I wish you would try. All is, I will not give sixteen cents for all the chestnuts you get in that way.

So, as I said, we wanted to make the time. Well, dear Miss Tryphosa said that she would put dinner at twelve, if we liked, and if we could coax the dominie to let us out of school then. So we asked Hackmatack to ask him, and Hackmatack did not dare to, but he coaxed Sarah Clavers to ask him. The old man loved Sarah Clavers, as everybody did. She was a sweet little thing, and she did her best! Old man, I call him! That was the way we talked. Let me see, he graduated in 1811, — I guess he was in Everett's class and Frothingham's. The "old man," as we called him, must have been thirty-seven years old then, — nineteen years younger than I am to-day. Old man indeed!

Well, little Sarah did her prettiest. But the old man — there it is again — kissed her and stroked her face, and said he had given the school a half-holiday, and he thought his duties to the parents forbade his giving any more. And when little Sarah tried again, all he would say was, that, if we would get up early and be dressed when the first bell rang, we might "go in" to school at eight instead of nine. Then school could be done at twelve, — Miss Tryphosa might do as she chose about dinner, but, if she chose, we might be off before one. This was something, and we made the most of it.

Still we wished we could make a little more time. And as it was ordered, — wisely, I have no doubt, — though, as I said, I do not pretend to justify the use we made of the order, — as it was ordered, — that very Tuesday afternoon, when we were all at work in the school-room, Brereton — that Southern boy, you know — was reciting in "Scientific Dialogues" to the Parson. I think it must have been "Scientific Dialogues," but I am not sure. Queer, I was going to say it was Pynchon, who has distinguished himself so about all those things since. But that is a trick memory plays you. Pynchon must be ten years younger than Brereton; I dare say he never saw him. It was Brereton — Bill Brereton — was reciting, and he was reciting about the pendulum. The old man told him about Galileo's chandelier, I remember.

Well, then and there I saw the whole thing in my

mind as I see it now. Singleton saw it too. He was hearing some little boys in Liber Primus, but he turned round gravely, and looked me full in the face. I looked at him and nodded. Nor from that day to this have I ever had to discuss the details of the matter with him. Only he and I did three things in consequence of that stare and that nod, — he did two and I did one.

What he did was to go into the dominie's bedroom, when he went up stairs after tea, take his watch-key from the pin it hung on, and put it into his second bureau drawer under his woollen socks. Then he went across into Miss Tryphosa's room, and hung her watch-key on a tack behind her looking-glass. He thought she would not look there, and, as it happened, she never did. Those were in the early days. Schoolboys had no watches then. I do not think they even wrote home for them. If they did the watches did not come.

I do not recollect that George then told me he did this; but I knew he did, because I knew he could. I had no fear whatever, when I went to bed that night, that the doctor would wind up his watch, or Miss Tryphosa hers. As it happened neither of them did. Each asked the other for a key, the master tried the old gold key which hung at his fob, which had been worn out by his grandfather when he was before Quebec with Amherst. Both of them said it was very careless in Chloe, and both of them went to bed.

We all got up early the next day, as we had promised. But before breakfast I did not go near the clock, — you need not charge that on me. I hurried the others, — got them to breakfast, — and ate my own speedily. Then I did go into the school-room ten minutes before the crowd. I locked both doors and drew down the paper-hanging curtain. I took a brad-awl out of my pocket, and unscrewed the pendulum from the bottom of the rod. I left it in the bottom of the box. I took a horseshoe from my pocket and lashed it tight with packthread about a quarter way down the rod, — perhaps two inches above the quarter. I put in a nail after it was tied, twisted the string round it twice, — and rammed the point into the knot. Then I started the pendulum again, — found to my delight that it was very good-natured, and ticked twice as fast as I ever heard it, — I shut and locked the clock door, rolled up the paper-hanging curtain, and unlocked the school doors. If you choose to say I went to the clock after breakfast, before school, that is true, — I do not deny it. If you say I went before breakfast, I do deny it, — that is not true. If you ask if it was right for me to do so, — as you implied you were going to do, — I do not claim that it was. I have not said it was right. All I have said yet is that the pendulum was good-natured. And I will always protest — as I have often done before — against these interruptions.

I suppose I was engaged three minutes in these

affairs. I cannot tell, because the clock had stopped, and, when we are pleasantly employed, time flies. I was not interrupted. Nobody came into that schoolroom before it was time. In the Boston schools now they hire the scholars to be unpunctual, giving them extra credits if they arrive five minutes too early. If they knew, as well as I do, what nuisances people are who come before the time fixed for their arrival, they would not bribe the children in that direction. Certainly dear old Parson Whipple did not. We went in when the clock struck, and we went out when it struck. He had no idea of improving on what was exactly right. If he had read Voltaire, he would have said, " Le mieux est l'ennemi du bon."

So when the clock struck eight we rushed in. Reverent silence at prayers. I suppose my conscience pricked me; I have very little doubt it did, — but I don't remember it at all. Little boys called up in Latin grammar. Luckily they were all well up, and gabbled off their lesson in fine style: —

" Amussis, a mason's rule.

" Buris, the beam of a plough," &c., &c.

The lessons went down — one exception to each boy — without one halt; the master nodded with pleasure, and passed up to the first boy again; down it went again, and down again. These were bright little fellows; not one mistake, — perfect credits all.

" It is a very good lesson," said the dear old soul. " It 's a pleasure to hear boys when they recite so well. This will give us a little time for me to show you — "

What he was going to show them I do not know. He turned round as he said "time," and saw to his amazement that the clock pointed to 8.30. He put his hand to his watch unconsciously, and half smiled when he saw it had run down.

"No matter," said he, "we are later than I thought. Seats, — algebra boys."

So we took our places, and very much the same thing followed. Singleton and I were sent to the blackboards, — for the dear old man was in advance of the age in those matters, — and we did our very quickest. But Hackmatack had not our motive, and perhaps did not understand the algebra so well, so that he stumbled and made a long business of it, and so did the boy who was next to him. That boy was still on the rack, too much puzzled to see what Singleton meant by holding up three fingers of one hand and one of the other, when the Parson said, "I cannot spend all the morning upon you; sit down, sir," sent another boy to the board to explain my work, looked at the clock, and was this time fairly surprised to see that it was already half past nine. He seized the opportunity for a Parthian lesson to Brereton and Hackmatack. "Half an hour each on one of the simplest problems in the book. And I must put off the other boys till to-morrow." The other boys were a little amazed at their respite, but took the goods the gods provided without comment. We went to our seats, and in a very few minutes it was quarter of ten, and we were sent out to recess. Recess, you know, was quarter of an hour; it generally began at quarter of eleven, but to-day we had it at quarter of ten, because school was an hour earlier. I say quarter of ten because the clock said so. The sun was overcast with a heavy Indian-summer mist, so we could not compare the clock with the sun-dial.

The little boys carried out their lunch as usual, going through the store-closet on the way. But there was not much enthusiasm on the subject of lunch, and a good deal of generosity was observed in the offer from one to another of apples and doughnuts, — which, however, were not often accepted. I soon stopped this by saying that nobody wanted lunch because we were to dine so early, and proposing that we should all save our provisions for the afternoon picnic. Meanwhile, I conferred with Clapp about the black mare. He said she was in the upper pasture, which was the next field to our sugar-lot; and he thought he would run across now and drive her down into the lower pasture, in which case she would be standing by the bars as soon as school was over, and he could take her at once, and give her some grain while we were eating our dinner. Clapp, you see, was a day scholar. I asked him if he should have time, and he said of course he should. But, in fact, he was not out of sight of the house before the master rang the bell out of the window, and recess was over. Even the little boys said it was the shortest recess they had ever known.

So far as I felt any anxiety that day, it was in the next exercise. This was the regular writing of copies by the whole school. Now the writing of copies is a pretty mechanical business, and the master was a pretty methodical man, and when he assigned to us ten lines of the copy-book to be written in twenty-five minutes, giving him five for "inspection," he meant very nearly what he said, as he generally did. I ventured to say to Hackmatack and Clapp, as we sat down at our form, "Let 's all write like hokey." But I did not dare explain to them, and far less to the others, why the writing should be rapid. Earlier than that, my uncle had taught me one of the great lessons of life, — "If you want your secret kept, keep it."

So we all fell to, — on

Time trips for triflers, but flies for the faithful,

which was the copy for the big boys for the day. The little boys were still mum-mum-mumming in very large letters. Singleton and I put in our fastest, — and Clapp and Hackmatack caught the contagion. The master sat correcting Latin exercises, and the school was very still, as always when we were writing. How lucky that you never could hear the old clock tick when the case was shut and fastened! I should not be much worried now by the stint we had then, but in those days these fingers were more fit for bats and balls than for pens, and the up-strokes had to be very fine and the down-strokes very heavy. Still, we had always thought it a bore to be kept twenty-five minutes on those ten lines, and so we had some margin to draw upon. And as that rapid, good-natured minute-hand neared the V on the clock I finished the *u* in the last "faithful," — having unfortunately no room left on the line for the *l*. Hackmatack was but a word behind me, and Clapp and Singleton had but a few "faithfuls" to finish. Why do boys think it easier to write their words in columns than in lines? Is it simply because this is the wrong way, — O shade of Calvin! — or that the primeval civilization still lingers in their blood, and the Fathers wrote so, O Burlingame and shade of Confucius?

We sat up straight, and held our long quill pens erect, as was our duty when we had finished. The little boys from their side of the room looked up surprised; and redoubled the vicious speed by which already their *mums* had been debasing themselves into *uiuiui* with the dots in the *i*'s omitted. Faithful Brereton and Harris and Wells — I can see them now — plodded on unconscious; I could see that none of them had advanced more than a quarter down his page.

For a few minutes the dominie did not observe our erected pen-feathers, so engaged was he in altering a "sense line" of Singleton's or somebody's. The "sense" of this line was, that "the virtuous father of Minerva always rewarded green conquerors," such epithets and expletives having suggested themselves from Browne's Viridarium. But the last syllable of "Palladis" had got snagged behind a consonant, and the amiable dominie was relieving it from the over-pressure. So we sat like Roman senators, with our quill sceptres poised, — not coughing nor moving, nor in any way calling his attention, that the others might have the more time. And the little boys fairly galloped with their *mums*. But our sedate fellows on the other form plodded painfully on, — and had only finished seven lines when Mr. Whipple looked up, saw the senators and the sceptres, and said, reproachfully: "You cannot all have hurried through that copy! the chestnuts turn your heads." With the moment he turned his, to see that the minute-hand had passed a full half-circle. "Is it half past?" he said innocently. "I beg your pardon; but among the Muses, you know, we are unconscious of time. Well, well, let us see. Rather shabby, George, — rather shabby; not near so good as yesterday;

'*Some strains are short and some are shorter*';

and you too, Singleton. I do not know when you have been so careless, — you both of you are in such haste. See, Wells and Harris have not yet finished their lines.

Wells and Harris I think were as much astonished in their way; for it was not their wont to come in sixth and seventh — fairly distanced, indeed — on any such race-course. But there was little time for criticism. That good-natured pendulum was rushing on. The little boys escaped without comment on those vicious *m*'s, and, if there were anything in the system, each one of them ought to write "commonwealth" now, so that it should pass the proof-reader as "counting-house." But there is not much in the system, and I dare say they are all bank presidents, editors, professors of penmanship, or other men of letters.

The clock actually pointed at quarter of eleven! Now at 10.30 we should have been out at recitation, translating Camilla well over the plain. We had thrown her across the river on a lance the day before. We shuffled out, and I, still in a hurry, had to be corrected for speed by the master. I then assumed a more decorous tone, his grated nerves were soothed as he heard the smooth cadences of the Latin, — and then, of course, just the same thing happened as before. The lesson was ninety lines, but we had not read half of them when Miss Tryphosa put in her head to look at the clock.

"Beg pardon, brother, my watch has run down. Bless me, it is half past eleven!" And she receded as suddenly as she came. As she went she was heard asking, "Where can the morning have gone?" and observing to vacant space in the hall, that "the potatoes were not yet on the fire." As for the dominie, he ascribed all this to our beginning the Virgil too late; said we might stay on the benches and finish it now, and gave the little boys another "take" in their arithmetics, while we stayed till the welcome clock struck twelve.

"Certainly a short morning, boys. So much for being quiet and good. Good day, now, and a pleasant afternoon to you." It is at this point, so far as I know, that my conscience, for the first time, tingled a little.

A little, but, alas, not long! We rushed in for dinner. Poor Miss Tryphosa had to apologize for the first and last time in her life! Somehow we had caught her, she said. She was sure she had no idea how, — but the morning had seemed very short to her, and so our potatoes were not done. But they would be done before long, — and of course we had not expected much from a picked-up dinner, an hour early. We all thanked and praised. I cut the cold corned beef, and we fell to, — our appetites, unlunched, beginning to come into condition. My only trouble was to keep the rest back till Miss Tryphosa's potatoes — the largest a little hard at heart — appeared.

For, in truth, the boys were all wild to be away. And as soon as the potatoes were well freed from their own jackets and imprisoned under ours, I cut the final slices of the beef. Hackmatack cut the corresponding bread; the little boys took galore of apples and of doughnuts; we packed all in the lunch-baskets, took the hard eggs beside, and the salt, and were away. As the boys went down the hill, I stopped in the school-room, locked the doors, drew the curtain, opened the clock, cut the packthread, pocketed the horseshoe, screwed on the bob, and started the pendulum again. A very good-natured pendulum indeed! It had done the work of four hours in two. How much better that than sulking, discontented, for a whole hour, in the corner of a farmer's kitchen!

Miss Tryphosa and her brother had the feeling, I suppose, which sensible people have about half the days of their lives, "that it is extraordinary the time should go so fast!" So much for being infinite beings, clad for only a few hours in time and clay, nor wholly at home in those surroundings.

Did I say I would write the history of that chestnutting? I did not say so. I did not entitle this story "The Good Chestnuts," but "The Good-natured Pendulum." I will only say to the little girls that all went well. We waited at the foot of the hill for a few minutes till Clapp and Perkins came up with the mare and wagon. They said it was hardly half an hour since school, but even the little boys knew better, because the clock had struck one as we left the school-house. It was a little odd, however, that, as the boys said this, the doctor passed in his gig, and when Clapp asked him what time it was he looked at his watch, and said, "Half past ten."

But the doctor always was so queer!

WELL, we had a capital time; just that pleasant haze hung over the whole. Into the pasture, — by the second-growth, — over the stream, into the trees, — and under them, — fingers well pricked, — bags all the time growing fuller and fuller. Then the afternoon lunch, which well compensated for the abstemiousness of the morning's, then a sharp game at ball with the chestnut burrs, — and even the smallest boys were made to catch them bravely, — and, as the spines ran into their little plump hands, to cry, "Pain is no evil!" A first-rate frolic, — every minute a success. The sun would steal down, but for once, though we had not too much time, we seemed to have enough to get through without a hurry. We big boys were responsible for the youngsters, and we had them safely up on the Holderness road, by Clapp's grandmother's, Tom Lynch driving and the little ones piled in — Sarah Clavers in front — with the chestnut-bags, when the sun went down.

By the time it was pitch dark we were at home, and were warmly welcomed by the master and Miss Tryphosa. Good soul, she even made dip-toast for our suppers, and had hot apples waiting for us between the andirons. The boys rushed in shouting, scattered to wash their hands, and to get her to pick out the thorns, and some of our fellows put on some of the chestnuts to boil. For me, I stepped into the schoolroom, and, in the dark, moved the hour-hand of the clock back two hours. Before long we all gathered at tea, — the master with us, as was his custom in the evening.

After we had told our times, as we big boys sat picking over chestnuts, after the little ones had been excused, Miss Tryphosa said, "Well, boys, I am sure I am much indebted to you for one nice long afternoon." My cheeks tingled a little, and when the master said, "Yes, the afternoon fairly made up the shortcomings of the morning," I did not dare to look him in the face. Singleton slipped off from table, and I think he then went and replaced the watch-keys.

The next day, as we sat in algebra, the clock struck twelve instead of ten. The master went and stopped the striking part. Did he look at me when he did so? He is now Bishop of New Archangel. Will he perhaps write me a line to tell me? And that afternoon, when Brereton was on his "Scientific Dialogues," actually the master said to him, "I will go back to the last lesson, Brereton. What is the length of a second's pendulum?" And Brereton told him. "What should you think the beat of our pendulum here?" said the doctor, opening the case. Brereton could not tell; and the master explained; that this pendulum was five feet long. That the time of the oscillations of two pendulums was as the square root of the lengths, Brereton had already said; so he was set to calculate on the board the square root of sixty inches, and the square root of the second's pendulum, 39.139. I have remembered that to this day. So he found out the beat of our pendulum, — and then we verified it by the master's watch, which was going that afternoon. Then with perfect cold blood the master said, "And if you wanted to make the pendulum go twice as fast, Brereton, what would you do?" And Brereton, innocent as Psyche, but eager as Pallas Athene, said, of course, that he would take the square root of five, divide it by two, and square the quotient. "The square is 1.225," said he, rapidly. "I would cut the rod at one foot two and a quarter inches from the pivot, and hang on the bob there."

"Very good," said the master; "or, more simply, you move the bob up three quarters of the way." So saying he gave us the next lesson. Did he know, or did he not know? Singleton and I looked calmly on, but showed neither guilt nor curiosity.

Dear master, if there is ink and paper in New Archangel, write me, and say, did you know, or did you not know? Accept this as my confession, and grant absolution to me, being penitent.

Dear master and dear reader, I am not so penitent but I will own, that, in a thousand public meetings since, I have wished some spirited boy had privately run the pendulum-bob up to the very pivot of the rod. Yes, and there have been a thousand nice afternoons at home, or at George's, or with Haliburton, or with Liston, or with you, when I have wished I could stretch the rod — the rest of you unconscious — till it was ten times as long.

Dear master, I am your affectionate

FRED. INGHAM.

PAUL JONES AND DENIS DUVAL.

[MR. THACKERAY seemed to lose no opportunity to show his interest in American history, after his first visit here. His admirable novel, "The Virginians," has never been appreciated in America as it deserves. I believe this is because we are not yet prepared for a careful or a conscientious study of our own Revolution, and the events which led to it. In my own estimate of Mr. Thackeray, his power as a philosophical historian was no less distinguished than his power as a novelist. I do not think it would be difficult to show that the imagination which enables a writer to create a series of characters, and move them to and fro over the checker-board of a romance, is the same power by which a true historian makes the dead bones of annals live, and move about as men and women again on the field of their old career. When Mr. Macaulay died, I could not but hope that Mr. Thackeray would undertake the continuation of the unfinished history of England. He would have carried out this work with more success than, in another generation, Smollett attained in his continuation of Hume.

True to his interest in American subjects, Mr. Thackeray brought his last hero, Denis Duval, to the edge of service against Paul Jones. I do not suppose Mr. Thackeray knew — probably he did not care — how indifferent America is to Paul Jones, his victory or his reputation. If he had written one more chapter of "Denis Duval," it would have been to describe the battle between the "Bon Homme Richard" and the "Serapis." To do this he had brought Duval on board the "Serapis," just before that battle took place. In the article which follows I have quoted the last words he wrote in that novel.

Supposing that some new interest had been attracted to Paul Jones by Mr. Thackeray's plan, and by the action between the Alabama and the Kearsarge, which had just taken place when this sketch was written, I attempted to write for landsmen, as a landsman might, an account of the action as it would have appeared to one viewing it from the English side. Of course I was not rash enough to take Denis Duval's pen. But I introduced him among the lay-figures, as I did Mr. Merry, the midshipman with whom Mr. Cooper makes us acquainted, as one of Paul Jones's companions. With the exception of Mr. Heddart, Mr. Merry, and Denis Duval's presence on the scene, the narration is purely historical, as far as I knew how to make it so, on a study of all the known authorities, which are strangely few.

The article was first printed in the Atlantic Monthly for October, 1864.]

INGHAM and his wife have a habit of coming in to spend the evening with us, unless we go there, or unless we both go to Haliburton's, or unless there is something better to do elsewhere.

We talk, or we play besique, or Mrs. Haliburton sings, or we sit on the stoop and hear the crickets sing; but when there is a new Trollope or Thackeray, — alas, there will never be another new Thackeray! — all else has always been set aside till we have read that aloud.

When I began the last sentence of the last Thackeray that ever was written, Ingham jumped out of his seat, and cried, —

"There! I said I remembered this *Duval*, and you made fun of me. Go on, — and I will tell you all about him, when you have done."

So I read on to the sudden end.—

"We had been sent for in order to protect a fleet of merchantmen that were bound to the Baltic, and were to sail under the convoy of our ship and the Countess of Scarborough, commanded by Captain Piercy. And thus it came about, that, after being twenty-five days in his Majesty's service, I had the fortune to be present at one of the most severe and desperate combats that have been fought in our or in any time.

"I shall not attempt to tell that story of the battle of the 23d of September, which ended in our glorious captain striking his own colors to our superior and irresistible enemy." (This enemy, as Mr. Thackeray has just said, is "Monsieur John Paul Jones, afterwards Knight of His Most Christian Majesty's Order of Merit.") "Sir Richard [Pearson of the English frigate Serapis] has told the story of the disaster in words nobler than any I could supply, who, though indeed engaged in that fatal action, in which our flag went down before a renegade Briton and his motley crew, saw but a very small portion of the battle which ended so fatally for us. It did not commence till nightfall. How well I remember the sound of the enemy's gun, of which the shot crashed into our side in reply to the challenge of our captain who hailed her! Then came a broadside from us, — the first I had ever heard in battle." *

Ingham did not speak for a little while. None of us did. And when we did, it was not to speak of Denis Duval, so much as of the friend we lost, when we lost the monthly letter, or at least, Roundabout Paper from Mr. Thackeray. How much we had prized him, — how strange it was that there was ever a day when we did not know about him, — how strange it was that anybody should call him cynical, or think men must apologize for him: — of such things and of a thousand more we spoke, before we came back to Denis Duval.

But at last Fausta said, — "What do you mean, Fred, by saying you remember Denis Duval?"

And I, — "Did you meet him at the Battle of Pavia, or in Valerius Flaccus's Games in Numidia?" For we have a habit of calling Ingham "The Wandering Jew."

But he would not be jeered at; he only called us to witness, that, from the first chapter of Denis Duval, he had said the name was familiar, — even to the point of looking it out in the Biographical Dictionary; and now that it appeared Duval fought on board the Serapis, he said it all came back to him. His grandfather, his mother's father, was a "volunteer"-boy, preparing

* Cornhill Magazine, June, 1864, Vol. IX. p. 654.

to be midshipman, on the Serapis, — and he knew he had heard him speak of Duval!

O, how we all screamed! It was so like Ingham! Haliburton asked him if his grandfather was not *best-man* when Denis married Agnes. Fausta asked him if he would not continue the novel in the "Cornhill." I said it was well known that the old gentleman advised Montcalm to surrender Quebec, interpreted between Cook and the first Kamehameha, piloted La Pérouse between the Centurion and the Graves in Boston Harbor, and called him up with a toast at a school-dinner; — that I did not doubt, therefore, that it was all right, — and that he and Duval had sworn eternal friendship in their boyhood, and now formed one constellation in the southern hemisphere. But after we had all done, Ingham offered to bet Newport for the Six that he would substantiate what he said. This is by far the most tremendous wager in our little company; it is never offered, unless there be certainty to back it; it is, therefore, never accepted; and the nearest approach we have ever made to Newport, as a company, was one afternoon when we went to South-Boston Point in the horse-car, and found the tide down. Silence reigned, therefore, and the subject changed.

The next night we were at Ingham's. He unlocked a ravishing old black mahogany secretary he has, and produced a pile of parchment-covered books of different sizes, which were diaries of old Captain Heddart's.

They were often called log-books, — but, though in later years kept on paper ruled for log-books, and often following to a certain extent the indications of the columns, they were almost wholly personal, and sometimes ran a hundred pages without alluding at all to the ship on which he wrote. Well! the earliest of these was by far the most elegant in appearance. My eyes watered a little, as Ingham showed me on the first page, in the stiff Italian hand which our grandmothers wrote in, when they aspired to elegance, the dedication, —

"To my dear Francis,

who will write something here every day because he loves his Mother."

The old English gentleman, whom I just remember, when Ingham first went to sea, as the model of mild, kind old men, at Ingham's mother's house, — then he went to sea once himself for the first time, — and he had a mother himself, — and as he went off, she gave him the best album-book that Thetford Regis could make, — and wrote this inscription in ink that was not rusty then!

Well, again! in this book, Ingham, who had been reading it all day, had put five or six newspaper-marks.

The first was at this entry: —

"A new boy came into the mess. They said he

was a French boy, but the first luff says he is the Captain's own neffew."

Two pages on: —

"The French boy fought Wimple and beat him. They fought seeventeen rounds."

Farther yet: —

"Toney is offe on leave. So the French boy was in oure watch. He is not a French boy. His name is Doovarl."

In the midst of a great deal about the mess, and the fellows, and the boys, and the others, and an inexplicable fuss there is about a speculation the mess entered into with some illicit dealer for an additional supply, not of liquor, but of sugar, — which I believe was detected, and which covers pages of badly written and worse spelled manuscript, not another distinct allusion to the French boy, — not near so much as to Toney or Wimple or Scroop, or big Wallis or little Wallis. Ingham had painfully toiled through it all, and I did after him. But in another volume, written years after, at a time when the young officer wrote a much more rapid, though scarcely more legible hand, he found a long account of an examination appointed to pass midshipmen, and, to our great delight, as it began, this exclamation: —

"When the Amphion's boat came up, who should step up but old Den, whom I had not seen since we were in the Rainbow. We were together all day,—and it was very good to see him."

And afterwards, in the detail of the examination, he is spoken of as "Duval." The passage is a little significant.

Young Heddart details all the questions put to him, as thus:—

"Old Saumarez asked me which was the narrowest part of the Channel, and I told him. Then he asked how Silly [*sic*] bore, if I had 75 fathom, red sand and gravel. I said, 'About N. W.,' and the old man said, 'Well, yes,—rather West of N. W., is not it so, Sir Richard?' And Sir Richard did not know what they were talking about, and they pulled out Mackenzie's Survey," etc., etc., etc.,—more than any man would delve through at this day, unless he were searching for Paul Jones or Denis Duval, or some other hero. "What is the mark for going into Spithead?" "What is the mark for clearing Royal Sovereign Shoals?"—let us hope they were all well answered. Evidently, in Mr. Heddart's mind, they were more important than any other detail of that day, but fortunately for posterity then comes this passage:—

"After me they called up Brooke, and Calthorp, and Clements,—and then old Wingate, Tom Wingate's father, who had examined them, seemed to get tired, and turned to Pierson, and said, 'Sir Richard, you ought to take your turn.' And so Sir Richard began, and, as if by accident, called up Den.

"'Mr. Duval,' said he, 'how do you find the variation of the compass by the amplitudes or azimuths?'

"Of course any fool knew that. And of course he could not ask all such questions. So, when he came on *practice*, he said, —

"'Mr. Duval, what is the mark for Stephenson's Shoal?'

"O dear! what fun it was to hear Den answer, — Lyd Church and the ruins of Lynn Monastery must come in one. The Shoal was about three miles from Dungeness, and bore S. W. or somewhere from it. The Soundings were red sand — or white sand or something, — very glib. Then —

"'How would you anchor under Dungeness, Mr. Duval?'

"And Duval was not too glib, but very certain. He would bring it to bear S. W. by W., or, perhaps, W. S. W.; he would keep the Hope open of Dover, and he would try to have twelve fathoms water.

"'Well, Mr. Duval, how does Dungeness bear from Beachy Head?' — and so on, and so on.

"And Den was very good and modest, but quite correct all the same, and as true to the point as Cocker and Gunter together. O dear! I hope the post-captains did not know that Sir Richard was Den's uncle, and that Den had sailed in and out of Winchelsea Harbor, in sight of Beachy Head and Dungeness, ever since the day after he was born!

"But he made no secret of it when we passed-mids dined at the Anchor.

"A jolly time we had! I slept there."

With these words, Denis Duval vanishes from the Diary.

Of course, as soon as we had begged Ingham's pardon, we turned back to find the battle with the Bon Homme Richard. Little enough was there. The entry reads thus, — this time rather more in log-book shape.

On the left-hand page, in columns elaborately ruled: —

Week-days.	Sept. 1779.	Wind.	Courses.	Dist.	Lat.	Long.	Bearings.
Wednesday, Thursday.	22.23	S. E.	Waiting for convoy till 11 of Thursday.	None.	54°9′	0°5′ E.	Flamboro H. N. by W.

The rest of that page is blank. The right page headed, "*Remarks, &c., on board H. M. S. Serapis,*" in the boy's best copy-hand, goes on with longer entries than any before.

"42 vessels reported for the convoy. Mr. Mycock says we shall not wait for the rest."

"10 o'clock, A. M. Thursday. Two men came on board with news of the pirate Jones. Signal for a coast-pilot, — weighed and sailed as soon as he came. As we passed Flamboro' Head two sails in sight S. S. W., which the men say are he and his consort."

Then, for the next twenty-four hours: —

Week-days.	Sept. 1779.	Wind.	Courses.	Dist.	Lat.	Long.	Bearings.
Thursday, Friday.	23.24	S.S.W.	E.S.E. W.S.W.	Nothing.	54.13.	0.11. E.	Flam. H. W.aftern. W. by N.

"Foggy at first, — clear afterwards.

"At 1 P. M. beat to quarters. All my men at quarters but West, who was on shore when we sailed, the men say on leave, — and Collins in the sick bay. (MEM. *shirked.*) The others in good spirits. Mr. Wallis made us a speech, and the men cheered well. Engaged the enemy at about 7.20 P. M. Mr. Wallis had bade me open my larboard ports, and I did so; but I did not loosen the stern-guns, which are fought by my crew, when necessary. The captain hailed the stranger twice, and then the order came to fire. Our gun No. 2 (after-gun but one) was my first piece. No. 1 flashed, and the gunner had to put on new priming. Fired twice with those guns, but before we had loaded the second time, for the third fire, the enemy ran into us. One of my men (Craik) was badly jammed in the shock, — squeezed between the gun and the deck. But he did not leave the gun. Tried to fire into the enemy, but just as we got the gun to bear, and got a new light, he fell off. It was very bad working in the dark. The lanthorns are as bad as they can be. Loaded both guns, got new port-fires, and we ran into the enemy. We were wearing, and I believe our jib-boom got into his mizzen rigging. The ships were made fast by the men on the upper deck. At first I could not bring a gun to bear, the enemy was so far ahead of me. But as soon as we anchored, our ship forged ahead a little, — and by bringing the hind axle-trucks well aft, I made both my starboard guns bear on his bows. Fired right into his forward ports. I do not think there was a man or a gun there. In the second battery, forward of me, they had to blow our own ports open, because the enemy lay so close. Stopped firing three times for my guns to cool. No. 2 cools quicker than No. 1, or I think so. Forward we could hear musket-shot, and grenadoes, — but none of these things fell where we were at work. A man came into port No. 5, where little Wallis was, and said that the enemy was sinking, and had released him and the other prisoners. But we had no orders to stop firing. Afterwards there was a great explosion. It began at the main hatch, but came back to me and scalded some of my No. 2 men horribly. Afterwards Mr. Wallis came and took some of No. 2's men to board. I tried to bring both guns to bear with No. 1's crew. No. 2's crew did not come back. At half past ten all firing stopped on the upper deck. Mr. Wallis went up to see if the enemy had struck. He did not come down, — but the master came down and said we had struck, and the orders were to cease firing.

"We had struck to the Richard, 44, Commodore Jones, and the Alliance, 40, which was the vessel they saw from the quarter-deck. Our consort, the Countess Scarborough, had struck to the enemy's ship Pallas. The officers and crew of the Richard are on board our ship. The mids talk English well, and are good fellows. They are very sorry for Mr. Mayrant, who was stabbed with a pike in boarding us, and Mr. Potter, another midshipman, who was hurt.

Week-days.	Sept. 1779.	Wind.	Courses.	Dist.	Lat.	Long.	Bearings.
Friday, Saturday.	24th, 25th.	S.S.W.		None.	As above.	As above.	As above.

"The enemy's sick and wounded and prisoners were brought on board. At ten on the 25th, his ship, the Richard, sank. Played chess with Mr. Merry, one of the enemy's midshipmen. Beat him twice out of three.

"There is a little French fellow named Travaillier among their volunteers. When I first saw him he was naked to his waist. He had used his coat for a wad, and his shirt wet to put out fire. Plenty of our men had their coats burnt off, but they did not live to tell it."

Then the diary relapses into the dreariness of most

ship-diaries, till they come into the Texel, when it is to a certain extent relieved by discussions about exchanges.

Such a peep at the most remarkable frigate-action in history, as that action was seen by a boy in the dark, through such key-hole as the after-ports of one of the vessels would give him, stimulated us all to "ask for more," and then to abuse Master Robert Heddart, "volunteer," a little, that he had not gone into more detail. Ingham defended his grandfather by saying that it was the way diaries always served you, which is true enough, and that the boy had literally told what he saw, which was also true enough, only he seemed to have seen "mighty little," which I suppose should be spelled "mity little." When we said this, Ingham said it was all in the dark, and Haliburton added, that "the battle lanterns were as bad as they could be." Ingham said, however, that he thought there was more somewhere, — he had often heard the old gentleman tell the story in vastly more detail.

Accordingly, a few days after, he sent me a yellow old letter on long foolscap sheets, in which the old gentleman had written out his recollections for Ingham's own benefit after some talk of old times on Thanksgiving evening. It is all he has ever found about the battle in his grandfather's rather tedious papers, and one passing allusion in it drops the curtain on Denis Duval.

Here it is : —

"JAMAICA PLAIN, Nov. 29, 1824.

"MY DEAR BOY: I am very glad to comply with your request about an account of the great battle between the Serapis and the Bon Homme Richard and her consort. I had rather you should write out what I told you all on Thanksgiving evening at your mother's, for you hold a better pen than I do. But I know my memory of the event is strong, for it was the first fight I ever saw; and although it does not compare with Rodney's great fight with De Grasse, which I saw also, yet there are circumstances connected with it which will always make it a remarkable fight in history.

"You said, at your mother's, that you had never understood why the men on each side kept inquiring if the others had struck. The truth is, we had it all our own way below. And, as it proved, when our captain, Pearson, struck, most of his men were below. I know, that, in all the confusion and darkness and noise, I had no idea, aft on the main deck, that we were like to come off second best. On the other hand, at that time, the Richard probably had not a man left between-decks, unless some whom they were trying to keep at her pumps. But on her upper deck and quarter-deck and in her tops she had it all her own way. Jones himself was there; by that time Dale was there; and they had wholly cleared our upper deck, as we had cleared their main deck and gun-room. This was the strangeness of that battle. We were pounding through and through her, while she did not fight a gun of her main battery. But Jones was working his quarter-deck guns so as almost to rake our deck from stem to stern. You know, the ships were foul and lashed together. Jones says in his own account he aimed at our main-mast and kept firing at it. You can see that no crew could have lived under such a fire as that. There you have the last two hours of the battle; Jones's men all above, our men all below; we pounding at his main deck, he pelting at our upper deck. If there had not been some such division, of course the thing could not have lasted so long, even with the horrid havoc there was. I never saw anything like it, and I hope, dear boy, you may never have to."

[*Mem.* by Ingham. I had just made my first cruise as a midshipman in the U. S. navy on board the Intrepid, when the old gentleman wrote this to me. He made his first cruise in the British navy in the Serapis. After he was exchanged, he remained in that service till 1789, when he married in Canso, N. S., resigned his commission, and settled there.]

The letter continues: —

"I have been looking back on my own boyish journal of that time. My mother made me keep a log, as I hope yours does. But it is strange to see how little of the action it tells. The truth is, I was nothing but a butterfly of a youngster. To save my conceit, the first lieutenant, Wallis, told me I was assigned to keep an eye on the after-battery, where were two fine old fellows as ever took the King's pay really commanding the crews and managing the guns. Much did I know about sighting or firing them! However, I knew enough to keep my place. I remember tying up a man's arm with my own shirt sleeves, by way of showing I was not frightened, as in truth I was. And I remember going down to the cockpit with a poor wretch who was awfully burned with powder, — and the sight there was so much worse than it was at my gun that I was glad to get back again. Well, you may judge, that, from two after-portholes below, first larboard, then starboard, I *saw* little enough of the battle. But I have talked about it since, with Dale, who was Jones's first lieutenant, and whom I met at Charlestown when he commanded the yard there. I have talked of it with Wallis many times. I talked of it with Sir Richard Pearson, who was afterwards Lieutenant-Governor of Greenwich, and whom I saw there. Paul Jones I have touched my hat to, but never spoke to, except when we all took wine with him one day at dinner. But I have met his niece, Miss Janet Taylor, who lives in London now, and calculates nautical tables. I hope you will see her some day. Then there is a gentleman named Napier in Edinburgh, who has the Richard's log-book. Go and see it, if you are ever there, — Mr. George Napier. And I have read every word I could find about the battle. It was a remarkable fight indeed. 'All of which I was, though so little I saw.'"

[*Mem.* by F. C. And dear Ingham's nice old grandfather is a little slow in getting into action, *me judice.* It was a way they had in the navy before steam.]

The letter continues: —

"I do not know that Captain Pearson was a remarkable man; but I do know he was a brave man. He was made Sir Richard Pearson by the King for his bravery in this fight. When Paul Jones heard of that, he said Pearson deserved the knighthood, and that he would make him an earl the next time he met him. Of course, I only knew the captain as a midshipman (we were 'volunteers' then) knows a post-captain, and that for a few months only. We joined in summer (the Serapis was just commissioned for the first time). We were taken prisoners in September, but it was mid-winter before we were exchanged. He was very cross all the time we were in Holland. I do not suppose he wrote as good a letter as Jones did. I have heard that he could not spell well. But what I know is that he was a brave man.

"Paul Jones is one of the curiosities of history. He certainly was of immense value to your struggling cause. He kept England in terror; he showed the first qualities as a naval commander; he achieved great successes with very little force. Yet he has a damaged reputation. I do not think he deserves this reputation; but I know he has it. Now I can see but one difference between him and any of your land-heroes or your water-heroes whom all the world respects. This is, that he was born on our side, and they were born on the American side. This ought not to make any difference. But in actual fact I think it did. Jones was born in the British Islands. The popular feeling of England made a distinction between the allegiance which he owed to King George and that of born Americans. It ought not to have done so, because he had in good faith emigrated to America before the Rebellion, and took part in it with just the same motives which led any other American officer.*

"He had a fondness for books and for society, and thought himself gifted in writing. I should think he wrote too much. I have seen verses of his which were very poor."

[*Mem.* by F. C. I should think Ingham's grandfather wrote too much. I have seen letters of his which were very long, before they came to their subject.]

The letter continues: —

"To return. The Serapis, as I have said, was but

* Gates was an Englishman, and has a damaged reputation. Lee was another, who has no reputation at all. Conway was an Irishman, and the same is true of him. But these men all did something to forfeit esteem. Jones never did. Montgomery died in the full flush of his deserved honors. He was Irish by birth.

just built. She had been launched that spring. She was one of the first 44-gun frigates that were ever built in the world. We (the English) were the first naval power to build frigates, as now understood, at all. I believe the name is Italian, but in the Mediterranean it means a very different thing. We had little ships-of-the-line, which were called fourth-rates, and which fought sixty, and even as low as fifty guns; they had two decks, and a quarter-deck above. But just as I came into the service, the old Phœnix and Rainbow and Roebuck were the only 44s we had: they were successful ships, and they set the Admiralty on building 44-gun frigates, which, even when they carried 50 guns, as we did, were quite different from the old fourth-rates. Very useful vessels they proved. I remember the Romulus, the Ulysses, the Actæon, and the Endymion: the Endymion fought the President forty years after. As I say, the Serapis was one of a batch of these vessels launched in the spring of 1779.

"We had been up the Cattegat that summer, waiting for what was known as the Baltic fleet.* If there

* Not bound to the Baltic, as Mr. Thackeray supposes. Cf. Beatson's Naval Memoirs, Vol. IV. pp. 550-553, where the language is, "He fell in with a British convoy from the Baltic." Jones's own despatch possibly misled Mr. Thackeray, for he says, on the 21st of September, he tried to get at two ships which were waiting "to take under convoy a number of merchant ships bound to the northward"; but those ships put back to the Humber, and it was not till the 23d that he fell in with the Serapis and her convoy.

A London newspaper, of the 28th of September, says: "Captain were room and time, I could tell you good stories of the fun we had at Copenhagen. At last we got the convoy together, and got to sea, — no little job in that land-locked sailing. We got well across the North Sea, and, for some reason, made Sunderland first, and afterwards Scarborough.

"We were lying close in with Scarborough, when news came off that Paul Jones, with a fleet, was on the coast. Captain Pearson at once tried to signal the convoy back, — for they were working down the coast towards the Humber, — but the signals did no good till they saw the enemy themselves, and then they scud fast enough, passing us, and running into

Pearson, who commands the Serapis, was coming *from off his station* in the North Sea, to go on board of the Endymion."

October 28th of the same year, "the Court of Directors of the Royal Exchange Insurance Company have generously voted a piece of plate, value one hundred guineas, to be presented to Captain Pearson of the Serapis, as a testimony of their approbation of his bearing and conduct in protecting the valuable fleet *from the Baltic* under his care."

Allen's History of York, at the year 1779, in the description of the battle, says: "A valuable fleet of merchantmen *from the Baltic*, under the convoy of the Serapis, Captain Pearson, hove in sight." My friend, Mr. J. C. Brevoort, has shown to me, among other very curious memorials of Jones, a handsome print, engraved by Peltro, from a painting by Robert Dodd, which is a representation of the action, dated London, December 1, 1781. The inscription on this print states that the fleet was *from the Baltic*.

These are wholly independent authorities, and leave no doubt as to the fact of which the only importance now is, that Mr. Thackeray should have shipped Denis Duval aboard his frigate a few months earlier than he did, and taken him into the Baltic before bringing him into action against Paul Jones.

Scarborough Harbor. We had not a great deal of wind, and the other armed vessel we had, the Countess of Scarborough, was slow, so that I remenber we lay to for her. Jones was as anxious as we were to fight. We neared each other steadily till seven in the evening or later. The sun was down, but it was full moon, — and as we came near enough to speak, we could see everything on his ship. At that time the Poor Richard was the only ship we had to do with. His other ships were after our consort. The Richard was a queer old French Indiaman, you know. She was the first French ship-of-war I had ever seen. She had six guns on her lower deck, and six ports on each side there, — meaning to fight all these guns on the same side. On her proper gun-deck, above these, she had fourteen guns on each side, — twelves and nines. Then she had a high quarter and a high forecastle, with eight more guns on these, — having, you know, one of those queer old poops you see in old pictures. She was, therefore, a good deal higher than we; for our quarter-deck had followed the fashion and come down. We fought twenty guns on our lower deck, twenty on our upper deck, and on the forecastle and quarter-deck we had ten little things, — fifty guns, — not unusual, you know, in a vessel rated as a forty-four. We had twenty-two in broadside. I remember I supposed for some time that all French ships were black because the Richard was.

"As I said, I was on the main deck, aft. We were

all lying stretched out in the larboard ports to see and hear what we could, when Captain Pearson himself hailed, "What ship is that?" I could not hear their answer, and he hailed again, and then said, if they did not answer, he would fire. We all took this as good as an order, and, hearing nothing, tumbled in and blazed away. The Poor Richard fired at the same time. It was at that first broadside of hers, as you remember, that two of Jones's heavy guns, below his main deck, burst. We could see that as we sighted for our next broadside, because we could see how they hove up the gun-deck above them. As for our shot, I suppose they all told. We had ten eighteen-pounders in that larboard battery below. I do not see why any shot should have failed.

"However, he had no thought of being pounded to pieces by his own firing and ours, and so he bore right down on us. He struck our quarter, just forward of my forward gun, — struck us hard, too. We had just fired our second shot, and then he closed, so I could not bring our two guns to bear. This was when he first tried to fasten the ships together. But they would not stay fastened. He could not bring a gun to bear, — having no forward ports that served him, — till we fell off again, and it was then that Captain Pearson asked, in that strange stillness, if he had struck. Jones answered, 'I have not begun to fight.' And so it proved. Our sails were filled, he backed his top-sails, and we wore short round. As he laid us athwart-hawse, or as we swung by him, our jib-boom ran into his mizzen-rigging. They say Jones himself then fastened our boom to his main-mast. Somebody did, but it did not hold, but one of our anchors hooked his quarter and so we fought, fastened together, to the end, — both now fighting our starboard batteries, and being fixed stern to stem.

"On board the Serapis our ports were not open on the starboard side, because we had been firing on the other. And as we ran across and loosened those guns, the men amidships actually found they could not open their ports, the Richard was so close. They therefore fired their first shots right through our own port-lids, and blew them off. I was so far aft that my port-lids swung free.

"What I said in beginning this letter will explain to you the long continuance of the action after this moment, when, you would say, it must be ended by boarding, or in some other way, very soon. As soon as we on our main deck got any idea of the Richard's main deck, we saw that almost nobody replied to us there. In truth, two of the six guns which made her lower starboard battery had burst, and Jones's men would not fight what were left, nor do I blame them. Above, their gun-deck had been hoisted up, and, as it proved the next day, we were cutting them right through. We pounded away at what we could see, — and much more at what we could not see, — for it was now night, and there was a little smoke, as you may fancy. But above, the Richard's upper deck was a good deal higher than ours, and there Jones had dragged across upon his quarter a piece from the larboard battery, so that he had three nine-pounders, with which he was doing his best, almost raking us, as you may imagine. No one ever said so to me, that I know, but I doubt whether we could get elevation enough from any of our light guns on our upper deck (nines) to damage his battery much, he was so much higher than we. As for musketry, there is not much sharp-shooting when you are firing at night in the smoke, with the decks swaying under you.

"Many a man has asked me why neither side boarded, — and, in fact, there is a popular impression that Jones took our ship by boarding, as he did not. As to that, such questions are easier asked than answered. This is to be said, however: about ten o'clock, an English officer, who had commanded the Union letter-of-marque, which Jones had taken a few days before, came scrambling through one of our ports from the Richard. He went up aft to Captain Pearson at once, and told him that the Richard was sinking, that they had had to release all her prisoners (and she had hundreds) from the hold and spar-deck, himself among them, because the water came in so fast, and that, if we would hold on a few minutes more, the ship was ours. Every word of this was true, except the last. Hearing this, Captain Pearson — who, if you understand, was over my head, for he kept the quarter-deck almost throughout — hailed to ask if they had struck. He got no answer, Jones in fact being at the other end of his ship, on his quarter, pounding away at our main-mast. Pearson then called for boarders; they were formed hastily, and dashed on board to take the prize. But the Richard had not struck, though I know some of her men had called for quarters. Her men were ready for us, — under cover, Captain Pearson says in his despatch, — Jones himself seized a pike and headed his crew, and our men fell back again. One of the accounts says we tried to board earlier, as soon as the vessels were made fast to each other. But of this I know nothing.

"Meanwhile Jones's people could not stay on his lower deck, — and could not do anything, if they had stayed there. They worked their way above. His main deck (of twelves) was fought more successfully, but his great strength was on his upper deck and in his tops. To read his own account, you would almost think he fought the battle himself with his three quarter-deck cannon, and I suppose it would be hard to overstate what he did do. Both he and Captain Pearson ascribe the final capture of the Serapis to a strange incident which I will tell you.

"The men in the Richard's tops were throwing hand-grenades upon our decks, and at last one fellow worked himself out to the end of the main-yard with a bucket filled with these missiles, lighted them one by one, and threw them fairly down our main hatchway. Here, as our ill luck ordered, was a row of our eighteen-gun cartridges, which the powder-boys had left there as they went for more, — our fire, I suppose, having slackened there: — cartridges were then just coming into use in the navy. One of these grenades lighted the row, and the flash passed — bang — bang — bang — back to me. O, it was awful! Some twenty of our men were fairly blown to pieces. There were other men who were stripped naked, with nothing on but the collars of their shirts and their wristbands. Farther aft there was not so much powder, perhaps, and the men were scorched and burned more than they were wounded. I do not know how I escaped, but I do know that there was hardly a man forward of my guns who did escape, — some hurt, — and the groaning and shrieking were terrible. I will not ask you to imagine all this, — in the utter darkness of smoke and night below-decks, almost every lantern blown out or smashed. But I assure you I can remember it. There were agonies there which I have never trusted my tongue to tell. Yet I see, in my journal, in a boy's mock-man way, this is passed by, as almost nothing. I did not think so or feel so, I can tell you.

"It was after this that the effort was made to board. I know I had filled some buckets of water from our lee ports, and had got some of the worst hurt of my men below, and was trying to understand what Brooks, who was jammed, but not burned, thought we could do, to see if we could not at least clear things enough to fight one gun, when boarders were called, and he left me. Cornish, who had really been captain of the other gun, was badly hurt, and had gone below. Then came the effort to board, which, as I say, failed; and that was really our last effort. About half past ten, Captain Pearson struck. He was not able to bring a gun to bear on the Alliance, had she closed with us; his ship had been on fire a dozen times, and the explosion had wholly disabled our main battery, which had been, until this came, our chief strength. But so uncertain and confused was it all, that I know, when I heard the cry, 'They 've struck,' I took it for granted it was the Richard. In fact Captain Pearson had struck our flag with his own hands. The men would not expose themselves to the fire from the Richard's tops. Mr. Mayrant, a fine young fellow, one of Jones's midshipmen, was wounded in boarding us, after we struck, because some of our people did not know we had struck. I know, when Wallis, our first lieutenant, heard the cry, he ran up stairs, — supposing that Jones had struck to us, and not we to him.

"It was Lieutenant Dale who boarded us. He is still living, a fine old man, at Philadelphia. He found Captain Pearson on the lee of our quarter-deck again, and said, —

"'Sir, I have orders to send you on board the ship along-side.'

"Up the companion comes Wallis, and says to Captain Pearson, —

"'Have they struck?'

"'No, sir,' said Dale, — 'the contrary: he has struck to us.'

"Wallis would not take it, and said to Pearson, —

"'Have you struck, sir?'

"And he had to say he had. Wallis said, 'I have nothing more to say,' and turned to come down to us, but Dale would not let him. Wallis said he would silence the lower-deck guns, but Dale sent some one else, and took them both aboard the Richard. Little Duval — a volunteer on board, not yet rated as midshipman — went with them. Jones gave back our captain's sword, with the usual speech about bravery, — but they quarrelled awfully afterwards.

"I suppose Paul Jones was himself astonished when daylight showed the condition of his ship. I am sure we were. His ship was still on fire: ours had been a dozen times, but was out. Wherever our main battery could hit him, we had torn his ship to pieces, — knocked in and knocked out the sides. There was a complete breach from the main-mast to the stern. You could see the sky and sea through the old hulk anywhere. Indeed, the wonder was that the quarter-deck did not fall in. The ship was sinking fast, and the pumps would not free her. For us, our jib-boom had been wrenched off, at the beginning; our main-mast and mizzen-top fell as we struck, and at day-break the wreck was not cleared away. Jones put Lieutenant Lunt on our vessel that night, but the next day he removed all his wounded, and finally all his people, to the Serapis, and at ten the Poor Richard went to the bottom. I have always wondered that your Naval Commissioners never named another frigate for her.

"And so, my dear boy, I will stop. I hope in God it will never be your fate to see such a fight, or any fight between an English and an American frigate.

"We drifted into Holland. Our wounded men were sent into hospital in the fort of the Texel. At last we were all transferred to the French government as prisoners, and that winter we were exchanged. The Serapis went into the French navy, and the only important result of the affair in history was that King George had to make war with Holland. For, as soon as we were taken into the Texel, the English minister claimed us of the Dutch. But the Dutch gentlemen said they were neutrals, and could not interfere in the Rebel Quarrel. 'Interfere or fight,' said England, — and the first clause of the manifesto which makes war with Holland states this grievance, that the Dutch would not surrender the Serapis when asked for. That is the way England treats neutrals who offer hospitality to rebels."

So ends the letter. I suppose the old gentleman got tired of writing. I have observed that the end of all letters is more condensed than the beginning. Mr. Weller, indeed, pronounces the "sudden pull-up" to be the especial charm of letter-writing. I had a mind to tell what the old gentleman saw of Kempenfelt and the Royal George, but this is enough. As Denis Duval scrambles across to Paul Jones's quarter-deck, at eleven o'clock of that strange moonlight night, he vanishes from history.

ROUND THE WORLD IN A HACK.

[THIS story mostly relates to a period early in Colonel Ingham's life, although, as will be seen, his own accurate knowledge of the facts came a generation later. It is necessary to observe to readers distant from Massachusetts Bay, that, in the language of that country, a "hack" is a hired carriage, not, as in the language of Mr. Todd, "a horse let out for hire." To Dr. Johnson, it seems, the word was not known in either sense.

The story was first printed in the Atlantic Almanac for 1869.]

IT is an old Boston story. One would never tell it at a dinner-party here, or in the Evening Transcript, because in Boston everybody knows it better than you know it yourself. But the Atlantic Almanac goes to Sceattle and Boothia Felix, which is your excuse for telling it in these pages at all.

I can hear Liston growl as he finds that seven good pages of his new Atlantic Almanac are consumed by a story which everybody heard in his cradle, or should have heard there. But, dear Liston, all babies were not lulled by an east-wind, and all school-boys did not wait on "Johnny Snelling" at "Mason Street."

Let it be understood, then, that I tell the story for the benefit of Sceattle, of Boothia Felix, and of Assiût, and the other outlying purchasers. Let it be understood that it is a story of a generation ago. And if any of the inhabitants here do not like the way I tell it, why, let them tell it themselves, only do not let us have any more of these beastly interruptions. How shall we ever get on, if we have to stop all the time to explain?

I. — Of Joshua Cradock.

A generation ago, then, kindest of naturalists in Sceattle, erst my fellow-laborer in the infants society of naturalists at Worcester, — a generation ago, O president of the rising college of those parts, — a generation ago, O foreman over the manufactory of teapots at Assiût, — a generation ago the people of Boston liked to know something. I fear that that generation has now passed, and is regarded as mythical. What I know of this generation is this, that it likes to be amused. It goes into raptures as well as any generation I ever heard of. It even knows the difference between the emotions produced on it by the overture to the second act of *La Belle Hélène*, and that of the first act of *La Duchesse*. But I do not find that it cares so much about being instructed. The last generation did, which is, perhaps, my dear young friend, the cause of a notable difference remarked in some circles between your mother and yourself. But let that go! The consequence was that, a generation ago, the public entertainment of Boston was found in solid lectures, of which the staple was instruction, — instruction given in good faith, from those who knew to those who did not know, — exactly according to the advice of the Dervish Nasr Eddin. Do not ask me for that story. If you want that story, take ship, and go ask the Consul.

So it was, that, one evening in the week, if you were of the blue blood of Boston, you went to the lecture-hall of the Masonic Temple, the same spot in space where we boys went to hear Mr. Hillard defend a pirate-boy in his young eloquence — "And Costa the cabin-boy, shall he die?" — and where, with his manly acumen, he now convicts any pirates who may happen to be brought under the bar of the law. Thus we change! I say you went once a week, in the evening, to this amphitheatrical lecture-room, where about five hundred of the very nicest people in the world met together, and there you were instructed. John Farrar, most entertaining of physicists, taught you of the steam-engine, with veritable models which worked, — and with sections which he worked, whose valves opened and shut before your eyes. John Webster poured acid into tall glass reservoirs of litmus-water, and it turned red; and then he poured in ammonia, and it turned green. George Ticknor illustrated Shakespeare. Ralph Waldo Emerson told of Mahomet; Edward Hitchcock explained as much as he knew about the crust of the earth. John Pickering told about telegraphs and language; James Trecothick Austin gave the history of the siege of Boston; Convers Francis, that of the French Huguenots. It had not yet occurred to any man boldly to lecture on the History of Form, or the Form of History; on the Substantiality of Shadows, or the Shadows of Substance; on the Decorum of Ideas, or the Ideas of Decorum. The formula of the modern lecture was first stated, long afterwards, by Starr King. "It consists," said he, "of four parts of sense and five parts of nonsense, and there are but ten men in New England who know how to mix the two." He was chief of the ten, as he was chief everywhere! This formula had not then been discovered, far less stated; and, as I say, people still went to lectures to be informed.

If, now, I should here insert a long excursus on what we learned, on the nice girls who went to learn also, and the very nice young men who went, particularly on the cosy family way in which the fathers and mothers went also; and then how you all went home in little knots, and had, after the whole, a few games of whist (euchre not yet known, far less Boston), and then some hot oysters at half past nine, not in a disreputable cellar, but brought in by John, on a waiter, into the drawing-room; and how you laid down the cards, while Amanda served you all round,

— if, I say, I went into this excursus, the editor would score it all out of the manuscript; so it is as well not to write it, although every word of it is essential to the true understanding of this story.

For it happened, one night, that, at the first or second lecture of an excellent course on astronomy, at the "Useful Knowledge," the lecturer, who must have been, I think, Professor Farrar, made the explanation, since then not unfrequent, that this world on which we live is round. In connection with the phenomena of eclipses, he had some excellent illustrations; and in connection with summer, winter, day and night, he had more; and there was a terrestrial globe, and on the globe, I think, a large ship, length several degrees of latitude, whose topmasts could be distinctly seen by a wooden man with a spy-glass, on a distant continent, while her hull was still far below the horizon. By way of illustration and entertainment, Mr. Farrar, if it were he, then told of the people who had sailed around the world, of Magelhaens and Captain Cook, and, likely enough, alluded to William Sturgis, who was probably present, and to our rights in the Columbia River. (Else, dear friends, how would you be in Sceattle in this living 1869?)

The lecture was excellent, as dear John Farrar's always were. The little clusters of people made themselves up, as I have told, Alice with Arthur, not arm in arm, following after Mr. and Mrs. Paterfamilias; and Clara, Dolly, and Emily giggling a little behind;

Fred and Grace, in like manner, decorously following Mr. Materfamilias and his wife; Horace, Impey, and John following, in eager discussion as to whether they would make their electrical machine with a junk-bottle, or try to persuade the boy at Brewer's to let them have for forty-two cents a cracked cylinder they had there. In a group of more advanced age, Joshua Cradock and Mrs. Champernoon walked up Park Street, and old Champernoon with Mrs. Cradock, and so down to the Cradocks' house in Beacon Street.

It was one of those comfortable old white marble houses on the south side of Beacon Street, of which I think there were none left the last time I was there. It was but a short walk from the Temple, but that they chose to go up Park Street with the lecturer and his party; not long, however, at the longest. They came home, had their whist, — Mr. Cradock lost all three games, which was unusual, and, as the Champernoons afterwards thought, was a little silent and meditative. But I do not believe they ever would have thought of this, had they ever seen his face again.

But this was their last whist-party. Seth brought in the oysters, with a decanter of old Juno. The Champernoons declined another rubber, and went home.

As Joshua Cradock took off his coat and vest that night (he took them off together, not being of Hebrew parentage), he said to his wife, "Mary, would not you like to go round the world?"

"O, I should be sea-sick," said she (inevitably a woman's first answer).

"But one might go by land, Mary?" For Cradock was not a Sturgis, nor a Dorr, a Woodbridge, Hale, or Worcester. He was in no sort a geographer. True, he descended, I suppose, from old Matthew Cradock, the Moses of our infant State, who, from the Pisgah of London Town, looked across the howling Jordan to the land of Medford, — milk and honey from hollow trees, — which, alas! he never saw. The first President of the Massachusetts Company was he. From him it must have been that Joshua Cradock inherited the adventurous disposition which lurked in him. But Joshua had been educated for and in the produce business. When he tasted a cheese, he knew whether, the week it was made, the Widow Somerby, who made it, had had visitors or no. But he did not know over what parallels of latitude the waves were flowing, and which parallels climbed crests of snow as they ringed in the solid land. He knew of the hoops of firkins, but not of the parallels of the earth. So he suggested to Mary that they might go by land.

"None of these people he spoke of went by land," said she, meditatively, — "neither Captain Sturgis, nor Captain Cook, nor the other man. And on the globe it was a ship, and not a stage."

"I think," said Joshua Cradock, "you could go by land!" And they went to bed.

Mrs. Cradock fortunately remembered this conversation the next day; not that Joshua himself alluded to it. They came down to breakfast, — poached eggs, steak rare, fried potatoes, cold hot-cakes, and hot bread-cakes, with two slices of toast red-hot, and two pats of choice Kinsman butter, a special present from Mrs. Kinsman to Mrs. Cradock, — coffee from Java, present from Mr. Balestier, — Seth waiting, — breakfast quiet and protracted. After breakfast, Mrs. Cradock went up stairs; Mr. Cradock did not go out; read his Advertiser, skipped Casimir Périer's speech, skipped protocol on Polish revolution, skipped Lord Brougham's address before the London University, read the price of hops, beans, pot and pearl ashes. Then he rang the bell; sent Seth to Niles's for a carriage, and bade him tell Hitty to go up stairs for his valise. Hitty brought down the valise. Mr. Cradock opened the lower part of his bookcase, and took out three little leather bags tightly tied; weight of each, say, ten pounds. These three he put in the valise. Seth announced the hack. Mr. Cradock put on his coat, and, from the foot of the stairs, said, "Good by, Molly. "Good by" came down stairs on a high key. They always bade each other good by. But when Mr. Cradock said good by to Seth, and bade him say good by to "the girls," Seth was surprised. He was also surprised at the weight of the valise. Excepting for these surprises,

Mr. Cradock's departure was as usual, when he did not choose to walk to North Market Street. He got into the carriage. The hackman stood a moment on the sidewalk, and then said, respectfully, "Where to, sir?"

And Mr. Cradock answered,

"ROUND THE WORLD."

So the hackman mounted the box. His horses were headed up the street, aimed, indeed, at North Market Street. But he quickly turned, drove down Beacon Street upon the Mill Dam; they passed the toll-house without stopping, only Mr. Cradock looked out pleasantly at the keeper, and said "Cradock," and this was the last word Boston ever heard from him from that day to this day. *

That is the way I have always heard the story told. It is generally told to illustrate the character of the Boston hackman of the best school, who is indeed the superior of any of his kind I have ever found in travel elsewhere, save in Sybaris; nor are the hackmen of the Sybarites any better than he. He is a wholly different man from the baggage-smasher of Babel, or from the cabman of London. When he takes his summer vacation, you meet him in the mountains with his wife and child, as much a gentleman in the essentials as you are yourself; and for non-essentials, as St. Augustine says, differing from you in that he drives a better horse, and drives him much better than you would. When he retires from business, he takes a nice house back in some mountain valley, and, if you visit him, he will give you his views of your old friends, your belles and your beaux, affected, it may be, by the punctuality with which they left their parties; for the hackman likes Cinderella better than her sisters. So, for that matter, did the Prince, and so do I.

The time may come when I shall have the leisure to edit what I have by me, — some "Passages from the Diary of a Hackman." But I do not propose to edit them now, but to stick closely to this story, — which, as I say, is generally told to illustrate the character of the high-toned Boston hackman; how he obeys orders without quarrelling with you or squabbling about his fare. "As Cradock said, 'Drive round the world,' and they started." That is the way the story is generally told.

But the story does not properly stop there.

II. — Of Mrs. Cradock.

Dinner-time came at the Cradocks'. Oyster-soup, sirloin of beef, — the second cut, — boiled apple-dumplings, shag-barks and raisins, almonds and dates; Juno again. But, as you know, Mr. Cradock did not come. Mrs. Cradock had been down in Federal Street, to take her turn at visiting at the Infant School. She had called on Mrs. Blowers on her way home. She had dressed for dinner, and at ten minutes of two was in the parlor, waiting for Joshua. But, as I said, he did not come. The clock struck two; at five minutes past she sent Seth out on the mall to see Park Street clock, because she felt sure the parlor clock was wrong. Her own watch had stopped, as is the custom of the watches of the more powerful sex. But Seth reported that the parlor clock was right, as it always was. Let Mr. Bond alone for that. At fifteen minutes past two Mrs. Cradock went to the window. No Joshua in sight. Then she rang for Seth again.

"Did not Mr. Cradock order a carriage this morning?"

"Yes, m'm, at Niles's."

"Did he go to the store?"

"No, m'm, I think not."

"Why not, Seth?"

"He took his valise with him, m'm. Hitty thought he was going to Providence, m'm. But I do not think he was."

"Why not, Seth?"

"Because I heard him speak to the hackman, m'm."

"And what did he say, Seth?"

"He said, 'Round the world.'"

Mrs. Cradock had felt it in her bones before. All through the movements of the children at the Infant School she had sat hardly conscious whether they were in the first position or the second; so sorry was she that she had, for the first time in her life, refused to Joshua something he proposed. So seldom did he propose anything! She always was glad to get him away from that horrid store. And now, when he had hinted at going away, she had thrown cold water on the plan. She had said she should be sea-sick. What if she were? — better be sea-sick than heart-sick; better be sea-sick with Joshua than land-sick alone. All the time Mrs. Blowers had been telling her about the cook's impudence and the second girl's marriage, she had been thinking, how, at dinner, she would bring up the plan of going round the world. She had thought what she would wear. She would wear that brown merino that Mr. Cradock had bought for her at Whitaker's. He had bought it, and it would wear well. She would only take the small black trunk; and in the bottom of it, for summer wear, she would put in that dress-pattern of seersucker which she had never made up. When she came home, she had told Hannah to have the cranberries strained for dinner, so as to make it seem more like a feast, and she had even had the best knives and forks put on, because he would notice that. And now it was too late. If only she had said "Yes!" Now he was gone! Poor Mrs. Cradock!

"Then we will not wait any longer, Seth. You can bring up dinner."

She did not say anything more. Silent women those Ipswich Brewsters, I have always noticed, when they were moved, — silent, but not the less decided. It must be the old Elder's blood.

She ate her beef alone, and pretended to eat cranberry. But Seth was not deceived. He knew she did not touch it. The table was cleared, and she ate her apple-pudding. Cleared again, and she had nuts and raisins on her plate. Then she rang up Seth again.

"Were they good horses, Seth?"

"The best Niles has, m'm, — the bay team you had last Monday."

"Then you need not go to Niles's this afternoon. Go down to Fullum's, in Bowdoin Square. Tell him I want a carriage at four; and, Seth, see that he gives us good horses. I am going round the world, Seth, after Mr. Cradock. Would you like to go?"

"Yes, m'm," said Seth. And that is the way he came to go.

"Mr. Cradock never drives after dark, Seth. I think if we drive late in the evening, we shall catch him in a day or two."

"Yes, m'm," said Seth.

And Mrs. Cradock went up stairs, and packed the little black trunk. She put the seersucker in the bottom. She put in the diamond necklace her husband gave her the day they had been married twenty-five years. She took the pocket-book which kept the quarter's housekeeping. She put in her Bible, and "Taylor's Holy Living and Dying," and the "Selections from Fénélon." Then she put in Mr. Cradock's best coat, which she found he had left, and some articles of apparel whose names I do not know.

She put on the brown merino from Whitaker's.

At four the hack came. Seth put the trunk on the driver's seat. The driver shut Mrs. Cradock in; and, like the other driver, said, "Where to?"

"Round the world," said Mrs. Cradock; and the driver mounted by Seth's side, and they started.

Niles's were good horses, but these were better. Seth had understood his commission. Perhaps he gave the driver a hint that a stern chase was a long chase. They took a good pace from the beginning, and they held it. They drove faster than Joshua did, I know, for I have both journals before me at this moment. But they did not catch him. It was a misfortune, — but they did not catch him. And this was the reason.

Seth had observed that Niles's horses headed up the street when they started and he shut the house-door. That was all he knew. So, when Mrs. Cradock said "Round the world," Seth bade her driver push boldly by the corner of Park Street. They passed the Thorndike house, the Bean's and the Dwight's, struck Hanover Street and Winnissimet Ferry; and, with a feeling they must continue east, crossed to Chelsea and the Salem turnpike. And when, that evening, after a very hard push, Mr. Cradock stopped at six, at the sign of Neptune, on Shrewsbury Hill, Mrs. Cradock was just driving out of Lynn. And her perseverance in keeping on till near eleven o'clock, which brought her even to the Wolfe tavern at Newburyport, only separated her twenty odd miles farther from her husband than if she had stopped when he did. Ah me! it was worse than Evangeline. For she, at least, was staying still while Gabriel sailed by her. But this man and this woman, under two motives, were going farther from each other with every differential of every revolution of their wheels.

Palmer, on the west, and Saco, on the east, marked their stopping-places of the second night; but, the third day, one of Mrs. Cradock's horses was amiss. She was fain to dine at Portland, and spend the night there.

Seth, I need not say, made inquiries from day to day in the stables. In the forgotten days of travel, when there were stables connected with inns, the people in the parlors knew nothing of what was passing till the people from the stables came in and told them. Seth got information at Portland, and came and told Mrs. Cradock, as she sat over her nuts and raisins again, that "they said" the best way round the world was to go by sea. Seth was an implicit believer in Mrs. Grundy, only, like most persons bred in a democratic country, he personified her as a noun of multitude. What "they said" — the voice of the people — was to Seth indeed as the very voice of God.

To Mrs. Cradock his remark was a sad one. It was only just what she had said only three short days before. And what wretchedness of separation had sprung from her saying it!

"Do they say so, Seth?" said she, sadly. "I said so once."

"Yes, m'm. They say there's oceans of people as goes round the world every year; but they goes in ships, — thousands on 'em. They call 'em 'whalers.' They goes for sperm oil and whalebone. Richardson keeps the best. We always has Richardson's."

"I know you *can* go by water, Seth. But Mr. Cradock preferred to go by land. They have not heard of Mr. Cradock, — have they?"

"All of 'em's heard on him, m'm. There is not a shop-keeper in the place but has heard on him. But none on them has seen him, nor knew he was travelling."

"I thought you did not inquire for him at the last toll-gate, Seth?"

But Seth declared he did. Mrs. Cradock's faith that they should overtake him held firm, though she was surprised that, while they paid toll steadily down the old turnpike, no one had seen Mr. Cradock's carriage, nor had they gained any clue to him at one of the inns. Yet her faith did not waver, and she still said, "We will go by land."

And the next morning Seth heated her soap-stones, folded round her a handsome bear-skin he had found in a furrier's shop: "The best skin they is in the State; keeps out cold, they say, five hundred times better than them buffaloes; they say the Indians makes them." He substituted a fur cap for the stove-pipe with which he had started, and again they pressed Down East. The same morning Mr. Cradock left the little tavern at Chester Factories, and began to pull up the hills. He was already on runners; but Mrs. Cradock, as it happened, did not have to take them till she came to Bangor. There she lay by three or four days in her first heavy snow-storm. She lost no courage, however. "If it stops me, it will stop him," she said; and, after the roads were broken out, she started again.

But this is not a diary of her journey nor of his; for I do not think it would be fair to print either his diary or hers. I will tell you, before I have done, how I came to have them. Her journey of that winter was her hardest, — harder, as it happened, than his. It was but a slow journey too, — for Seth was very careful, and not over bold; if the weather were too cold, he invented endless reasons why they should not go on. Who does not know how completely a traveller is in his courier's hands? — most of all when that traveller is a woman, innocent of geography, and without a guide-book; and, if that courier have always managed her household, hard for her indeed! A horrid business they had pulling across from Bangor to Eastport. And there Seth made a long stop. Once and again he suggested the ocean experiment. But Mrs. Cradock answered, as before, that Mr. Cradock proposed to go by land, till she had come to the very end of the peninsula of Nova Scotia, had bravely crossed the Gut of Canso to the island of Cape Bréton, drove into hospitable Sydney, and there looked eastward on the sea. How should she go by land now?

For my part, I should be well pleased, if, as she had hoped, she had found Mr. Cradock also sea-bound in Sydney, and if this story had ended there. I do not know if there is better place for a story to end than there, where so many stories have begun. Is it the eastern point of a southeastern branch of the Laurentian hills? Then it is, if I understand Agassiz, the first spot of this world that lifted itself above the hot water.

> "When the young sun revealed the glorious scene
> Where oceans gathered, and where fields grew green."

A good deal began when that bit of lowland beach first put its nose for air above the brine! And so a good many hundred million of years afterwards (ask Darwin and Lesley how many), when "the time was come" for John Cabot and his son to open up North America to England and to the world, this same old shore was the "New-Found-Land" that peered out from the fog to them on St. John's morning. Not the island of Newfoundland, but Cape Bréton. So Mr. Deane tells me, and, if he does not know, nobody does. A good deal began then; and so if you want to get either to the beginning of all things American, or to the veritable jumping-off place either, you may go to Sydney. And are there not some such charming people there? And do I not wish I was there at this living moment when I write these words? A good place to celebrate St. John's day! Here, at all events, Mrs. Cradock came, and found, of course, that she could travel east in a hackney-coach no longer. "Nothing, madam, but the sea between you and Ireland," as the native guides say so proudly on so many sea-shores.

"And has no one seen Mr. Cradock, Seth?" No: no one had seen him. How should they? Mr. Cradock had arrived that night, after a good many chances and crosses, at his fourth station in the prairies west of Detroit. He had been welcomed by a stray Canadian who had made himself a log-cabin there the year before. Neither of them could understand a word of the other's language. But in that cabin he stayed till the frost of that winter was wholly out of the ground.

III. — Of Him.

I asked dear old Robert Owen once what we should all do, when he had the whole world successfully divided off into "Family Unions" of 2,500 people each, — all the Peruvians, Patagonians, Chinchillas, and Cattaraguses happily ordered under the same order of society, each with its own cotton-factory and its own lyceum, — and all the babies nursed in central nurseries by the most approved system, with night-gowns worn in the daytime all cut by one cosmopolitan standard.

"What shall we all do, when the world is well adjusted?" asked I.

And the dear old man's face beamed with a happy smile of transfiguration, as he thus contemplated the new mathematical paradise, grateful to me for recognizing its possibility, even by conjecture; and he answered, "Do? we will *travel!*"

There is a good deal in it. When education has completed itself at home, travel is a first-rate university; and the poor, stunted freshman of Life College, who at first dares not say his soul is his own, or, if he dares, says what is not true, after a little travel through the different courses of this beneficent Alma Mater's direction, — proceeds "Bachelor at Arts."

That means, he gets "the power of speaking as often as anybody asks him to," — a very great power, as I have observed men.* A few years more of travel, and he is "Master of Arts," which means, he receives the power of professing that he is acquainted with things, if anybody asks him. This power, as the world goes, is also a considerable one.†

Many is the well-trained Bostonian who will admit that a course of travel of much less compass than Joshua Cradock's has opened his eyes mightily to the

* "Cum privilegio publice prælegendi, quotiescumque ad hoc munus, evocati fueritis." These are the words which accompany a Bachelor's degree.

† "Cum privilegio publice profitendi, quotiescumque ad hoc munus evocati fueritis." These make one a Master of Arts, if spoken with authority.

size of the world and to his own duty and place in it. And Joshua Cradock, as I remember this experience of his life, stands out to me, not as a disappointed adventurer following a phantom, ruined by his own ignorance, and homeless because too proud to make inquiry in time; but rather as a true, brave man, who, in his narrow life at home, found one chance for an outlook on the larger world, used that chance, and was himself changed in the using, and so saved, — converted. He was faithful in such little duty as he had in North Market Street; but he did not make the one great mistake of thinking that duty was all. In his ignorance, even, of the world without, there seemed to open to him a chance for enlarging his study of it, and that chance he took; because he took it, his life also became what it did, and he knew the honors, if he knew the sufferings, of a true, unselfish child of God.

I do not pretend to say that I can unravel all his journal; it was kept originally in a book ruled for a ledger, of which one end had, in fact, been used for posting the book-accounts of some customers of his in some early adventure. Mixed right up with the diary are memoranda of accounts, draughts of letters, one sketch of a speech he made to some Indians on the Plains, a very curious and original calculation of the longitude from his notes of the great lunar eclipse of 1832, and I know not what beside. In the first winter, as I said, he came as far as Michigan; but then mud stopped him, who had not faltered before snow. The journal, brief like all journals, when there was anything to tell, becomes, like other journals, voluble when he had nothing to do. Evidently he fascinated the Canadian's children. He taught them to read and write, and to talk English; and Hubert, the oldest of them, held to him for years afterwards.

Farther on, when they had worked along to the southern end of Lake Michigan, there are the traces of a long stay he made there, in which he must have devoted himself to the fortunes of the new slab city of Rochambeau. Rochambeau has gone to its reward before now, — at least I cannot find it on the map, far less on the spot, — but here was Cradock, learned in the lumber trade, disentangling those poor settlers from the snares into which they had been led by a sort of Dousterswivel who gloried in the name of Dodwell, and making clear to them how they were to get their timber at fair rates; nay, waiting there till the first cargo came; if, in fact, he did not himself command the craft that bore it. Here he lost or gained a great deal of time; and, indeed, all the slowness of his Western progress is to be accounted for by his determination to see wrong righted in many such an enterprise. At last, after the burning of the prairies, or before, or at the possible time, whenever that was, — Flagg and Staples and the rest of them will explain to you, — he struck the Mississippi quite low down, got his craft on a steamer which was exploring the upper river, then so little known, made some northing, and then, in the freshness of one early spring, they pushed across, he and the faithful driver and Hubert, by the Great Pipe Rock to the upper Missouri. From that time it is wild adventure indeed. The getting the carriage through was of course now a mere piece of pride. But they had all the time there was. They conciliated all those roving tribes, even of Yellow-Stones. Who in this world does not such a man as Cradock conciliate? and there is something racy in the triumph with which he announces the running of successive cañons as they work down what I suppose to have been Lewis's River.

"*October* 27. — Fair, — water not so high, but high enough. Sighted the wheels to-day, after a good deal of doubt whether they had not passed in the night. Hubert lassoed the raft and hauled it in. All right.

"*October* 28, 6 A. M. — Rainy, — cleared afterwards. Started the old booby (by this name the carriage-body has been called for some months) at six, and the wheels at eight, following with Hubert still on the south side. Lost sight of the little raft at once; but there is a red hide trails behind the big raft, which we saw on the foam for half a mile. Road on the south side very hard, but this pony would go anywhere.

"*October* 29. — Fair. Did not make two miles. Vorse must have gone some other way. If he did not, we shall never see the booby again.

"*October* 30. — Rain with thunder. Dead lost.

After a day's work, struck the river half a mile *above* last night's camp!

"*October* 31. — Rain. Found the trail. Pushed twenty miles and came into camp. Vorse had made a good fire, and had biscuits baking. Best of all, he had sighted both rafts in the back-water yesterday, and had hauled them both in. They are floating just off shore now. The Mission is only two hundred miles below."

At this Mission I suppose they spent that winter; for it is not till the 4th of July of next year that I find them in Walrussia, spending that day in Sitka. And this man, who left his home simply an honest produce merchant, who had tried hard to believe that the Boston schools were the only schools, the Boston streets the only streets, the Boston newspapers the only newspapers, and the Boston Society for promoting Useful Knowledge the only possible society, — this man had, since he left Boston, taught one Western town how to save its children's children from epidemic in reorganizing their drainage; had watched in another through all the horrors of a relapse of the first cholera invasion; had attended to that little matter of the lumber at Rochambeau; had made certainly two treaties, and I know not how many more, between squabbling tribes of Indians, who, but for him, would have cut their throats, — and here at Sitka, at last, he gives a public dinner to the Russian Governor and the agents of the North American Company, to Captain

Taganoff and the other naval officers in port, and actually makes them a speech in French (acquired from Hubert), on the relations between the two great powers which divide the northern zones. Mr. Seward would like to print that speech in the archives of Alaska.

IV. — Of Lake Baikal, or the Sea so called.

For myself, the way I came to have these papers before me, and to be able to tell you what Seth and the rest said and did, and what they did not do, is easily told.

In one of the inter-acts of the drama of a somewhat varied life, I had taken the contract for laying the Inter-Hemispheric wire, on the fourth section of the Siberian Telegraph Division, and this led me to spend the better part of two years not far from the Chinese Wall, between Krasnoyarsk and Yakoutsk. Properly speaking, our part of the line began at Krasnoyarsk, though, for reasons I need not name here, we took from Section 3 one hundred and eleven wersts this side of that place, beginning at Post Station 87. The first time I went over my line, in company with my dear friend Bolkhorinitoff of the Imperial engineers, the country was as new to me as it is to you, dear reader. And then came that delicious first visit at Irkutsk, where every visit has been so delicious. Is there any traveller who does not bless the Mouravieffs with a full heart, and remember them every night as he puts his head on the pillow? Well, we had all the fun there, — such coasting as there is not in all Russia beside, nor even in New Bedford. Dancing, music, — what did we not have that was charming in a wilderness? We arranged our head-quarters there, and then with Bolkhorinitoff I pushed on to determine the eastern line.

Of course there must be a station at Irkutsk. It is the capital of Eastern Siberia. Beyond that was the question. I was rather for clinging to the Chinese frontier, and carrying it right through Kiachta. But the reader will understand that the difficulty was with Lake Baikal. Before the ice broke up, we pushed across once to Posolskoi, and so down to Kiachta on the snow, and back again. A magnificent expedition it is. You have the best horses I ever rode behind, and you know and they know what is the wager as you cross the ice. You leave and they leave the western shore at ten in the morning. You are on ice which is so clear that you cannot believe you are standing on anything; — thick, who knows how thick? On — on — you push across, are turned here by a ridge which has formed itself after some storm, get the eastern line there, holding your landmark in sight steadily, — on and on — seventy-five wersts, — fifty miles, — you have driven in four hours, with the thermometer at the point of frozen mercury! That is a good match against time for you, and the stakes are worth considering.

If only the ice would last all through the year, there, of course, would the wire go, but for six months this sea of glass, dear Mr. Calvin, is a sea of water; and where shall our wires go then? We went to Kiachta, came back round the southern end of the lake, and were dissatisfied.

Bolkhorinitoff and I agreed that, as soon as the navigation was opened, he should go north by post on the west side, I would go up by boat over the lake to Nofpo Staun, — a new place which none of them had seen, at the very northeastern point, — we would meet there, and see if the lake might not be doubled better on the northward. The lake, (Heaven forgive me, I have called it so three times!) I mean the sea, is, you see, as long as Lake Superior.

So, when we got into May, poor Bolkhorinitoff left me; and early in June I went down to the sea, — it is forty miles from Irkutsk, — and chartered a queer craft for the voyage. She had just come in with omully, or omoulé, the herring of that region. She smelt of the cargo after it was gone, as vases do of attar. I made friends with the skipper, and had a chance to learn to speak "Russia-in-Asia," if I had never had it before; for we were windbound there ten days. He did not want to beat to windward, and, after I knew better, I did not want to either.

The Irkutsk people say that no man knows how to pray from his heart till he has been on the Baikal Sea in autumn. I can understand the proverb very well from my experience of that spring. We stayed in shore for ten days, the skipper and I playing a detestable form of sledge on the villanous pack of Russian cards he had, whiling away time by his teaching and my learning to talk "Russia-in-Asia," as I said, and I working up my journal with some notes I have never published, on the traces of Sandemanianism in the architecture of the parish churches of the Ural. At last we got to sea, — and such a sea!

It is from forty to sixty miles wide. It is certainly five hundred miles long. When the wind blows the wrong way, the best thing you can do is to get out and wait, if you can. But sometimes you cannot, the conditions being severe. We started too soon; the wind hauled round into the northeast when we were thirty miles off-shore, and we had to take it, cold and heavy, — very cold and very heavy.

With the help of my dictionary I asked the skipper if there were no shelter on the east side of the lake, thinking we might claw a little to windward, and gain something in distance. I was amazed as he begged me to be still; — if I could say nothing better than that, to say nothing; and, somewhat snubbed, I went below. After the gust was over, he apologized. I had called the Baikal "*osero*," a lake, instead of "*morè*," a sea. Now this was an insult to the ruling powers. He told me with perfect seriousness, that an ungodly fellow, years ago, swore it was a lake, and lake it should be called. So he called it "a lake."

"But," whispered the skipper, "whichever way that man sailed, the wind was always against him. Six weeks, two months, it blew always ahead; no matter how he tacked, the wind tacked too; till at last he swore a terrible oath, and said it was a sea, and should be a sea; and, before the words were well out of his mouth, the fog lifted and he was on shore."

I told the skipper coolly that this must be a Dutchman; and he said he was; — quite innocent of my satire. And I found the story afterwards in Gmélin's Travels. He tells it of a countryman of his. This was the reason the skipper wanted me to mind my *p*'s and *q*'s as I talked upon such risky water.

I confess I had some sentiment all this time. Have not you a sentimental feeling about some parallels of latitude and meridians of longitude? Yes? well, so have I, — a great deal of it. Here is this dear old meridian of 71° runs right through Boston Harbor. I feel as if I could kiss it every time I cross it on Hough's Neck, and I walk my horse if I drive over it on the Salem turnpike. Do you wonder at Wendell Phillips's interest in Toussaint? Why, the meridian of Boston crosses the middle of Hayti! how can a Boston boy help feeling himself at home there? And I never wondered why they thought Valparaiso was the Valley of Paradise, when they found out that, so far as the longitude went, they were under this blessed Boston meridian. And when you complete the great circle, and come on the other side of the world, you feel it all the more. That is the reason why Coram enjoyed Java so much; because this meridian of 109° east, just half-way round, as the sun moves, makes everything seem so natural. Six o'clock here when it is six o'clock there, only here it is night when there it is morning.

So I was a little sentimental in the old herring-boat, for I was on or about 108° east, and knew I was nearing 109°. Did they think of me at home? I was almost as far from them as on that parallel I could go, and after that point I should be coming nearer. Perhaps it was this; perhaps I took cold by getting wet when we shipped those heavy seas the fourth day out, for it was very slow work.

I had all the tortures in my lower jaw, left side; I did not know there was a bad tooth there, but there was something. O, what a night that was! Miss Martineau says we do not remember pain. I should like to try her on that toothache. I smoked some wretched Chinese tobacco, — no good. Then I took some nostrum of the skipper's, — no good. Then I dropped fifty drops of laudanum, — no good. Then I thought I might as well die one way as another, and I raked out some *Cannabis Indica* (hasheesh, you know) that was in Orloff's medicine-chest; I chewed that, — no good. Finally I put myself to sleep with ether, and lay like a log till, long after dark, I waked, found the skipper had covered me warm, and that we had made a splendid run. It was just midnight, and we were running up to the wharf, or slip, of Nofpo Staun.

I said I would go ashore. The skipper tried to make me wait till morning. "No: I had had enough of the lake, — I begged his pardon, — of the sea." I wrapped myself warmly, stepped on the wharf, and found it a little peninsula connecting with another, just as the T connects with the old Long Wharf of Boston. And up this other longer wharf I walked, under the silent moonlight, into the little town. Was I asleep? I knew I was not drunk! was it the hasheesh? was it the ether? or was there in fact a little old State House at the head of the street? and was there the dome of another State House beyond it, only very small? There was nobody to tell me; but, as I went up and on, I found I was in a quaint, queer, old-fashioned little Boston. Was it Duchesne's model, which had grown a little? or was I still dreaming in the skipper's cabin? Up State Street I went, — up Court Street I went, — I passed the funny little Tremont House and the funnier Tremont Theatre. I passed the Deblois House, where our Horticultural Hall is now. When I came to the little Park Street Church and the little Common, I was convinced I was crazy. I walked sadly back to the little Tremont House, went up the low steps, made a row at the door, and was admitted by a sleepy Buraet, who looked like the half-Chinaman that he was. A little pantomime and a little Russia-in-Asia gave me a good bed any way; and I went to sleep, and slept off twelve hours more of toothache, cannabis, laudanum, and nostrum.

When I crawled down to breakfast the host came, attentive, as Chinese as his waiter; but he talked a little German. So did I. Two littles in language may not fit very closely, however, and our "littles" were not the same "littles," and to my joy he soon sent for an interpreter; for he wanted to be attentive. And in fifteen minutes an indubitable Yankee, gray-haired and smiling, appeared, who was, as it proved, no other than Seth, of whom I have been telling you. He had lived in this place, he said, for nigh thirty years. "There wa' n't nothin' when I came," said he; "but Mr. Cradock liked to stay here, and he went into the lumber business, and we make the town as much like the old place as we can." And so he launched me on the story I have been telling you.

V. — Of Mrs. Cradock again.

For Mrs. Cradock never turned back from Sydney. Not she. She stayed till summer, making friends of high and low in her gentle, tender way. But she only waited for a chance to go farther. A little French fishing-vessel ran in for doctor's help for the skipper's wife, who was on board. Dear Mrs. Cradock helped her more than all the faculties; and when she was better, and the little schooner started for St. Malo, the Boston hack was hauled upon her deck, covered with a tarpaulin, the horses were sold, and Madam and Seth and Nimshi Jehusson, the driver, took passage eastward. Madam was deadly sea-sick; but she said, "If I could only bè sea-sick and he here," for she remembered. The French people could not understand a word they said, nor they the seamen. But they understood that Madam was a saint, and that the others were her familiars. So when they came to Brest, before running up to St. Malo, the French people told all comers that here was a Lady Abbess from a great American convent. And Madam smiled and was courteous, and Seth was voluble and unintelligible, and Nimshi said nothing. A Lady Superior came down to see them. She found Madam on deck reading her Selections from Fénélon and her Bible. The Lady Superior was not strong in literature, but she knew the word "Bible" when she saw it, and she knew the word "Fénélon" when she saw that, and she knew the little gold cross which Madam Cradock wore because Joshua gave it her on her birthday. So the Lady Superior took them with all the honors to her convent, all officers of customs bowing respectful, and here they stayed till Nimshi and Seth had bought little Bréton horses that suited them, and then they started on what the Lady Superior called, properly enough, their "*pèlerinage sainte.*" She directed them to the next holy house, and so, by good luck, they started east with a better introduction than all the savans and all the diplomatists in the world could have given them. It was very droll to hear Seth's account of how they got a passport. A "sport" he always called it, rejecting the first syllable, and it was long before I found out what he was talking about. The Lady Abbess had used some pretty stiff influence, I fancy; at all events, what with the American Consul at Brest, and the Abbess, and some ecclesiastics whom Seth designated as "them priests," something was arranged which answered the purpose for two continents.

And once, as they rode from one holy house to another, Madam Cradock took into that Boston hackney-coach, at which the village children stared so, a little waif of an orphan, for whom the sisters were caring, who was supposed to need change of air. She promised to deliver her safely to the sisters at Grand Lucé. And this little puss, with her French questions, which Mrs. Cradock could not answer, and with her relish of Mrs. Cradock's store of bonbons, and with dropping asleep hot afternoons in Mrs. Cradock's arms, and laying her head resolutely in Mrs. Cradock's lap as evening drew on, became so dear to the good lady that, when they came to Grand Lucé, she could not bear to part with her. And after they had rested there the accustomed three days, Madam begged her of the sisters that she might carry her on to Bonnelles; and at Bonnelles, she begged that she might take her on to Rampillon. Now the child was nobody's child but the good God's, so far as man knew or nun knew, and at Rampillon there was no difficulty in letting her go to Bruyères. And at Bruyères she started again with them to Weil, and so to Ellwangen and Bruck, and indeed never left Mrs. Cradock more. Whether, indeed, the nuns, any of them, understood one word of the pantomime by which Madam Cradock told the story, I think may be doubted. For she and Seth and Nimshi resolutely held, all the way through, to the language to which they were born.

I have sometimes thought that those people who know nothing of a foreign language fare better, in the parts where it is spoken, than those who think they know something. They are put through by the courtesy of the natives, while the people who insist on doing their own talking are e'en left to care for themselves. So was it, at least, with Seth, and Nimshi, and Mrs. Cradock. And by the courtesy of the nuns to the child, Mrs. Cradock became proprietor of this little Adèle, without any apprentice-papers or act of sale.

So from convent to convent they fared on. Nimshi and Seth made their sets of acquaintances among horse-people ; Mrs. Cradock and Adèle made theirs in chapels and ghostly parlors. If winters came, they made long pauses. If summer came, they drove toward sunrise. Little they knew of the politics of the countries they passed through ; but there were love and faith and hope inside the carriage, and resolution and courage outside ; and little Adèle, who sat now within and now without, became, in those long stages, mediator and interpreter between the two.

And so it happened at last, one bright September day, as they were crossing the flat at the northern end of the Baikal Sea, that Seth pointed to Nimshi a tandem team approaching them far distant; three Lapland reindeer scampering down with a heavier carriage behind them than the usual low Russian post-coach, and asked him what he would give to boot, if the post-boy offered to swap the three deer against their half-blood Tartars. Nimshi replied with some good-natured chaff; but as they approached the stranger, he admitted that the heavy-clad post-boy kept his wild team well in hand, and that they were a handier set than he would have supposed. They drew up off the road for the "little beggars" to go by; not expecting conversation, for which, indeed, they were not prepared. But the stranger was more communicative. By a wild Lapland cry he threw the little creatures back on their haunches, and in three or four words addressed the Yankee.

"Irkutsk shipko glübnik?" asked he.

And Seth said: "We speak English, if you please."

"English," cried the bearded Laplander; "who are you? I said to myself that the driving was like the driving of Nimshi Jehusson, — are you Seth Corbet?"

And by this time a woman's head was out of one window of the Eastward hack; and a man's out of one of the Western.

"Joshua!"

"Molly!"

They had met half-way.

VI. — Of Noffo Staun.

At the spot where the carriages met I found them still standing, thirty years after, as a monument of the happy rendezvous.

Just above it rises the mimic State House, below is the mimic Common, around which their travels ended; here they founded the New Boston, which was their after home.

FRIENDS' MEETING.

[MR. INGHAM visited the Friends' Meeting here described, at the Franklin Street Meeting-house, Philadelphia, on the 16th of May, 1847. His report of it was first published in "The Rosary," a collection of poems and essays, in 1848.]

I HAD been to a Friends' meeting before. But that was when I knew that a distinguished English Friend would be present. I went with a crowd of others, who went to hear him. We knew he would speak, or thought we knew it, because the streets were placarded with announcements that he would be there. And we heard him.

But this day — my only Sunday in Philadelphia for a long time — I wanted to go to a real, *usual* Friends' meeting. And therefore we had gone without especial expectation to hear any one. I wish everybody could go to meeting, always, as free from that sort of association. Here, at least, the Friends have the better of the rest of us Protestants.

It was a beautiful Sunday, — most beautiful in May; — and, in beautiful Philadelphia, "*May*" means

May. Fortunately enough, we were very early at the meeting, so that the doors were not opened; and we walked once and again, as we waited for the service, around Franklin Square; in which the fountain was flashing in the sun, the grass and foliage green and fresh and bright as fairy-land; and the crowds of people, men, women, and children, as cheerful, though as quiet, as Sunday.

And thence we walked on, and arrived a second time at the meeting-house, together with others, so that the gradual gathering showed that this was the right hour. One after another the Friends came, almost all stopping in the outer square, to bid each other good day, and to drink a little of that sparkling water from the can which is chained there. As I sit I can see the little boys drag their fathers aside to the hydrant, if they pass it without this draught; and then each sips a little, so that one would half fancy it was a preparatory rite; the boys whisper a little, while their fathers say "good day" to each other, and then all walk into the house together. Is it fancy or not, that they come in with a more natural, unaffected air than worshippers into temples of more pretension? Is there a sort of formal pace for our carpeted aisles, — as if the organ voluntary, like a military tune, demanded a movement of its own? I hardly know. Perhaps I never before looked thus at the different people scattering into church. I cannot help watching them here. Indeed, I do not care to help it. These people all come in, reverently indeed, but not more reverently than they walk the streets every day. At least, there is no sombre look on their faces.

Every one is in. No! there is one of the world's people creaking in at the end door. How can he make that noise in the midst of this silence? Why could he not come in time? But now he is seated,— and the silence— No!—there is another and another. But they sit nearer the door; I am glad of that. I hope nobody will come in now. This silence,—real silence,—while one has the perfect consciousness of communion, is refreshing, truly. I remember how utterly a lonely silence always impressed me.

This is like it, but I had rather be here than there. I sat in one of the long halls in the cave of Schoharie. C. and the rest of them had gone by, and I had only my lamp for company. They were quarter of a mile in advance,—and the world quarter of a mile above me, and nothing but thick rock between. I remember the instant when I put out my lamp, that I might be quite alone. I was never less alone;—a familiar thing to say,—often said,—but how wonderfully felt when one feels God with him, in the fearlessness, the trust, the excited enthusiasm, of one of those cave or mountain solitudes! Great God! whose lessons, whose handwriting, whose voices are like those of thine?

What is that bird? O, I *am* in the Friends' meeting! How they sing,—those cheerful little fellows on those branches which will swing to and fro across the open doorway! One, two, and then a third strikes in, to show that he can sing as well. They understand Sunday wonderfully well. Or, better, I suppose they keep Sunday every day. There is no inconsistency between their Sunday and their week-day lives. Sing away, little fellows; there are no better masses than those, to-day, all round the world! As the world turns to-day, there is sounding something better than a perpetual morning drum-beat. To-day, as land after land flashes into the sun, there is a perpetual morning prayer going up to God, from that Church which he sees as one, though we subdivide it so. And every day, as the lands turn to meet the sun, there is poured upwards *this* chorus of praise, which does not know, perhaps, that it is praise, — and yet is perpetual, — has been, ever since Adam was. An eternal hymn, of bird and beast, going up to the God of life! Great God! — how beautiful this world is! Sound and sight always delighted, never bewildered. Spring crowded with wonders, which we say we never felt before; nay, which we never did feel before. For, thank God! if one power of our nature does grow as we grow older, it is this with which we so enjoy nature. Was ever anything before so beautiful to me as the trees in Franklin Square to-day, and that rich grass, and the willows hanging over the basin, — green fountains as they seemed, — and the bright sparkles of the other fountains, — that delicate spray!

— and the beautiful rainbow, when we walked round so as to catch the right light of the sun! Certainly, I never enjoyed anything in the world more. Why, the very May-flower hunt, of last Tuesday, in Massachusetts, has made me enjoy Franklin Square to-day! Thank God that we do gain so, — that every spring, every walk, teaches Sterling's lesson of the night: —

"As night is darkening o'er,
And stars resume their tranquil day,
They show how Nature gives us more
Than all she ever takes away!"

Why, there is the dancing shadow of the branch on the wall yonder! Never, till this moment, have I noticed such easy gracefulness of movement in a shadow. It is on one side of the doorway. I do not see the branch itself.

But here, of course, I must not move. I had forgotten I was in meeting. Nobody has spoken yet. — I do not wonder. Why should they speak? . . . . How simply arranged everything here is! They carry their simplicity too far. Because they would be simple, their house need not be ugly. That window would have answered the same purpose if it had been of agreeable proportions. How the eye seeks for something graceful, — nay, must have it! That is the reason that mine, so unconsciously, has been resting on that cord with which they pull up the curtain. They forgot to stretch that tight when they arranged the room. And so, of itself, as we blasphemously say, it has fallen into that graceful curve. It is the only graceful thing inside the building on that side on which I am looking. It is the only thing which men have left alone. Curiously graceful that catenary curve in which it hangs! You cannot draw one by your eye. Not the truest artist! And yet, the world over, there is not a loose cord but is hanging in that delicately graceful way. Why, even those that they stretch the tightest — that they say are *perfectly* tight — really bend a little, a very little, and in this exquisite curve. The world over, they are obeying the same law. And because it is God's law, that form, in which they fall obedient, pleases my eye, pleases every one who looks on it. The same here, there, and everywhere; the same arrangement that makes Leverrier's planet sweep around in an orbit of such consummate grace; the same makes the trough of the waves of such sweep as it is; the cordage of a ship so beautiful; yes, and that law has been strong enough to defeat this mistake of my Friends (they are Friends, though I never saw one of them) here in their meeting-house. Strong enough for that? Why, yes. I remember, that men prove by the calculus, — by its highest flight and best, — which is, as always in the mathematics, the highest and best flight of poetry, — I remember, that by the most elaborate and recondite of calculation, they prove, that, in fact, no human power, no finite power, can strain a cord that it shall be absolutely straight; that it shall not have something of this beautiful God-ordered curve. The highest power of man, his best calculation, shows, like his weakest and his poorest, that God has ruled all things in beauty, and that all man's twitchings and struggles are powerless, when they act against this eternal Law. God of order! God of beauty! how can we thank thee for such daily miracles? How can we learn — grow — to prize as we ought life and its wonders? Strengthen us, Father! strengthen us! that our free lives, also, may accord better and more often with thy Eternal Life; — that we may labor with thy laws, with thy power, — thou in us, and we in thee!

Some one spoke! No; it was the moving door which startled me. I hope it will not swing to. I must see still that shadow of the branch flitting to and fro on the outer wall there. What a handwriting it is! So graceful! and with every new motion so different from that before! beautiful, and infinite, like all the rest! Must these inner walls around us be left so bare, and coldly white, and unornamented? Surely we should not be made more worldly if the memory of God's love came to us from the inner as well as that outer wall of this house. And could it make us more worldly to see him in the pure works of brave men, made strong by his strength, than it does to see him in the shadow there, or the leaf, or the bough?

If that dead white wall which is opposite me, beneath the little windows, and above the elders' seats, bore some representation of one of the victories of God when he works in the soul of man? Suppose it were of the very beginning of this gathering which is here to-day? The first day that William Penn, a gentlemanly, courtly, spirited young fellow, went with his college companions to hear Thomas Loe, the Quaker itinerant, as they called him, preach in Oxford, — what a day that was for this Pennsylvania, for us here, nay, for the whole world! I can figure them out for myself on the large blank wall, — Loe preaching that which he remembered these college sprigs of nobility and gentility needed. Plainly dressed he, but nobly moved; feeling that the spirit is on him. I can see his face as it would lighten up, as he spoke to that crowd around him of wondering citizens, growing more and more cordial to him, and to that group of students, who have gone there to laugh, to ridicule, or, in one word, to "see fun." Why, on the picture, even their faces should be growing grave, beneath his solemn spirited, gospel eloquence! And what ought to be the face of Penn? At this moment he is receiving the influence which shall last through his life, — the preacher is fanning into a flame the sparks which have always been in his heart; and those words, that spirit of that man, are mastering him; are compelling him to listen; are compelling him to obey; and, from this moment forward, he will be the true-hearted, God-seeking friend of man! It is a moment to study expression. As he leans on John Locke's shoulder there, — as he listens with more ardor and more, — his face must lighten with the most intense light. It is fervent devotion, resting on grave thought. Penn, ardent and moved, resting on Locke, — thoughtful, but perhaps no less touched in his own way. What a pair these, to stand among these flaunting laughers, gay dressed and half listless, and those sober, undemonstrative citizens, in their simpler aspect, to be listening to such a preacher as Thomas Loe! What a triumph of the true sincere spirit of Loe, if he could have only known what should come from that moment! Penn did stand by his death-bed, remember, a few years after, and the dying saint knew then that here was a young man all ready to go forward in his own work. But he could not know that that young man should be the beginning of a nation; the visible symbol to all time of the uselessness of war, whose name should be synonymous with peace; and he did not know — who does know? — how far that day's preaching rested on Locke's conscience, and made him the true man he was. Unconscious genius! how brave is this working in faith when there is no sight! — this preaching to those who seem scoffers, perhaps, — who are the regenerators of the world! It is God's work again. Faith, noble faith, — so much more noble than knowledge — like all things noble, it leads us up to Him of whom it tells us! Father! let it do more; as it brings us up to Thee, let it inspirit us also, and make us also alive, that, though we see nothing of the harvest, we may still forever sow the seed; that, though the heaviest thunders are above us, and the blackest clouds and the darkest day, we may still scatter it on the field; and do Thou, by the lightning itself, and these very storms which overwhelm us, give it life and strength; that, though long after we have left our work, it shall still spring up, and yield abundantly!

But there is no picture! The wall is only white. I wish there were! I wish George Wall, the Quaker painter, would paint one there. I should be glad to be reminded oftener of these brave men, God's true children; and, by their deeds, of their Father. What picture could we have on the other side, — the woman's side? There is a blank wall also. It matches this: there should be a woman's picture too: one of woman's Christian victories. Such resolution as they have, in all their weakness! Such wisdom as they have, coming straight from their unlogical simplicity! Such power as they have, from their mere quiet truth, unconcealing, unconcealed! Ready, if they think there is need, — ready as the stoutest man, — to go even to the scourge or to the stake! Poor Jane Darc! Her only fault that she loved her country and her countrymen too well, and acted out her love in the crude language her time had; in that brutal outer fighting, the only way she knew of; as brave as the bravest of them; and stronger and more hopeful than the strongest of them, because she trusted in the Eternal Truth, in Eternal Righteousness, — trusted in God! You almost say that it never happened in fact! — that the picture of her would be only a type of what is always true. Faith like hers should be mounted on the charger of victory; yes, and it should be clothed with that helmet and breastplate, that heavenly armor, of which Paul tells. How natural to represent that Spirit in her form, — and around her the group of soldiers, wondering, fearing —

I forget myself! Jane of Orleans must not be in a Friends' meeting-house. Some one else must be painted on that panel. Mrs. Fry, perhaps, in a prison? Or some Quaker mother here among the Indians? Or some of the sufferers among the English, or New English? — the martyrdom of a later saint? No, not that; we will not preserve the memory of the persecutions. That shall die, as other old forms die, and old languages, when men have done with them. But the true spirit of all these, — that must be preserved. That spirit of perpetual confidence, — unshrinking faith in the secret conscience call of God, — that is immortal. The picture shall show that! It was in all of them, just as it was in the young, steel-clad French maiden. I can see her, I can almost hear her, with its supernatural eloquence, exciting starved and fearful soldiers. Or, in that little minute, when men's awe of death leaves even a convict wholly free, just before he dies, to speak all he will, — I can see her, as she stands chained to the stake; her face alive with more than earthly life; her eyes flashing with heavenly fire, and yet soft with heavenly love, as she speaks her last words to those dull persecutors!

But I forget myself again. A warrior, a woman of the sword, must not be in a Friends' meeting-house! No. But who shall be? Not Judith, — not Deborah, — not the Queen of Sheba. She was coldly intellectual; no! it shall be a Christian woman, who gives life to the scene with Christian faith, with Christian endurance, and Christian power. It shall be one of the martyrs among women who have consecrated the church which has so often made saints of them; who have carried forward, so often and so far, the gospel, which spoke to the first of them so truly, though they were in anguish, in a woman's tears, — and suffering with all a woman's sympathy, when he looked down upon them from the cross. They also have been apostles, though unnamed; they also have been preachers, whether they spoke aloud or not; they also have been Christian soldiers, whether they have girt on armor or not. The heroine of France, in rallying the soldiers, is only an outward exhibition of what so many of them have been before. We see her do — what so many of them have done, unseen — lead on thousands by the word of faith. We hear her say — what so many of them have said, unheard — that the call of God makes the weakest powerful. We see her suffer, — as so many have suffered, unheralded, — a true, brave woman ; — true to the last, and brave in the midst of torture.

I *will* think of Jane Darc! I will draw out her picture there on the wall, as I look at it. This is not a vague wandering of thought that brings me back to her ; and she and her sufferings are not unfit associates of the place. For one does not think of the fighting ; it is not of that sad bloodshed that I am reminded. Their memory has gone ; it is lost to me as is the old dialect in which she spoke ; or the fashion, indeed, of any of the outward dresses which she wore ; of any of the outward seemings through which her spirit spoke. God be praised for that! God be praised that the bitter form of fighting and bloodshed does seem old and gone! that these Friends here have helped to push it away, — to bury it in rust! But the spirit which spoke through it — the trust in God, the consciousness of God's inner voice, which enlivened it — will never die. That is immortal! And it is the one Spirit which enlivened all those other martyrs. God be praised for that! God indeed be praised! I thank thee, Father, for this also, — that in all the past which is gone, as in this present, thou art unchanging, unchanged; that as time passes by, God's spirit does not pass by, but is Right Eternal, Truth Immortal! Do thou, the Eternal God, — the unchangeable I Am, — enter my heart with all the power of thy presence, that in me the right and the truth may not falter, may not yield; make me *to be* thine forever!

Hark! some one speaks. It is one of the elders beneath the narrow windows. "They who wait upon the Lord shall renew their strength. They who wait upon the Lord shall renew their strength. I am glad, my friends, that there is still a company of those who are willing to wait upon the Lord, although in silence, knowing that he will renew their strength. I am glad, that in this time, when there are so many voices, and so many men who oppose him and his people, there is still a company of those who are willing to meet, as their fathers did, and wait for the influence of his Spirit. When all philosophy tells us that even of dead matter there is no end, — that its atoms separate but to unite in other forms, and never perish, — how can it be that the spirit, which gives all its life to matter, shall end, or be of no worth or of no account? And how can we forget to seek the Eternal Spirit; the Spirit of spirits? — to wait for it in prayer, and in communion, that it may inspirit our lives?"

How can we, indeed? — how can we? I hope he will say nothing more! No! he has sat down. How can we go through the world as if it were a dead world, a giant corpse, and talk of dead philosophies as if we were dissecting it, and studying the anatomy of it as it would be if there were no Spirit to give order and law? How can we do this, and talk of this, and think of this forever? And that God is so near us, speaking to us, if we will only hear; calling us, if we will only listen; his spirit knocking, if we will only receive it; every pulse, every fibre of this corpse, as I called it, alive; and alive because it is his will! God of life! now, at least, I do remember thee; now, at least, I do seek thee! O, seek me, Father, when I am dead, or sleeping! seek me in the living voices of truth and love, that I may wake again, and live again, in Christ's life, — in thy life, — in the life which thy goodness has made eternal!

There is a woman speaking! "They that wait upon the Lord *shall* renew their strength; they *shall* mount up with wings of eagles; they *shall* run and not be weary; they *shall* walk, and not faint." She says nothing more. But what an answer is here to prayer! Before it is offered, before it has conceived itself, God has promised thus to hear it and to bless it. God finds us thus the moment that we seek him. He is with us when we try to be with him.

O God! direct my wandering thought
  To centre upon Thee;
Direct my eyes to look through aught,
  Till Thee, their God, they see!

In every leaf of every tree,
  In all the world around,
My wandering eye has looked, — till Thee,
  The God of love, it found.

In every work where labors man,
  With true or selfish mood,
My wandering thought finds God sustain,
  And crown each toil for good;
My wandering thought finds all in vain
  The toil which turns from God.

Praise God, for wandering eyes his world of love to see!
Praise God, for thought which wanders always free!
Praise God, for faith which bends a willing knee,
Draws me to Him, the while He smiles on me.

Ah! One of the elders is standing up! See! he shakes hands with another. And there, those others are shaking hands. They are beginning to go away. The meeting is done.

DID HE TAKE THE PRINCE TO RIDE?

[After Mr. Ingham first retired from naval service, — and after his first rebuff in the Sandemanian ministry, — having established his residence in the minister's lot, No. 9, in the 3d range in Maine, — he then assumed a position of modest usefulness in the city of Boston, which compelled him and Mrs. Ingham to reside here for some years. To this period of his life belongs the year 1860, and Mr. Haliburton's adventure which is here recorded. My impression is that Mr. Haliburton was at that time connected with the Methuselah and Admetus Life Company.

The narrative was first published in the Atlantic Monthly for May, 1868.]

Did he take the Prince to ride? How should I know? The Prince never told me anything about it. I never saw the Prince but twice, — once was out by the old Francis House, in Brookline, where I rode into a pasture that 'Zyness might pass by with his suite, — and once was as he came in from Cambridge on the old Concord Turnpike, when I and my wife sat in the buggy and joined in general enthusiasm. There is a photograph of him in the tray there; but he never told me, nor did the photograph, whether Haliburton took him to ride. Don't ask me.

Haliburton does not know himself. He thought he took him to ride; and he came to our house and told me and my wife he had done so. But when he read the "Advertiser" the next day, the "Advertiser" said the Prince went with the City Government to see the House of Correction, the Insane Hospital, the Mount Hope Cemetery, or some of the other cheerful entertainments which are specially provided for distinguished persons. So Haliburton was a little dashed, thought perhaps he had been sold; and to this hour when we want to stir him up a little, we ask him, "Did he take the Prince to ride?"

This is the story: —

The afternoon of the day when his Royal Highness, Albert Edward, Prince of Wales, Duke of Saxony, Prince of Saxe-Coburg and Gotha, Grand Steward of Scotland, Duke of Cornwall and Rothsay, Count of Chester, Count of Carrick and Dublin, Baron Renfrew, Lord of the Isles, visited the University at Cambridge in New England, left his autograph in the Library, and inspected a room or two in Holworthy, — of the day when, as above, I backed the buggy into a corner for 'Zyness to pass, and attempted vainly to entice the burghers of Cambridgeport into a unanimous cheer, — this day, I say, he visited, with a few friends, the beautiful Library of the Historical Society in Tremont Street; the most attractive public book-room, let me say, in New England, and therefore the best public lion in Boston. There he saw the Dowse

Library, the pen that signed the Articles of Confederation, the Manchester velvet small-clothes of Franklin, and the curious swords from Prescott's library. These are the swords of the English Captain Linzee, who first opened fire on Bunker Hill, and of the Yankee Colonel Prescott, who had thrown up its fortification. Prescott's grandson, the historian, married Linzee's granddaughter; and so, in that household, the two swords worn that day by the two chiefs came lovingly together. Blessed be the omen! These curiosities, and others, the Prince saw; he expressed a kind interest in them; asked for an autograph of Washington for his brother Alfred, which some gentleman gave him, and went away.

Haliburton happened to be there, — or says he was there, — and it is there that the story begins. How Haliburton came to be there I am sure I do not know. He is not a member of the society, and probably never will be. We tell him he smuggled himself in from the street, and was mistaken by his hosts for one of the delegation from Prince Edward's Island. But being there, — if he were there, — and talking with one of those thoroughly intelligent gentlemen of the Prince's suite, who have left behind them such pleasant memories here, — Haliburton said that it was a pity the Prince should see only those things in which America could not, from the nature of the case, rival other countries, and in which, of course, she had least that was individual or of special interest. "History," said

Haliburton, must, of course, "be the element of least interest of all in the country whose past is the shortest of any." And so he went on to say, that, almost from the nature of the case, the Prince, like all other travellers, was seeing just those things in which nations most resemble each other, and was seeing least of the peculiarities of domestic life which make nations what they are, and different from each other.

This gentleman, whose name Haliburton never told me, if he knew, — and if he had I would not tell you, — said this was true enough; but he did not see how the matter could be mended. Only the Caliph Alraschid could get into the private life of his people; and it might be doubted whether the Vizier Jaffir had not sold the Caliph in each of the celebrated visits of inspection. As Haliburton had said, private life, because it was private, could not be seen in a public visit of ceremony.

As to this, Haliburton said, where there was a will there was a way. If the Prince, or any gentleman of his suite, wanted to see private life in Boston, almost any man of sense in Boston could show it to him. Whether that was what the *cortége* was here for Haliburton did not know. He had sometimes doubted whether princes saw much of domestic life outside of palaces at home, — or if they wanted to.

His friend laughed, and said he could not say. But he did think that, abroad, a traveller, as keen as his Royal Highness, wanted to see what there was; and he ventured to say that he would be very much obliged to any American gentleman who could put him in the way of seeing how people lived. And so their talk ran on, rather more into detail; and it ended in Haliburton's promising to call in his buggy at the side-door of the Revere House at ten o'clock the next day, and see if there was anybody who cared to drive round Boston with him. Not a word was said to the Prince, or the Duke of Newcastle, nor to General Bruce. The visit to the Library was ended, and they all went home.

The next morning Haliburton had Peg harnessed, and, at the stroke of ten, drove up at the Bulfinch Street door. Then, he says, as sure as Peg is a living horse, at the moment, before he had time to get out of the carriage, the door of the hotel opened, and a slight young man, of fresh, ruddy face, with a very shiny hat, looking as if it had been bought that morning, stepped quickly down, looked up brightly in his face, asked if he were Mr. Haliburton, and stepped in, — Haliburton making room for him, but actually not leaving his seat. If he had said, "Are you the Prince of Wales?" there could be no question now like that at the head of this article. But he did not say anything of the kind. Either he was dashed by the presence of royalty *in posse*, or he felt too certain of his passenger to ask, or he felt modest and thought it would be impertinent. The young gentleman took the left side of the seat. Haliburton lifted the reins. Peg started, and they drove through Bowdoin Square into Green Street, and the expedition had begun.

After a word or two of mutual civility, Haliburton asked his friend how much time he could give him. He said it was arranged that they were all to lunch together at three, and till that time he would be at Haliburton's service. Haliburton then said that he had undertaken to show him how people lived, — that, if he might direct the morning, he would try to bring into it as much variety as possible. He would show his friend how an Irish emigrant lived in the first month after his landing. He would show him how another Irish emigrant lived after he had been here five years. He would show him how a Vermont mechanic lived, who had moved here from the country, and was at work on wages. He would show him how the same man's cousin lived, who had been twenty years in active life, and had made his fortune. He would show him as well how another emigrant family lived when the father took to drink and went to the dogs. And he would show him how the staid old Bostonian lived who had Copley's pictures of his great-grandfathers hanging in the hall and the dining-room, — who had other grandfathers who sold stay-laces in Pudding Lane, — but who, for all that, descended from higher families, who came over in Winthrop's fleet. "This is a small town," said Haliburton, "and I think we can do this, though not in this order perhaps, before the time you name."

I asked Haliburton once how he called his incog. companion, — whether he said "Uryness" to him, or

"Prince," or assumed the familiar "Albert." But Haliburton said, "Do I call you 'Ingham' all the time, or 'Colonel,' or 'Parson,' or 'Fred,' or do I say 'you'? I said 'you' to the young man, whoever he was, and he said 'you' to me."

I may not get the order of their morning calls rightly. I ought to say, to Haliburton's credit, that, whenever I have heard him tell the story, he has told it at very great length, and with much detail. I hope this is not important; for what with not listening always, and with forgetting, I am not very strong on the details. But I am sure as to the general drift of the expedition.

They brought up first, say in Seneca Street, or one of the parallels, at a three-story tenement-house. Haliburton jumped out, fastened the horse by his iron weight, which he wound around the lamp-post, and which was a novelty to his companion, who inspected the simple machinery, and asked about it with interest. Haliburton bade him follow, opened the front door without knocking, and pushed up two flights of stairs. The passage was dark, and had that odious man-smell which most school-houses and prisons have, some hospitals even, and the halls of all tenement-houses which are not kept under very strict *régime*. A few of the banisters were knocked out from the balustrade.

Arrived at the third story back, Haliburton knocked. "Come in!" And they went in. A room twelve by fourteen. The floor white with sand and elbow-grease, and a six-foot-square bit of worn carpet in the middle. A Banner stove, size No. 3½, well cleaned with black lead, without fire, in front. On the mantel, a china image of St. Joseph with the infant Saviour; a canary-bird, in wax, fastened on some green leaves; a large shell from the West Indies; a kerosene lamp; three leather-covered books without titles on their backs; a paper of friction-matches; and a small flower-pot with a bit of ivy in it, — placed in the order I name, going from right to left. On the wall behind, a colored lithograph of Our Mother of the Bleeding Heart, — her bosom anatomically laid open that the heart might be seen, — and the color represented accurately by the artist; another colored lithograph of Father Mathew; and a Connecticut clock, with the fight of the Constitution and Guerriere. Between the windows another colored lithograph, "Kathleen Mavourneen"; table under it; a rocking-chair; four wooden chairs; another table between the doors; small bedstead in one corner. All this I can describe so accurately because I was often there, and recollect the room as well as this I am in.

Mrs. Rooney rises, as they enter, from a settee on rockers, across two thirds of the front of which is a rail, — convenient cradle and rocking-chair joined, — puts by Rooney *fils* into the cradle part, and steps forward cheerfully, neat as wax, trig and bright.

"How d' ye do, Mrs. Rooney?"

"Very well, Mr. Haliburton; and welcome to you. Won't you gentlemen take seats?"

"This is my friend Mr. Edward; Mrs. Rooney; he is riding with me to-day."

Mrs. Rooney quickly, a little clumsily, takes the shiny hat, with Haliburton's felt, puts them both on the table, quite unconscious that she is serving the son of her sovereign (if, indeed, that day Haliburton *did* take the Prince to ride). That was the first and last that passed between her and him during the call. He kept his eyes open; beckoned to little Phil Rooney, who stood in the corner with his thumb in his mouth, but the boy would not come. Not that he knew a Saxon from a Kelt. Duke of Saxony was all one to him with Brian Boroghue; he would have come to neither. The Prince (if it was the Prince) had no pence or lozenges, or did not know enough to produce them. The conversation was all between Haliburton and Mrs. Rooney.

"Children well?"

Yes, pretty well; Phil there cutting some back teeth; Terence, a bad cold, but wanted to go to school again; and Miss Cutter had been round, and wanted him to go, and so he had gone.

"All three at school now?"

"Yes, Delia — Bridget, that is, but she likes us to call her Delia — is at school still. If I found a good place at service, I would take her away. But she is particular, and so am I. Terry, he would be glad enough to be out; but his father says, 'No; if there 's a chance for learning, the boy must have it.' And the boy, if he is my boy, is a good boy to mind; and, if he is fond of play, he does well at school too. Yonder is his last certificate, and there is the other which he had in Miss Young's room."

Delia, it seems, or Bridget, has three certificates; but her father has sent them all to Borriscarra, County Mayo, province of Connaught. Terry's are framed in mahogany, and hang above the Prince's head (if indeed it were H. R. H.).

"And how did the children stand the summer?" They had not stood it too well. Dreadfully close some of those hot nights! Delia made a visit of a week at Malden, and Terry made friends with a boy whose father sailed from Beverly for mackerel, so that he was away all the vacations; but for Mrs. Rooney and the little children it was hard. Indeed, Mrs. Rooney often thought of the bit cottage, a mile outside Borriscarra, as you go to Ballintubber, and could not but wish that her children had the chance to run outdoors that she had there. On this, H. R. H. (if it were he) showed signs of curiosity, and Haliburton, having waited in vain for him to ask the question he wanted to, put it himself.

"And would not you like to go back again, Mrs. Rooney, and show them the children, and live in the old cottage again?"

"Indade, no, your honors. Dick has just sent out fifty-five dollars for the old people, and we expect them before Christmas here. What should we do at

Borriscarra? The times are harder there than iver. Nothing has gone well with them since the Queen took the spinning-wheels away!"

(Expression of surprise on the younger man's face. But he says nothing.)

"Then why does not Dick go up country, take a bit land there and a house, and let the children play about as you and he did?" persisted the persevering Haliburton. And for an answer he was told that indeed Dick would be glad to do so, and that he had had a good deal of talk with a man they dealt with at the yard, who owned a marble-quarry near Rutland. But Bridget must be at service soon. She could not yet find a good place for her; and they were very well off as they were, and so on and so on, and so forth and so forth. Haliburton knew too much to make a fuss with his advice, seized his felt, gave his companion his stove-pipe, and they retired.

"What did she mean about the spinning-wheels?" said the Englishman, as they started again. And Haliburton told him that there was a popular superstition among five or six millions of her Majesty's subjects, to the effect that the decline of house-spinning was due to an edict of the Queen, that spinning should be done in factories rather than at firesides. And as they talked thus they came into Osborn Place, (not Osborn House, Uryness,)—and Haliburton took his friend into an up-stairs parlor of one of the pretty suites of a "model lodging-house."

It is very odd how this word "model" is changing its meaning, when you apply it to such places. Often and often it is given to some wretched huddle of crowded rooms, which never should be model or pattern for anything. I am not sure but its technical use in connection with lodging-houses is due to some model houses of Prince Albert's, this boy's own father. However this may be, the houses in Osborn Place are models which I wish the cities of the world would largely follow. Up stairs and up stairs, a good many flights, they ran, Haliburton leading. He rang at the door-bell when they reached the right landing, and pretty Caroline Freeman opened to them, and ushered them in.

"I beg your pardon," said the voluble Haliburton, "for calling before hours, but you and I are not formal, you know. My friend was shy of coming up, but I said you would not mind. Mr. Edward, Miss Freeman," — and she offered them chairs, in her pretty parlor, and they sat down. A bright view — I know not how many miles — through the vines and other greenery of her windows; a cheerful glow from the bright carpet; a good water-color by her brother, — scene in the harbor of Shanghae, or Bussora, or somewhere outlandish, no matter; and a good chromolith. But to my mind, always the prettiest ornament was Caroline herself, and I believe her visitors thought so then.

Haliburton's real object was accomplished when

they had sat long enough to give his companion a chance to see the room, but he had to make an excuse for coming at all. He was going down to Buzzard's Bay for some shooting. Could not Fred come with him? Say start on Thursday and be back Tuesday?

Caroline would ask Fred, but doubted. Wished Fred would go, for Fred was low-spirited and blue. He had been disappointed about the opening at Naguadavick; they had determined, after all, not to start their steam-mill this winter. Fred had had full promise of the charge of the engine-room there, as Haliburton knew; but this threw him out again, — and times were dull everywhere, and he said he was fated to get nothing. He had been talking with the chief at the navy-yard, who was an old friend of his; but there was no chance there, and no chance that there would be a chance. She would rather Fred should go to sea again; he was always better at sea.

"And how is your mother?" — at which moment that lady appeared.

I never can describe people, but you all of you know just one nice person, who, at forty, looks for sweetness as if she were seventeen, and for serenity as if she were seventy. Well, Mrs. Freeman, Caroline's mother, is the one I know. She would not own she was ill, though she was; she said she was a great deal better than she had been, and would be a great deal better the next day, — for all which it was clear enough that both of them were delicate. A pity they should have to rough it through here in this *vilain* winter. But she parried all talk about herself, and in a moment was making "Mr. Edward" talk; had he been travelling far? was it his first visit West? was he fond of sporting? were the Western grouse like the Scotch? and, before he knew it, the young Englishman was talking rapidly; Haliburton chuckling, and withdrawing with Caroline into an aside, showing her a memorandum he had in his note-book. This done, the other two were not done. So Haliburton and she kept on; — her maiden article in "Merry's Museum"; Ingham's (that 's my) sermon of Sunday at the chapel; the Philharmonic programme for the winter; Lucy Coleman's new piano, which Lucy said should be at Caroline's use for the winter while Lucy was in Cuba, and so on, and so on. At last Haliburton looked at his watch, and told the young gentleman they must go; and so tore him away while he was telling how they ran the rapids at the mouth of the Ottawa.

"Those are nice people," said he; "what class of society are they of?"

"'Umph," mused Haliburton aloud. "Classes do not divide themselves quite so distinctly with us as with you. That is the class of widows in delicate health; who live in an upper story of a model lodging-house, supported by the earnings of a son and daughter, neither of whom is of age. That girl will to-night be at an evening music party of fifty of the nicest people in Boston, and to-morrow morning she will be in the basement of the first house we went to, teaching her scales on the piano to the daughter of a well-to-do Irish stone-mason, who wants his girl to learn to play, at fifty cents a lesson. I never thought," added Haliburton, laughing, "that Caroline Freeman would make a good duchess; she has not weight of guns enough, *aplomb*, or self-assertion for a duchess; but, say for a viscountess, she would do nicely, or for a schoolmistress in Dubuque, Iowa. I am not sure which class in society she belongs to."

They both laughed, and Haliburton, following his hand, rather than the plan which he had laid out in the morning, crossed the town, passing the Common, and called on Lucy Coleman, to see what she could tell him about Mrs. Freeman's cough. It is a way Haliburton has of doing one thing at once, — he calls it making one hand wash another; he says he learned it from John Jacob Astor, who told him, the only time Haliburton ever saw him on business (Haliburton's father had a lot of otter-skins), that he should like to settle the matter there and then, that he never might have to think of it again, or see Haliburton himself more. So, I say, Haliburton, forgetting his plan, drove through Charles Street, between the Public Garden and the Common, and called on Lucy Coleman.

"I had not meant to come here," said he to the Prince (if it w. t. P.), as they left the carriage, "but it is as well as if we had gone to see the Copleys. If there are no Copleys here, — and by the way there are, — there are others as good, — Allstons and Champneys."

"You forget that I do not know what Copleys and Allstons and Champneys are. What are they? — people, or things to eat, or fashions of clothes?"

"Oh! I forgot; they are pictures. Copley was a bright boy here, — went to the Latin School, where you were Tuesday, and painted first-rate portraits a hundred years ago; then went to England, and died there twenty years before you were born; left a son you have seen, your old Chancellor, Lord Lyndhurst. Allston was a Carolinian, who lived and died with us, painted such landscapes, and such lovely faces! Look there! — " and his friend was by this time absorbed in the exquisite dream of beauty before him.

Miss Lucy came running down stairs. "I saw your carriage, and I would not keep you waiting," she said, and then paused, seeing the stranger, welcomed him, and made no further apology. It was still long before calling-hours, but she had bravely run down in her exquisite morning cashmere. Haliburton was, I think, rather glad that he had been moved to come round here. He had meant fairly to show the Prince what should make a fair average of life, and to put no best foot foremost. He knew, however, that he had lapsed from grace in going up to the Freemans' rooms, — that there were ten people in Osborn Place, not near so pretty as Caroline, where he had an equal right to call. But here he had called fairly. And if the parlors were perfectly furnished and hung, if the half-dozen pictures, all on the line of the eye, were of the choicest, yes, in the world; if the little low book-cases were tempting in what they revealed, and tempting in what they concealed; if the two or three pamphlets and the three or four books that lay loose were of just the latest freshness, and most appetizing qualities; if the cannel coal had just crusted over so that the room was not a bit heated by it, yet so that one dig from the steel poker would wake it to a frenzy of light and life, — was this any fault of his. Had he chosen to come here? or was there not an irresistible destiny which compelled him? Once more he intimated that he brought his friend up, rather than leave him in the carriage; the young man sank in an easy-chair, with a volume of Darley's prints, and Haliburton and Miss Lucy fell to talk about the Freemans.

Had he heard? Did she know? Yes, he knew this, and she knew that, and both knew this and that, and she had not heard thus, and he did not understand the other, and so on. What had made Haliburton forget the Prince's ride was his uneasiness about Caroline's flushed face, — which had made her look so pretty, by the way, — and his determination to see whether something could not be done about that and her mother's cough. So, in that wild, impulsive way of his, instead of writing a note to Lucy Coleman, he had slammed right over there, before she had even got her morning-dress off, to consult with her.

But nothing could be done about it. Lucy had been more eager than he; Lucy had been begging Caroline to go with her to Charleston, and so to Cuba, and then to Santa Lucia and St. Thomas. Mr. Coleman himself had been interested about it, — knew how much pleasure it would give Lucy, and had been down to call on Mrs. Freeman. But they said they could not break up their establishment. Fred must not be left adrift so little while after he had come home; Fred had himself tried to persuade them, but they would not think of it. As to the cough, Mrs. Freeman was sure it would be better the next week; and as for the flush, Caroline would not have it talked of at all. So Haliburton had had his ride for his pains. "I wish you could manage it," said the bright young lady, "for I shall lose my journey if something does not come to pass. Papa is discouraged already, and would give it all up in two seconds, if anything else happened amiss. And yet he will not go unless there is somebody I like who will go with me. As if I could not take care of myself! True enough, I dread the idea," she said, rather sadly, and Haliburton knew she was thinking of her last journey.

And this was all their *tête-à-tête*. She laughed at him because he never called unless he had an axe to grind, said he had not heard her new piano, and never came to her little musical parties. He said he never was asked; and she said he never came when he was, but had a general invitation. He said there was no time like the present, and went to the piano, and opened it. She readily enough consented to play, asked what she should play, and they both turned to their silent companion, who had put down his "Margaret," and crossed the room.

Then it is that the first bit of evidence as to the question you have asked me comes into the story. For when the young man was asked what Miss Lucy should play, he stammered and blushed, and ha-haed, and bothered generally, and finally screwed himself up to saying that there were some very nice waltzes by Strauss.

Lucy Coleman did n't even let her eyes twinkle. She took care not to look at Haliburton, said "O yes," very sweetly, and blazed away, — two, three, four good brilliant Strauss waltzes. Then the gentlemen thanked her, she rewarded Haliburton by a little scrap of Mozart; he said they must not stay, and tore himself and his young friend away. But when, afterwards, she was told that this young man was the Prince, she said "No." And to this moment, red-hot pincers would not persuade her that the Prince of Wales, the son of Prince Albert, would ask her to play one of Strauss's waltzes. It is in vain that we tell her of the glories of Strauss's own orchestra; it is in vain that we dwell on a young boy's early enthusiasm for the Coldstream Guards and their band; in vain that we hint at a fondness for dancing. "Never," she cries; "the blood-royal never asked me for Strauss." I even sent her a stray programme of a concert given at Windsor, when Saxe-Meiningen came on a visit, in which was a selection of these waltzes played for his delectation. She will not be persuaded, nor will my wife, nor will Annie. So much for the high classical!

They went away from Lucy's, crossed the town again, where was a corduroy road two hundred years ago, and, by way of contrast, they went into one of those man-sties that there used to be in Orange Lane, running back to the railroad. Thank God, that nuisance is abated now! there are wild beasts hard by, but no wild men there; and I will not tell you what they saw. John Gough would tell such a story better than I should. The man had not been three weeks over from Ireland. He had been drinking the spirits of the new country as he drank the beer of the old, and was wallowing there on the pile of straw on one of those dark back-bins, without a window, dead asleep, if you call that sort of thing "sleep," after last night's "spree." And his wife was in the dirty ten-foot room front, that did have one window, offered her only chair to the son of her Queen (if it were he), and apologized that it had no back, cuffed the child with the dirtiest face, and laid the baby on the straw by its father, that she might render the hospitalities that the position permitted. Ask Mr. Gough for the detail.

Haliburton forgot what sent him there, as he saw the wretchedness. She looked wholly broken down; and he, of course, had no word of reproach for her. But she said she could not keep things nicer, and nobody who saw him would let him have any better room, — how could she leave the children? and what could she do, indeed, but die? What indeed? I do not think Haliburton knew. The younger man wanted to give her money, but Haliburton would not let him. "If you like," said he, "we will send them some meal and potatoes; but money is the most dangerous of drugs, as it is the cheapest, for the relief of suffering. I had no idea things would be so bad, or I should not have brought you here. This place, you see, is a little neater, and this and this quite nice in comparison," as they passed one and another of the open doors of that old rookery.

"Now let us get a little air at the least"; and they drove across the Dover Street Bridge, and came out to my house. I was then living in D Street, over in South Boston. Unfortunately, I was out, and so was Polly. We, as I have said, had seen the Prince in Cambridgeport; so, if we had been in, we could have answered the question. But I was at a meeting of the Board for providing Occupation for the Higher Classes (*mem.* "Boards are made of wood, — they are long and narrow"); and Polly was — I know not where. Haliburton ran in without ringing, upset Agnes and Bertha, found we were out, opened the cake-box himself, and got out doughnuts, and gave an orange also to his companion, besides taking one for himself. Thus refreshed, they started again, — this time, I believe, to hunt up his Vermont mechanic who had lived here twenty years. But, just as they left the house, Wingate Paine came running by; and Haliburton stopped him, and introduced him to Mr. Edward. Mr. Edward was studying tenement-houses, he said. Could Paine take him in the buggy over to Washington Village, and show him how some of their operatives lived there?

Certainly, Wingate could and would, if Mr. Edward would stop a moment at the works. He was already late with his errand there, — but the horse and buggy would correct all that. So they both got into the carriage. Haliburton told Paine to keep it as long as he chose, and betook himself to playing with Agnes and Bertha, and cutting pussy-cats out of paper for Clara and the babies. The clock struck one as these delights engrossed him, — struck two, indeed, before the fifty-second cat had been added to the long procession, and before the rattle of wheels announced the young men's return.

"We took you at your word," said Paine. "I have shown your friend the tenement-houses, and half the rest of the town." Haliburton said he was satisfied, if they were, — that there was still full time to meet the latter end of their appointment. Paine bade good by, and Haliburton resumed the reins. His companion told him that, when they came to the iron-works, he had been interested by the processes he saw there, which were, strange to say, new to him; that Mr. Paine offered at once to show him the varieties of South Boston iron-work. They had been in at Alger's to see cannon cast; they had seen wire drawn at another mill, and, I believe, rails. "Oddly enough," he said, — "though the world is very small, after all, — we met Mr. Coleman at their first establishment, the father of your pretty friend. I think, indeed, Mr. Paine said he was President of their Company." Haliburton said "Yes." "He talked to Mr. Paine about his proposed journey," said the other; "he seemed a little annoyed at the delay; said to Mr. Paine that, if he could get off, he should want to place him in the counting-room in town, and send some one else out to the works; hoped he would like that, for he should be much more at ease if the correspondence were in Paine's hands. Then he was very civil to me, though he did not know me from Adam. He took us across to the Cronstadt Works, and was at the pains to stop one of the rollers for me, that I might see how the power was applied. So I took my first apprenticeship in iron-work. George! it does one good to see those brave fellows handle those hot blooms, push them up so relentlessly to the rolls, and compel the rolls to bite them, whether they will or no! I should have got mad with the machines, but the men seemed to have gained the imperturbability of the great engine itself. And then, when the bloom is once between the rolls, there is nothing more for it but to succumb.

'Fine by degrees and beautifully less,'

with a vengeance; for, before you are done with it, you see the great stupid block transformed into a spinning, spitfire serpent, hundreds of yards long, writhing all over the floor."

This was the longest speech which anything drew from this young gentleman. After following through the various iron-works, giving up Loring's iron ship-yard for lack of time, they had gone to the new tenement-houses, and so back to D Street. As Haliburton crossed the bridge again, his friend reminded him of the meal and potatoes; they stopped at a shop, and ordered these to be delivered to Michael Fogarty, and drove on, with Haliburton's last call in view, when —

Ge-thump; ge-thump again; once more ge-thump; a sharp strain on the reins, pulling Haliburton over the dasher; dasher, Haliburton, and friend then all rapidly descend into the street, — horse, reins, front-axle, and wheels depart at the rate of 5.20, hind wheels, gentlemen, and buggy-top picking themselves up as they could. There had been something amiss in the paving, the king-bolt had parted, and the buggy had broken in two.

"What I thought of," said Haliburton, "was this,

What is the name of this man's oldest brother? For, if I have broken his neck, I have broken the succession. But I had not broken his neck at all. He was up on the other side as soon as I was. His nose was bleeding, but he was laughing. I made a thousand apologies, led him out of the crowd upon the sidewalk, terrified lest we should be recognized; saw to my joy that we were on Adoniram Newton's doorstep; rang, and after waiting two or three minutes we were let in."

Curious feature that of half the doorsteps in New England! South of Mason and Dixon's line, the instinct of curiosity sends the black servant to the door in two seconds, when the bell rings, to know what has turned up. But with us, Bridget, hard worked, not looking very trig, loiters and loiters, — hopes, indeed, that something may turn up. Carter has a clever little sketch-book, of street incidents, which he has drawn while waiting on doorsteps. He keeps it in his ticket pocket outside. Indeed, it was always said that Wetherell and his wife made each other's acquaintance, and were engaged, on Boston doorsteps. Some malicious gossip had started the story that they were engaged, when they did not know each other by sight. They went round to contradict it. The town was smaller than it is now; and they spent so much time on different doorsteps, that, before the report was contradicted, he had offered himself to her, and it was true!

At last Haliburton and friend got into the hall at

Adoniram's. Then, with great difficulty, Bridget got the parlor door *unlocked!* It was dark, and had the smell of seven years before on it, as if it had not been opened since Thanksgiving of 1852. Haliburton bade Bridget call her mistress, pulled up the green shades and the other shades with unnecessary indignation, thrust open one set of blinds, and revealed a magnificent velvet carpet of very positive colors, and very large figures. Upon the walls, covering their part of the gilded paper-hangings, were two immense mirrors and four prints, selected for their size, so that they might conceal as much as possible. Two china dancing-girls and an Odd Fellows' Manual made up the ornament of the room. Here again they soon completed their survey of the ornaments; Haliburton stood at the window watching the policemen who watched the wreck of his carriage, chafing as he waited for Mrs. Adoniram; his companion's handkerchief grew redder and redder, and at last she came, radiant in wine-colored moire-antique, gold chain, eye-glass tucked in her belt, showy cap, and so on.

Haliburton made "short explanations," as Neptune said on an occasion not dissimilar. He begged for a basin of water; and so at the very moment when Mrs. Newton was internally fretting because the school-committee men of their ward had refused her a ticket to the Music Hall, so that she could not hear the thousand children sing "God save the Queen" to the Prince, — at that moment, I say, had she but known it, her hands were occupied in unbuttoning his wristbands for him, and in holding the towel, as he chilled the wounded blood-vessels, and stopped the blood of Egbert as, after a thousand years, it dropped from his nose; for that this was the blood of Egbert is certain, whether this were the Prince or no! "Whoever you are, reader," says Dr. Palfrey, wisely, "whose eye lights upon these lines, if you be of Anglo-Saxon lineage, it is certain that the blood of King Egbert runs in your veins! It is as certain that it meets there with the blood of Egbert's meanest thrall!" Haliburton saw the bathing process well started, and then rushed out to find officer No. 67 leading back Peg after her run, the wheels still whole. The box under the seat furnished a new king-bolt, a New Worcester wrench fitted the new nut, and by the time the Egbert blood was stopped, and the hands were washed, the renovated carriage was at the door. I would give sixpence to know what Mr. Edward had said to Mrs. Adoniram meanwhile, and what she had said to him. Whether he found out how people live in those desolate bowling-alley parlors, or whether he found that they never live there, I do not know. I do not believe that centre-table was ever put to half such useful service before.

"We must give up our last calls," said Haliburton, after he had apologized once more for the accident, and holding Peg in hand a little more carefully; "I had other varieties of home to show you."

"Of course," replied the other, "no two homes are alike, — but, really, what we have seen has interested me immensely. I was thinking," he added in a moment, "that the young man we did not see holds the key of the position."

Haliburton did not understand, and had the sense to say so.

"Why, don't you see, if this young Mr. Freeman — Fred, his sister called him — should get a position at sea again, his mother would go to Rehoboth to her sister's, and Miss Caroline could join the Cuba party."

"Of course," said Haliburton.

"If Miss Caroline would say she would go, that impetuous Mr. Coleman and your bright Miss Lucy would sail next week for Charleston."

"I know they would," said Haliburton.

"In that event, Mr. Paine, here, would be promoted into the city counting-room, and his salary would be raised. He would be married, I know ; for, though he said no word of it, I could see that he is engaged to somebody."

"It is to Sybil Throop, over in the Arbella School," said Haliburton.

"I think," continued the other, "that such a couple as that, moving into the Freeman's suite of rooms, would like to take Delia Rooney to service, and, if it were my business, I should advise Mrs. Rooney to place her there."

Haliburton stared aghast at these words of wisdom from lips so young.

"Then the Rooneys could go up to the stone-quarry, as she evidently wanted to; and I should think you might arrange that that drunken beast and his wife might be transferred from their den one peg up to the other's better quarters. If I have read to-day's lesson well, it is the lesson of keeping open the lines of promotion. That, Mr. Haliburton, is the duty of a free country!"

And here they came to the private entrance of the Revere again. Haliburton had no moment to answer this address, or even to comment on it. His companion asked him to come in. He declined, and the clock struck three.

Haliburton drove slowly home, meditating on the plan of promotion which the youngster had blocked out for him. He was himself not then married. He was in a Life Office, I think, and had begged a holiday for the day, borrowing Danforth's horse and carriage for this expedition, — as we all did, whenever Danforth was stationed here. He came over at once to our house, and astonished us by telling us, "How he took the Prince to ride!"

But the next morning, as I said, when we read the "Advertiser," it taught us how a guard of police had marched the Prince to the City Hall, and how he and the mayor and aldermen had spent the day in visiting penitentiaries and hospitals.

How could this be?

I do not know. Haliburton does not know. If

you write to England they will say General Bruce is dead, and that they do not know themselves. Only the Prince knows, and it is not proper to write to him. Polly and I, who had seen the real Prince, quizzed Haliburton unmercifully. We said he had spent the whole morning with a Canadian dry-goods clerk from Toronto, who had come East, for the first time, to buy an assorted stock of winter goods, and mistook Haliburton for a drummer whom he had met in the hotel reading-room the night before, — and I believe myself it was so.

But the next Tuesday Haliburton had the laugh on us. The Prince bade good by to Boston, went to Portland, and embarked. And, the evening of the day he got to Portland, Haliburton received from Portland an immense envelope, with an immense seal. Opened, it proved to contain a warrant: —

"For Mr. Frederic Freeman of Boston, appointing him first assistant engineer on her Majesty's steamer Stromboli, with instructions to report at Halifax."

Fred reported at Halifax, and is in the Queen's service to this hour.

Mrs. Freeman broke up housekeeping, and went to Rehoboth or Swansea, and Caroline went to Cuba with the Colemans.

Wingate Paine was promoted to a salary of two thousand dollars, and married Sybil Throop, and went to live in the Freemans' rooms in Osborn Place. They took Delia Rooney for their maid of all work.

The Rooneys went to Chittenden, above Rutland. He owns a marble-quarry in that region now, and gratefully sent Haliburton a present of two grave-stones last week.

Haliburton got Mr. Way to let the Rooneys' two rooms to the Fogartys; made Fogarty take the pledge in compensation. He took the place below Rooney in the stone-yard; and really, the last time I was there, they were all so decent that I called the oldest girl Delia instead of Margaret, as if she were a Rooney, forgetting that nine years had gone by.

The only person whose condition could not be improved, of all they saw that morning, was Mrs. Adoniram Newton. For she lived in a palace already.

All this I know. But, as I said, I cannot answer, when you ask me, "Did Haliburton take the Prince to ride?"

HOW MR. FRYE WOULD HAVE PREACHED IT.

[THIS sermon was first published in the "Atlantic Monthly" for February, 1867. My friend, Mr. Robert Collyer, in a public criticism of it, takes issue with Mr. Frye for saying that extra wages had worked him woe. Mr. Collyer says it has not been so with him,—that "extra money" has been a great comfort to him. This I can well believe. But he adds, that to many workmen it is a snare and delusion. Mr. Frye, many of whose failings are studied from the life, is one of them.

The sermon, which Mr. Frye heard the strange minister preach in the new church was printed in the "Christian Register" the week that Mr. Frye's was printed in the "Atlantic." It has since been reprinted by the American Unitarian Association.]

MR. FRYE and his little wife live at our house. They took a room for themselves and their little girls, with full board, last December, when the Sloanmakers went to Illinois. This is how it happened that one Sunday, after dinner, in quite an assembly of the full boarders and of the breakfast boarders also, all of whom, except Mr. Jeffries, dine with us on Sunday, Mr. Frye told how he would have preached it.

What made this more remarkable was, that the Fryes are not apt to talk about themselves, or of their past life. I think they have always been favorites at the table; and Mrs. Frye has been rather a favorite among the "lady boarders." But none of us knew much where they had been, excepting that, like most other men, he had been in the army. He brought out his uniform coat for some charades the night of the birthday party. But till Sunday week, I did not know, for one, anything about the things he told us, and I do not think any one else did.

Every one had been to church that Sunday in the morning. Mrs. Whittemore gives us breakfast on Sunday only half an hour late, and almost all of us do go to church. I believe the Wingates went out to Jamaica Plains to their mother's, but I am almost sure every one else went to church. So at dinner, naturally enough, we talked over the sermons and the services. The Webbers had found Hollis Street shut, and had gone on to Mr. Clarke's, where they had a sort of opening service, and a beautiful show of fall flowers, that some of their orphan boys had sent. Mr. Ray is rather musical. He told about a new *Te Deum* at St. Peter's. The Jerdans always go to Ashburton Place. They had heard Dr. Kirk. But it so happened that more of us than usual had been to the new church below Clinton Street. We had not found Dr. Willis there, however, but a strange minister. Some said it was Mr. Broadgood, one of the English delegates. But I knew it was not he. For he said, "If you give an inch they take an ell," and this is a sentence the English delegates cannot speak. The sexton thought it was Mr. Hapgood, from South Norridgewock. I asked Mr. Eels, one of the standing committee, and he did not know. No matter who it was. He had preached what I thought was rather above the average sermon, on "The way of transgressors is hard."

Well, we got talking about the sermon. My wife liked it better than I did. George Fifield liked it particularly, and quoted, or tried to quote, the close to the Webbers; only, as he said, he could not remember the precise language, and it depended a good deal on the manner of the delivery. Mrs. Watson confessed to being sleepy. Harry said he had sat under the gallery, and had not heard much, which is a less gallant way of making Mrs. Watson's confession. The Fryes were both at church. They sat with me in Mrs. Austin's pew. They were the only ones who said nothing about the sermon. Mrs. Frye never does say much at table. But at last the matter became quite the topic of after-dinner discussion; and I said to Frye that we had not had his opinion.

"O," said he, "it was well enough. But if I had had that text, I should not have preached it so."

"How would you have preached it?" said Harry, laughing.

Oddly enough, Frye's face evidently flushed a little;

but he only said, "Well, not so, — I should not have preached it that way."

I did not know why the talk should make him uncomfortable, but I saw it did, and so I tried to change the subject. I asked John Webber if he had seen the Evening Gazette. But Harry has no tact; and after a little more banter, in which the rest of them at that end of the table joined, he said: "Now, Mr. Frye, tell us how you would have preached it."

Mr. Frye turned pale this time. He just glanced at his wife, and then I saw she was pale too. But whatever else Frye is, he is a brave man, and he has very little back-down about him. So he took up the glove, and said, if we had a mind to sit there half an hour, he would tell how he would have preached it. But he did not believe he could in less time. Harry was delighted with anything out of the common run, and screamed, "A sermon from Mr. Frye! — a sermon from Mr. Frye! — reported expressly for this journal. No other paper has the news." Poor Mrs. Frye said she must go up and see to her baby, and she slipped away. A gentleman whom I have not named said, in rebuke of us all, that we might be better employed, and he left also. He is preparing for a Sunday paper a series of sketches of popular preachers, and it is my opinion that he spent that afternoon in writing his account of the Rev. Dr. Smith. I do not know, but I used to think he was a correspondent of the New York Observer, for I noticed once that he spoke of Jacqueline Pascal as if Jacqueline were a man's name, and as if she wrote the *Pensées*. When they were gone, Mr. Frye told us

How he should have preached it.

"I should have said," said Mr. Frye, "that when Jenny and I were married, fourteen years ago, at Milfold, there was not so good a blacksmith as I in that part of Worcester County. To be a good blacksmith in a country town requires not only strength of arm, and a reasonably correct eye, but a good deal of nerve. And when I first worked at the trade, and afterwards here, once when I worked in Hawley Street for good Deacon Safford, I got the reputation of being afraid of nothing. And I think I deserved it as far as any man does. Certainly I was not easily frightened. So it happened that I was at work for the Semple Brothers, in Milfold, at the highest journeyman's wages, and with lots of perquisites for shoeing the ugly horses. For a circle of fifteen miles round there was not a kicking brute of the Cruiser family who, in the end, was not brought to our shop for Heber Frye to shoe. I have shod horses from Worcester, who came down with all four of their shoes off because nobody dared touch them. Now in the trade all such work is well paid for. As I say, I had the highest journeyman's wages. And in any such hard case I was paid extra; and as likely as not, if they had had trouble, I got a present beside. The Semples liked the reputation their shop was getting; and so, though I was a little fast, and would be off work at working hours sometimes, they kept me; and if I had chosen to lay up money, I could have made myself — what I never did make myself — a forehanded man.

"Well, I fell in with Jenny there. And while we were engaged she took care of me, and made me stick to work, and kept me near her. I did not want any other excitement, and I did not want any other companion. She would not go where I could drink, and I would not go anywhere where she did not go. And for the six months of our engagement I was amazed to find how rich I was growing. When we were married I was able to furnish the house prettily, — as nicely as any man in Milfold, — though it was on a baby-house scale, of course. But, as Tom Hood's story says, we had six hair-cloth chairs, a dozen silver spoons, carpet on every room in the house, and everything to make us comfortable."

But here Mr. Frye stopped and said: "This is going to be a longer sermon than I supposed, and those of you who are going to meeting had better go, for I hear the Old South bell." But nobody started. Even Mrs. Whittemore held firm, only moving her chair so that Isabel might take the dirty plates. The rest of us moved up a little way, and Mr. Frye went on.

"We were married, and we lived as happily as could

be, — a great deal more happily than I deserved, and almost as happily as my wife deserves, even. But, I tell you, there is nothing truer than the saying, 'Easy earned, easy spent'; and I believe that perquisites and fees, unexpected and uncertain remunerations, are apt to be rather bad for a man. At least they make a sort of excuse for a man. I never could be made half as careful as Jenny is, or as I had better be. I spent pretty freely. I liked to spend money on her. And then I would get short; and then I would find myself hoping some half-broken, kicking beast would be brought in, which nobody could manage but me. And if one came, and I managed him, and shod him, instead of feeling proud of the victory, as I fairly might, I would feel cross if the owner did not hand me a dollar-bill extra as he went away. Then I knew this was mean; and then I would be mad with myself; and then, as I went home, I would stop at Williams's or Richards's, and get something to drink; and then, when I got home, I would scold Jenny; and after the baby came I would swear at the baby if she cried; and then Jenny would cry, and then I would swear again; and I would go out again, and meet some of the fellows at Edwards's, and would not know when I came home at night, and would be down at the shop late the next morning, and, what was worse, had not the nerve and grit which had given me the reputation I had there. Dutch courage, for practical purposes, ranks with Dutch gold-leaf or German silver.

"Well," said Frye, rather pale again, but trying to laugh a little, "perhaps, my beloved hearers, you don't know what this sort of thing is. If you don't, lucky for you. When they asked that Brahmin, Gangooly, if he believed in hell, he said he believed there were a good many little hells, as he walked through Washington Street to come to the church that evening. If he had come into my house almost any evening, he would have found one. Poor Jenny did her best. But a woman can't do much. It is not coaxing you want. You know it 's hell a great deal better than anybody can tell you. It is *will* you want. You can make good enough resolutions about it; the thing is to keep them. All this time the Semples were getting cross. At last they got trusteed for my wages. And old Semple told me he would discharge me if it ever happened again. Then one day, Tourtellot's black mare got away from me, knocked me down, and played the old Harry generally in the shop; and the other hands said it was because I did not know what I was doing, which, by the way, was a lie. It was because my hand was not steady, nor my eye. What is it we used to speak at school, about failing brand and feeble hand? It was not that night, but it was some other night when I was blue as Peter and cross as a hand-saw, that I stopped to take something on my way home. I remember now that Harry Patrick, who was always my true friend, tried to get me by the shops. He did get me by the hotel, for a strong man can do almost anything with a broken one; but after I had promised him I would go home, he was fool enough to leave me, and then I stopped somewhere else, — no matter where, — you do not know Milfold, — and when I got home, it might as well have been anybody else. I don't remember a thing. If the Prince Camaralzaman had gone there, I should now know as little what he did from my own memory. But what I did, — or rather what this hand, and arm, and leg, and the rest of the machine did, — was, to kick the baby's cradle over into the corner; to knock poor Jane down with a chair, on top of it; to put the chair through one window, and throw it out of the other; then to scream, 'Murder! fire! murder! fire!' and then to tumble on the 'hair-cloth sofa,' which was to make us so comfortable, and go into a drunken sleep.

"This was what I learned I did, the next morning, when I found myself in a justice's court; and for this the judge sent me up to Worcester to the House of Correction for three months. It was a 'first offence,' or it would have been longer. As for poor Jenny and the baby, neither of them could come and see me."

By this time Frye was done with pretending to smile. He stopped a minute, drank a little water from his tumbler, and said: "Now you would think that would cure a man. Or you would think, as the law does, that three months in the House of Correction would 'correct' him. That is because you do not know. At the last day of the three months I thought so.

There is not a man here who dreads liquor as I did that day. Harry Patrick, who, as I said, was my best friend, came to meet me when I went out. Richardson, the sheriff, as kind a man as lives, took pains to come down and see me, and said something encouraging to me. Harry had a buggy, that I need not be seen in the cars. And as we went home, I talked as well to him as any man ever talked. Jenny kissed me, and soothed me, and comforted me. The baby was afraid of me, but came to me before night; — and so, before a month was over, we had just such another scene again, and went through much the same after-scene, but that this time I went to Worcester for six months. For now it was not a first offence, you see.

"Well, not to disgust you — more than I can help," — and the poor fellow choked for the only time in the sermon, — "not to disgust you more than I can help, — this happened three times. I believe things always do in stories. This did in fact. The 'third time' you go for twelve months. And one Sunday Harry had been over to see me, and had brought me a dear kind letter from poor Jenny, who was starving, with two children now, in an attic, on what washing she could get, and vest-making, and all such humbugs, — one Sunday, I say, we were marched out to chapel, — they have a very good chapel in Worcester, — and a man preached; and he preached from this very text you talk about, 'The way of transgressors is hard.'

"What the man said I know no more than you do.

I don't think I did then. Indeed, I do not think I cared much when he began. But it is a great luxury to hear the human voice, when you have been at work on shoes for a week in a prison on our Massachusetts system, which they call the Silent System, where you have heard no word except the overseer's directions. So I sat there, well pleased enough, — even glad to hear a sort of yang-yang they had for music, — and very glad to have some good souls who had come in sing. I remember they sang Devizes, which my father used to sing. So I got into a mood of revery as this preacher went on, and was thinking of Harry, and old Deacon Safford, and father, and Jenny, and what we would call the baby, when to my surprise the minister was finished. And he ended with the text, as some men do, you know. And he said, 'The way of transgressors is hard.' And I caught Wesson's eye, — he was my turnkey, — and Wesson half laughed; and, in violation of all order, I said across the passage to Wesson, 'Damned hard! Wesson.' Mrs. Whittemore, I beg your pardon, but I did say so.

"Wesson nodded, and looked sad. If he had informed on me, I don't know where I should be now. But he looked sorry, — and I have not touched liquor since.

"I was discharged the next Wednesday. Harry came for me again, as he always did. I told him I did not want to go on in Milfold. And the good fellow agreed. He brought me and Jenny and the babies down here to Boston. I 'll tell you where we lived. We took two rooms in the third story in Genessee Street, and we began life again.

"Now any of you who are tired can go away. But this is only one head of the sermon."

Nobody went, — only Mrs. Whittemore made us leave the table, — and we moved up to the windows. Isabel took off the cloth, and put on the tea-cloth, and went off, I suppose, to the half-Sunday which was one of her "privileges." Mr. Frye went on.

"People always have an excuse. Perhaps if we had not used the cars more or less, I should not have had this head in my discourse; I know it all began with these Metropolitan tickets. I would not work at shoeing any more. I got a place in that shop where your firm are now, Mr. Webber, — the Beals were there then, — as a machinist. I had no difficulty ever with tools and iron. Pay was good enough. Work was steady, though rules were much stricter than at Milfold. But I had not got away, I have not till this hour, from that passion for extras. It is so much easier to earn an extra than to economize; and it is a great deal easier still to plan how you will earn one, — and to think that is the same thing. I was tearing a strip of Neck car-tickets in two, one day, to give Jenny half, when it occurred to me that there was a great moth of money. We spent twenty or thirty dollars a year on these tickets, and should be glad to spend twice as much. I think the fun of the thing at first, and then curiosity about it, set me on the business. I know I did not tell her. And before I had got my little hand-press started, and had succeeded in my electrotypes to my mind, and had spoiled a dozen blocks of wood in cutting my pattern, I had spent as much money five times over as all the car-tickets I ever printed would have cost me."

"You printed car-tickets?" said Mrs. Webber. "I don't understand."

"O," said poor Mr. Frye, blushing. "I forgot that all people do not look on things as a machinist does, to see how they were made. Yes, Mrs. Webber, for two or three years I printed all the Metropolitan tickets my wife and I used in riding. And eventually we rode a good deal. I satisfied such conscience as I had, by never selling any. And, as I said, I never told my wife. I tried to persuade myself it would be an economy after the plant was paid for. But it never was an economy. What was the worst part of it was, that I had the plant. I had this little handy printing-press. You did not think why I got it, Mrs. Whittemore, when I printed your cards for you. That is rather a tempting thing to have in the house. And that little Grove's battery, that I gilded your silver thimble with, Mrs. Stearns, is more of a temptation. Both together, I can tell you all, they start a man on more enterprises than are good for him.

"There is no danger," he added, rather meditatively, "of the kind people call danger, if a man will only be reasonable, and be satisfied with what is good for him. It is the haste to be rich which is dangerous in that way, to people who would never have been 'detected,' as they call it, if they were willing to be reasonable and comfortable. But it is not the detection and punishment which play the dogs with a man. It is the meanness and lying, after the first excitement of the enterprise is over. As I said, I never sold any car-tickets or stage-tickets. I just made enough for my own use and Jenny's. I did give away a lot of concert-tickets one week at the shop; and I told the men that I had them for printing them. It was the off-part of the season, and the Music Hall was not half full as it stood. I have sometimes thought the Steffanonis, or whoever it was, may have thanked me in their hearts for the audience. No. The trouble is, you see, you have to do things on the sly. I thought it would be a satisfaction to me to have five or six books out of the library at once; and I got up my own library cards, — easy enough to fill them out with the names of dead people. But I never took any comfort in those books. George Fiske went into the gift-concert business. He knew I had this battery up stairs, and I used to gild his watch-backs for him. Well, George always paid me fairly, and I never told the lies at the counter and office and in the newspapers; but I never saw a man take out his watch in the street, but I felt I was lying. I should not have stood it long, I suppose, any way; but I got tripped up at last pretty suddenly."

"You were arrested?" said little Lucas.

"Arrested, my dear fellow? No! Whose business was it to arrest me. You do not keep your police to arrest people, do you? No. The first breakdown was all along of the war. Look at that quarter-dollar."

And Mr. Frye handed us a well-worn American quarter.

"I carry that for a warning to transgressors. But I never told its story before. Now see here."

And he lighted the gas at his side, balanced the quarter on his knife-blade, held it over the jet a minute, and the two silver sides fell on the table, while a little puddle of melted solder burned the "Living Age," which he held in his hand beneath.

"There," said he, "did you ever see a worse quarter than that? Yet five minutes ago you would all have said it was worth thirty-seven cents in currency. Now, do you think, I had deposited with that battery, night after night, at last, eleven hundred and fifty-two silver eagles like that, and eleven hundred and fifty-two reverses like that, — twenty-four to a frame; and I set the frames forty-eight times. I had just adjusted my lathe for polishing the backs, — if this thing was not so hot, I could show you, — when the banks suspended in 1861. And before I could get the backing in, and the soldering done, and the milling, and the tarnish well on, — you have to tarnish them, Mrs. Whittemore, in a mixture of lapis-lazuli and aqua-regia, — why, silver coin was at a premium of ten per cent. Not a quarter was offered by anybody in the shops; and if anybody got one, it was sent somewhere where it was weighed within twenty-four hours. So all that speculation of mine flatted out. I kept two or three as a warning, like this one. But for the rest, — I had to melt down my silver to pay my little bills for turning-lathes and acids and lapis-lazuli, Mrs. Whittemore."

And this time he laughed rather more good-naturedly.

"I laugh," said he, "because this is the beginning of the end. We were living in Tyler Street when this happened; and I had just enough persistency in me to say that if I could not have one quarter, I would another. But currency is a great deal harder. No! Mrs. Webber, you can't print bank-bills on a hand-press like that I have up stairs. It is not very easy to print them at all. But I was just so mad at my failure about the silver, that I went into my largest enterprise of all. I moved away my lathe to the shop; I fitted up the closet in the attic for my chemicals; I bought that pretty Voigtlander camera I showed you the other day, Mr. Barnes; I sent out to Paris for the last edition of Barreswil's book on Photography; and that was where my skill in portraits began. I had to give up my place in the machine-shop. You can mill silver quarters at midnight; but you need sunshine to photograph currency. And then I had to open a photographic establishment, to satisfy the butcher and baker, and Jenny's friends, and the mild police of the neighborhood generally, that I had something to do, and was entitled to have black fingers. I bought a show-case full of pictures of a man in Manchester, New Hampshire, — and horrid things they were. I hung that out at the door. Sometimes, to my rage and dismay, a sitter would come. I took care to be cross as a bear, to charge high, and to send them off with wretched pictures. They never came a second time. But I had to have some come, because of the mild police as I said; and I had to take Jenny's friends for nothing. A photograph man has a good many dead-heads, as well as one or two lay-figures. All this set me back. Then the government kept changing the pattern of its quarters. Worst of all, I had to let Jenny know this time, because it changed my life so entirely. I was, you see, roped into it by accident, I did not really know how. I promised her that, as soon as I was well out of debt, and the things all paid for, I would give it all up. But we were pretty badly in debt, and I should have to get more than two thousand dollars to make things square. And I had my pride up, and went on, till I did have, though it is a poor thing to boast of, as handsome a set of sheets of that second issue, and of their reverses (they were printed for security on thin paper to be pasted together), as Mr. Chase himself ever looked upon. Now, you need not look so frightened, my dear Mrs. Webber, for that was the end!"

"How was it the end?" said she.

"Why, my dear Mrs. Webber, as the minister said this morning, 'The wicked flee when no man pursueth.' That comes into my sermon as it did into his. I had these lovely sheets, — they were lovely, though I say it, — three thousand sheets, twelve bills on a sheet, and the reverses too. I had just got up the gold sizing for the blotch round the face, when the door-bell rang. It was eight in the evening. Now we often had evening visitors; but it was arranged between Jenny and me, that, when they were all safe, Jenny should just touch a private bell that came up into the attic to my work-room. I heard the door-bell, but after the entry, no *ting* on my own.

"Who in thunder was it? I slipped down one flight, and could see and hear nothing. I bolted the double doors. I put those precious negatives into my coal-stove, and opened the lower draught. I took those precious sheets and laid them in the two full bath-tubs that stood ready. That saint, Jenny, still kept the officers down stairs. They must be searching the cellar. If I only could get three minutes more! The glass of the negatives ran out in a puddle in the ashes. So far so good. The different piles of paper softened; and, pile by pile, I rolled them and rammed them into the open waste-pipe which for months had been prepared to take them in such an exigency to the sewer. I have not, — no, Mrs. Webber, — not one of those bills to show you. In seven minutes from that happy door-bell ring the last shred of them was floating, in the condition of double-refined *papier maché*, under ground, in Tyler Street, to the sea; and I walked down stairs to see where Jenny was, and the officers.

"Officers! there were no officers. Only her nice old uncle and his wife had missed the train to Melrose, and had come to take tent with us.

"Jenny saw that I was nervous. But what could I say? O dear! we talked about early squashes and Old Colony corn, and the best flavor for farina blanc-mange; and then he and I talked politics, Governor Andrew, and the fall of Fort Henry, and what would happen to General Floyd. Till at last, after ten eternities, bed occurred to them as among the possibilities, and the dear old souls bade good night. His wife made him go. He had just got round to Jeff Davis; and his last words to me were, 'The way of transgressors is hard.'

"'Hard indeed,' said I, as I turned round to Jenny. I was too wild with rage to scold. She did not know what was the matter. I spoke as gently as if I were asking her to marry me. And she — all amazement — declared she had struck my bell!

"She had tried to. But as we tried it again, it was

clear something had happened. It had been a piece of my own bell-hanging, and a kink in the wire had given way. Jenny had sent her signal, but the signal had not come. And I had sent my currency down to the sea for the sculpins to buy bait from the flounders with!

"'Jenny,' said I, as I took down the candle from the ceiling, 'you and I will go to bed. "The way of the transgressor is hard," beyond a peradventure.'

"And as I looked at Jenny, I saw she was still too much frightened to begin to be glad. For me, I was not mad any longer. Do none of you fellows know what it is to feel that a game is played through, wholly through, and that you are glad it is done with? Well, I can tell you what you do not know, — that if that game has required one constant lie, — or, what is the same thing, a steady concealment of real purpose, — and if it has forced you to lead some little saint like my poor wife into the lie, — the relief of feeling that it is through is infinite.

"'Jenny, darling,' said I, 'don't be afraid to be glad, — don't be afraid of me. I was never so much pleased with anything in my life.'

"And she looked up — so happily! 'Heber,' said she, 'the way of the transgressor is hard'; — and we went to bed.

"That is the end, brethren and sisters, of the second head of this discourse. Let us go into the parlor."

So we went into the parlor.

Nobody said much in the parlor. But I noticed that all of them came in, which was unusual. Some of us lighted our cigars; — I did. But Frye said nothing; and I, for one, did not like to ask him to go on. But George Fifield, who, with a good deal of tenderness, has no tact, and always says the wrong thing, if there is any wrong thing to be said, blurted out, "Go ahead, Mr. Parson, we are all ready."

"Does any one want to hear the rest of such madness?" said poor Mr. Frye.

"Not if it pains you to tell us," said good Mrs. Webber. "But really, really, you were very good to tell us what you did."

And Mr. Frye went on.

"If I had been preaching the sermon in my way," said he, "I should have told you, what you could have guessed, that, having played that act through, I did not care to stay in Boston more than I liked to stay in Milfold. I had been married ten years, and I had learned two things: first, that a man can't live unless he keeps his body under; next, that he can't live and lie at the same time, — that he can't live unless he keeps his ingenuity under, and his cunning and snakiness in general. To learn the first lesson had cleaned me out completely, and I hated Milfold, where I learned it. To learn the second had cleaned me out again, and left me two thousand dollars and more in debt, — so much worse than nothing. And, very naturally, I hated Boston, where I learned that too.

"What did I do? I did what I had always done in trouble. I went to Harry Patrick, who happened to be here on business at the time. Harry had fought for me at school. He had coaxed my father for me when I was in scrapes. He took care of me when I was an apprentice. I have told you what he did for me in Milfold. He established me here. He sent his friends to see my wife. He had me chosen into his Lodge. He lent me money to buy my tools with. He introduced me at the Beals'. When I wanted my cameras and things he helped me to my credit. So of course I went to him. Well, I thought I was done with lying; so I told him just the whole story. There was a quarter's rent due the next Monday. All the quarter's bills at the shops were due, and some of them had arrears behind the beginning of the quarter. My winter's overcoat, my best clothes, indeed, of every name, were at the Pawners' Bank, where they keep your woollen clothes from the moths as well as those people on Washington Street do, but where they charge you quite as much for the preservation. Then I had borrowed, in money, twenty-five dollars here, five there, a hundred of one man, and so on, — old fellow-workmen at the machine-shop, — saying and thinking that I should be able to pay them in a few days. This was the reason, indeed, why I had hurried up the negatives, and printed off the impressions as steadily as I had, — because the 1st of October was at hand.

"No. I was glad I did not have to write to him. I told him straight through, much as I have been telling you. If it has seemed to you that I was talking out of a book, it has been because once — though of course never but once — I have been all over this wretched business in words before. I told Harry the whole. They say a man never tells all his debt. I suppose that is true. I did not tell him of some of the meanest of mine, and some that were most completely debts of honor. I said to myself that I could manage those myself some day. But then I told no lies. I said to him that this was about all. And he, — he did, as he always does, the completest and noblest thing that can be done. He gave me three coupon bonds which he had bought only the day before, meaning them for a birthday present for his mother. He gave me three hundred and twenty dollars in cash, and he went with me to the office of the photographic findings people, with a note of introduction Mr. Rice gave to him, and gave a note, jointly with me, for the chemicals and the cameras. So I was clear of debt that night, except the little things I had not told; and I had near fifty dollars in my pocket.

"'And what now?' said he, when I went to thank him again the next morning, — and he spoke to me as cheerily as if I had never caused him a moment's care.

"Well, he wanted me to go on with the photograph room. But I hated it. I hated Boston. I hated the old shop. I hated the Tyler Street house. I hated the very color on my hands. I begged him to let me go with him to Washington. Perhaps I thought I should do better under his wing. I am ashamed to say that I had not then any special wish to serve the country, — God bless her! — though I knew he was serving her so nobly. Nor did I know the whole meaning of the way of transgressors. Simply I hated Boston.

"So he told me to leave the forty-three dollars with Jenny, and to come with him the next day to Washington. I had never been even to New York before. And at Washington not once did he fail me. For two or three weeks that I was hanging round, living at his charges, and hopelessly unable to do a thing for him, seeming like a fool, I suppose, because I know I felt like one, not once did he forget himself, nor speak an impatient word to me. And when he came unexpectedly back to our lodgings one day, an hour after he had gone out, to say that the head of the Department had that morning given him an appointment for me, or the promise of one, in the Bureau of Special Supplies, he was more glad than I was, you would have said. Not really; but he was gentle about it, and took no credit to himself, and would have been glad if I could have believed that 'The Chief' had heard of me from my own fame, and had sent to him to find out where such a rare bird could be caught.

"So pleasant days began again. Jenny and the

children came on. Washington is, to my notion, the pleasantest city in America, if you have only the wherewithal. Always, you see, the great drama is going on before your eyes, and you are one of the chorus. You see it all and hear it all, before the scenes and behind, and yet are even paid for standing and hearing the very first performers in the world. Tragedy sometimes, comedy sometimes, farce how often! melodrama every day. If you only obey Micawber, and insure the 'result — happiness.' But I could not do that, you know. Jenny could, and would, if I had let her. But I would buy books, — and I would take her on excursions, — I don't know, — Harry went off and I got in debt again. But I worked like a dog at the bureau. I brought home copying for Jenny. Always these odd jobs were my ruin. I was always hoping to help myself through. But I was early at work, and at night I screwed out the gas in the office; and so I got promoted. That helped, but it ruined too. Promotion, too, was an 'odd job.' I ran behind again, and I got promotion again. But when I ran behind a third time, no promotion came, and I —

"O, no! dear Mrs. Webber. I did not do as Floyd or those people do. I did what was a great deal worse, — as much worse as the sin of a being with a heart can be than the sin of a being with only a brain.

"In my new post I had the oversight of all the

accounts from the Artificers' Department in the field. By one of the intricacies, which I need not explain, they were in the habit of sending over for us to use, from the Quartermaster-General's, the originals of all the reports they received, for us to see what we wanted by way of confirming our vouchers; and we then sent them all back to them. This was because we were ahead of them. They were some weeks behindhand, and we were "fly," as our jargon called it. So it happened that I used to see Harry's own official reports to their office, even before they read them themselves. They opened them, you know, and sent them to us, — we copied what we wanted, and sent them back again.

"Of course I was interested in what he was doing. I need not say that he was doing it thoroughly well. He loved work. He loved the country. He believed in the cause. And off there, at that strange little post, curiously separated from the grand armies, and in many matters reporting direct to Washington, he was cadi, viceroy, commissary, chief-engineer, schoolmaster, minister, major-general, and everything, under his modest major's maple-leaves. It was a queer post, — just the place one dreams of when he fancies himself fit for everything, — just the place for an honest man, — yes, just the place for him.

"Strictly speaking, I had no right to read his reports. But then I did read them. I liked to know what he was doing. At last, one infernal day, I happened to notice that he had misunderstood one of the service regulations about returns, which had made us infinite trouble when I was in the large room with Blenker. I knew all about it. But it had confused Harry. I was glad I observed it before they did, and I wrote to him at once about it. I knew it might save him money to notice it; for they would stop his pay while they notified him. I wrote. But he never got the letter. The next week and the next this same variation in his accounts-keeping came in. Nothing wrong, you know; but — look here — if I had a blank I could show you. Well, no matter, — but just one of those things which you world's people call 'red tape.' Really, one part of it sprang from his not understanding where the apostrophes belonged in 'Commissaries' wagoners' assistants' rations. I wrote to him again and again and again. Four letters I wrote; but Sherman and Hardee and Benham and Hayes, and I do not know who, were raising Ned with the communications, and he never got one of my letters. And when the sixth of these accounts of his came, — well, I was in debt, I wanted a change, — well, — your Doctor to-day would have said the Devil came. I wish I thought it was anybody's fault but mine. What did I do, but send over to the Quartermaster's for the whole series, which we had sent back; and then I went up to the chief, I sent in my card, and I said to him that my attention had been called to this obliquity in accounts, — that I had warned Mr.

Patrick, because I had formerly known him, that he was not construing the act correctly, — that he persisted in drawing as he did, and making the returns as he did, — and that, in short, though strictly it was not my business, yet, as it would be some months before the papers would be reached in order (this was a lie, — they had really come to the first of them), I thought it my duty to the government to call attention to the matter. As we both knew, I said, it was an isolated post, and an officer did not pass under the same observation as in most stations.

"Yes, I said all that. It was awful. I can't tell you wholly how or why I said it. I did not guess it would turn out as it did. I did hope I should be sent out on special service to inspect. But I did not think of anything more. But a man cannot have just what he chooses. The chief, — not his old chief, you know, who appointed me, but a new Pharaoh, a real Shepherd King who did not know him or me, — the chief was one of those chiefs who makes up for utter incompetency in general by immense fiddling over a detail, — the chief, I say, had his cigar, and was comfortable, and knew no more about this post than you do, and asked me, in a patronizing way about it, not confessing ignorance, but as a great man will. That temptation I could not resist. Who can? You know a man's business better than he knows it himself; and he asks you to tell it to him, and sits and enjoys. I say, not Abdiel nor Uriel in the host of heaven would have been pure enough to have resisted that temptation, if the Devil had feigned ignorance, and asked advice about keeping the peace in Pandemonium. At all events, I could not resist. I stood, — I sat at last, when he asked me, — and told him the whole story, adorned as I chose.

" The next day he sent for me again; and I found more than my boldest hopes had fancied, — that he was thinking of displacing poor Harry, and putting me there as his substitute. Of course I blocked his wheels, you say, and explained. No such thing. I snapped at the promotion! Was not promotion what I must have? I played modest to be sure. 'I had not expected — but if the government wished — there were reasons — our bureau — my own early training,' — this, that, and the other. Don't make me tell the whole; it was too nasty. The end was, that I was ordered to leave Washington with a colonel's commission, outranking Harry two grades, the right to name my staff when I got upon the ground, and a separate commission making me military governor of the district of Willston, Alabama, to report in duplicate to Washington and to the district head-quarters. Poor Harry was to report in person to the Department, in disgrace.

" Here was a prize vastly higher than I had sought for. I was not very happy with it. But I had the grace to say to myself that I could pay my debts now, and would never go in debt again. I would even pay poor Harry, I thought; but then I had another qualm, as I remembered that there were near three thousand dollars due him, and that even a colonel's pay and allowances would not stand that, in the first quarter. I did not go back to my own office then. I went home and told Jenny. I did not tell her where I was going. I only told her it was promotion, and high promotion. I bade her take comfort; and that very afternoon I turned over my papers and keys and hurried away.

"I went on to Willston. I wish I were telling you how; but that is not a part of the sermon. I got there. I found Harry. He was amazed to see me. He was delighted. He took me right into his own little den, asked if there was bad news, asked what brought me, and — well, my friends, the worst thing of the whole, the worst thing in my life, was my telling him I had superseded him!

"And now, do you believe I had the face to say to him, that it was the saddest moment of my life? That was true enough, God knows! But I said more. I dared tell him that I had had no dream of what was in the wind. That I did not receive my orders till I had left Washington, and that I had not a thought or suspicion who could have been caballing against him at the Department! I told him this, when I knew I had done the whole!

"Good fellow! He cried. I believe I did. He said, 'I can't talk about it'; and he hurried away. I did not see him again till the war was done. I went out and found the gentlemen of his staff. Of course they hated me. By and by I had my own staff. They did not love me. The people hated me. Did you hear that man read to-day, 'The citizens hated him, and said, We will not have this man to reign over us'? But I am ahead of my story. It was Saturday night that I arrived. Sunday I dressed up and 'attended religious worship with the garrison.' Do you believe, the chaplain, a little wiry Sandemanian preacher, chose to tell those men, 'The way of transgressors is hard.' And I had to stand and take it, without the consolation I am giving myself to-day.

"It was not he that told me, — what I found out the night before, when I quailed under Harry's eye, — that it is the *way* that is hard. I had always tried to think that it was a hard station that you got to, — a lock-up or a bankruptcy. But as I lied to Harry, and then as I met the staff, and now again behind this chaplain, I knew that what was hard was the *way*. And from that moment till I had to resign my commissions, I knew every second of life that the *way* was hard. I had good things happen, some, and lots of bad ones; but I never got that feeling about the way out of my heart. I said just now my own gentlemen did not love me. I don't know why I say so, but that I thought so. For I thought nobody liked me or believed in me, — just because I hated myself after I stood there with Harry, and did not believe in myself.

I tell you it was very hard for me to go through the routine of life there. As for success, — why, if Vesuvius had started up next door to us and overwhelmed us, I should not have cared.

"I suppose you know what did happen. If you do, the sermon is ended. There never should have been any post at Willston. We were there to 'make Union sentiment.' In fact, the Rebels lived on us, laughed at us, and hated us. Harry did conciliate some people, I think, and frightened more. I conciliated nobody, and frightened nobody. I had begun wrong. 'Sinful heart makes feeble hand,' — and it makes feeble head too, Mr. Marmion; and, worse than that, a man can't make any friends of himself or anybody else with it. I tried a great diplomatic dodge. There was a lot of rice on a plantation, and I started a private negotiation with one Haraden who owned it, — not for myself, really, but for government. We wanted the rice. Then my chief woke up one day from a long sleep, and sent us a perfectly impossible string of instructions. Then I heard that Dick Wagstaff, one of the enemy's light-horse, was threatening my outpost at Walker. I did not know what to do. How should I? But I put on a bold face, and marched out the garrison, and went part way to Walker; and then I thought I had better go down to Haraden's; and then, — I tell you, it was just like a horrid dream, — then I remembered that the gunboats might have been sent up to help us, and I sent an express for them, and marched that way; but then news came that we had been wrong about Walker, and I thought we had better cross back there. But while we were crossing, there came an awful rain. We could not get the guns on, and had to stop over night, not only in the wettest place you ever saw, but in the only place we ought not to have been in at all. And there, at the gray of morning, before my men could or would start a cannon, down came Dick Wagstaff's flying squadron. What is worst is, that we found out, afterwards, there werè but forty of them, and yet, in one horrid muddle of confusion, we left the guns, left what rice we had got, left ever so many men who had not time to tumble up, and, indeed, we hardly got back alive to Willston. If Dick Wagstaff had known his business half as well as he was thought to, not one of us would have seen the place again. But the queer thing of all this shame and disgrace to me was, that it almost comforted me. I remember my mother used to flog me when I was sulky, and say she would give me something to cry for. As we trailed back through the mud, it fairly pleased me to think that now, if I looked like a cursed hang-dog, people would not wonder. My outside was as bad at last as my in. I remember, as we came to the last bridge over the Coosa River, I, who was riding after the rear of the column, overtook McMurdy, — this chaplain I told you of. He was walking, leading his own horse, on which sat or crouched a man faint as death, so he could hardly hold on. I made

McMurdy take my horse and trudged beside him for the rest of the way. 'This is pretty hard, Doctor,' said I.

"'Hard for us,' said the grim little man, 'but not so hard for us as for the Graybacks.'

"'I don't see that,' said I. But in a minute I saw that the little man was clear grit, and true to his cloth.

"He set his teeth, and said: 'Not so hard for us, because we are right, and they are wrong. Every dog has his day, Colonel. They are bound to come to grief when the clock strikes for them.'

"Poor little Doctor. He preached at me harder, when he said that, than the first day I saw him, when he was 'secondlying it,' and 'in conclusioning it,' to the men. I made my mouth up to say, 'The way of transgressors is hard, Doctor.' But the cant stuck in my throat. That would have been too steep. Who was I, to say it? I said nothing. He said nothing. But I trailed after him, up to my knees in that Alabama mud; and I said to myself, It is the way that 's hard, by Jove. It is not the consequence that is hard, nor the punishment. That is rather easy in comparison. And I spoke aloud: 'It 's the way.' Just then a contraband's mule pitched into me, — almost knocked me down, — and the little nigger said to me: 'Beg pardon, massa; Jordan mighty hard road to trabble to-night.' I did not swear at him. I stood by and let him pass. And I said to myself: 'Mighty hard. It is the way that 's hard, and not the bed you lie on at the end of it.'

"Indeed, at that very moment of misery, utter failure, beastly defeat, I felt the first reaction from the misery that had galled me ever since I lied to Harry's face. This was the end at last. All that was the way.

"As soon as they heard of all this, of course I was relieved, in disgrace. I was bidden to report at Washington, just as Patrick had done. I swear to you I was a happier man than I had been since the day he left me there."

Mr. Frye stopped. And then he walked up and down the room. It was long since he had smiled, or pretended to. But he rested on a chair-back now, and said: "That is all the sermon. I shall feel better now I have told you. I shall never tell any one again. But one revelation of such a thing a man had better make, where it costs him something. So I am glad to have told you."

Mrs. Webber had her eyes full of tears. "You don't tell us all," said she, — "you don't tell how you came here."

"That hardly belongs to the sermon," said he. "Yes it does. When I met Jenny, I told her the whole thing right through.

"'Poor boy,' said she; 'it is hard,' meaning to comfort me.

"'Jenny,' said I, 'it is hard. Drinking is hard; cheating is hard. You and I found that out before. And this infernal intriguing — politics, I believe they call it — is the hardest of all. It's a hard way, Jenny.'

"'Body, mind, and soul,' said poor Jenny: 'it is hard any way';—and she cried.

"So did I. And then I went across, and sent in my name to Harry. He was all right again, and brevetted brigadier. And I said, 'Harry, ten times you have lifted me out of the gutter; ten times I have gone in deeper than before. This time I help myself. This time I have found out, what till now I have never believed, that I carried failure with me,—that I was therefore bound to fail, and had to fail. Harry,' said I, 'the very God in heaven does not choose to have a broken wire carry lightning, nor a lying life succeed. That 's why I 've failed. Now see me help myself.'

"Harry gave me both his hands, shook mine heartily, and we said good by. I came on here, because here I had been in the mud. I started this little patent about the clothes-brushes. I let the results look out for themselves. For me, all I care for now is the way. I pay as I go; and I take care that Jordan shall be an easy road to travel. Harry came on last fall, and we ate our Thanksgiving together at Jenny's father's.

"That is all my sermon."

And now Frye lighted his cigar.

We agreed among the boarders that we would not mention this. But last Sunday, at a church I was at in Boothia Felix, the man led us through three quarters of an hour of what my grandfather's spelling-book would have called "trisyllables in ality, elity, and ility," and "polysyllables in ation, ition, etion, and otion." It was three dreary quarters of abstract expression. When the fourth quarter began, he said, "History is full of illustrations of our doctrine, but I will not weary you by their repetition."

"Old Cove," said I, "I wish you would. If you would just take that lesson from Mr. Frye!" Or I should have said so, had the ritual and etiquette of that congregation permitted.

THE RAG-MAN AND THE RAG-WOMAN

[I WAS tempted to write out this passage of Mr. Haliburton's memoirs by a few words which fell from one of our most distinguished students of social order. He told me of the hint he had received from a great paper-maker, of the wastefulness of burning paper stock which cost $ 220 a ton. And he urged some of us whom he supposed interested in publication, to start a magazine for the people, which, in teaching them how to live, — which the American people do not know, — should inculcate at the same time the lesson of frugality, which, in the unheard-of bounty of nature throughout the land, the American people has yet to learn. Whoever shall undertake that magazine will have it in his power to teach a great lesson to our people, if he can make them read it. Not waiting for its appearance, I offered as my contribution to the first number of the Atlantic Almanac the really tempting results of the honest frugalities of Mr. and Mrs. Haliburton. — F. I.]

"IT was a downfall indeed, — or it seemed so then.

"There was I, as comfortable a young fellow as wore nice kid gloves in Boston. My place was easy enough and hard enough. My salary was eighteen hundred a year. I had a reasonable vacation. I liked the other clerks and they liked me. I understood my business, as it proved, only too well. Best of all, perhaps, I had fitted up my two rooms at Mrs. Thayer's as prettily as heart could wish. The bed was large enough, and you could air the bedroom. The carpets were ingrain, of small figure; they were cheap, but of that dark claret and black which give a warm tone and make things feel comfortable. Not too many pictures, — but those hung low enough. Not too many books, but the free list at the old Boston Library, four or five cards at the Public Library, and three or four friends on the staff there, a minister's right at the Athenæum, and a pleasant intimacy with Loring. I owed no man a dollar. I had no enemy in the world. I was at home in a dozen nice cordial families of friends; and what more could man require?

"Of a sudden the bolt fell! Or is it a sword that falls? I believe it is a sword. Make it 'sword,' Mr. Proof-Reader. Of a sudden the sword fell!

"Thus: —

"The office that I was in was the newly established 'Methuselah and Admetus Life-Assurance Company.' To say Assurance, instead of Insurance, is rather natty; it sounds English, and people fancy the Barings and the Bank of England pay the bills. 'Methuselah' was to attract the biblical, and 'Admetus' the classical gudgeons. For, though the great hope of the man who insures his life is that he may be beloved of the gods and so die young, yet practically people insure in the vague feeling that they thus take a bond against

Death, or turn him the cold shoulder. It is somewhat as you carry an umbrella in the hope of preventing rain.

"We had got our advertisements and prospectuses out, and really we had a great many new features. If you held our scrip eleven years and four months, and then did not sell it for two years and one month more, at the end of that time we declared a dividend of four nineteenths of all the profits before undivided, after striking a balance between two elevenths of the risks, and seventy-three per cent of the premiums, reserving, of course, $37,273,642.17 to secure the cousins of the bondholders. That feature may have been in some other companies, but I never saw it. We had a very fine sign in front of our office in Queen Street, with a picture of Methuselah kissing Admetus, and Alcestis crying in the corner, because her husband could not die, I believe. Within, we had a velvet carpet for the President's room, a tapestry carpet for the Directors' room, English brussels for the Secretary's, American brussels for ours, and that nice, clear Russian mat, that smells so pleasantly of tar, for the customers. We had comfortable chairs, and all the newspapers.

"I should have been there to this hour, I suppose, but that one day a very stupid customer came in. Not but this often happened. But, this day, the President found his velvet lonesome, and had come forward into our office. I thought he was reading the 'Cornhill,' but, as it happened, he was listening over his spectacles to me. That sentence is not quite right, but I cannot alter it. People do not listen over their spectacles, — they listen over their collars; they 'peek' over their spectacles. Perhaps he did that too.

"Well, I explained and explained to the customer, who finally went away without customing. He took the little pink book, and the large blue pamphlet, and the card with the head of Methuselah, and both the little cards, but he did not take out a policy, and he did not say he would. I am sure I did not wonder, but it seems the President did.

"'What did you say to that man?' said he.

"'I explained the system of Life Insurance, — I mean Life Assurance,' said I, 'as well as I could.'

"'Yes,' said the President. 'But what did you tell him about invalid lives?'

"'O, I had shown him the Northampton tables, and the Carlisle tables, and the Equitable tables, and I repeated to him Cowper's lines to the Registrar.'

"'I know, I know,' said the President, who is a little hasty, though he is my aunt Lucy's brother-in-law, which accounts for my being there indeed. 'I know all that, but what were you saying about invalid lives?'

"'Why, I explained to him that nothing was so certain as the average law of death. We had these tables, — and so we knew, on an average, just how long people would live. And we fixed our risk accordingly, so as to meet the average. And he asked me why he was to go to a medical examiner then. And I told him that it was because we only wanted to insure healthy lives. And he asked me whether only healthy lives came into the tables of mortality, — whether they were only healthy people who lived in Carlisle and Northampton and the rest, — and why we did not do our business on our own principles, and take healthy people and sick people together. And I told him that if the company did not make any profit, we could not keep up the office. And he asked me why we did not say so in the prospectus, and what was the use of making so much talk about the certainty of the average of mortality, when we had nothing to do with the average of mortality, but only with some of the best lives in the community. I told him that was our business, and not his. And he said he thought the profit of the business ought to come to the people who paid the money. And I said if he thought that, he had better go to a mutual company, he would find one the other side of the street. And then he went away.'

"It was the longest address I ever made to my aunt's brother-in-law, and it did not seem to be satisfactory. He scowled and said, 'I don't wonder.' And then he went away.

"The next day I received a note informing me that my services were no longer needed. He enclosed a check for the balance due me, — fifty-seven dollars and eleven cents, — and that was all. I took my umbrella and my office coat, bade the clerks good by, and went home. And I have never been there since."

We were sitting in Haliburton's smoking-room in his nice house on Commonwealth Avenue, when he told me the story above repeated. It is the only house I thoroughly like in Boston. He bought eight lots, and so got a front of near two hundred feet. Then he was able to extend his house on the floor, instead of running it up into sky-parlors. He was able to have the air on every side, as they have in Sybaris, — and a little garden on every side too. If I had been he, I would have had no staircase, but those which went into the cellars. But he yielded to the popular taste enough to have his house two stories high. If you care to look for it, I think you will find it between Fairfield Street and George the Third Street, — if that is the next in the alphabetical order.

We had just dined, — the girls had gone up to see the babies, and Haliburton told me this story. It was a bad tumble, I said, and I asked how he got out of it.

"Well," said Haliburton, "they say everything is an accident. For me, I say nothing is. You shall judge. I went home to my pretty crimson and black ingrain carpet, and I thought I looked my last on it. The rent was paid till the end of that month. And what was I to do then? I could not dig, and the one thing I was sure of was, that I would not borrow. I was a little blue, I can tell you, when George Plunkett, whom I had met at Lebanon not long before, came in. He was down in Boston, it seemed. I tried to be hospitable, found two chairs for him; we talked over the Columbia House and the rest, — what had become of the partners of the summer, — and I offered him a cigar.

"As it happened, I twisted up the back of a letter for him to light it with, and so it happened that you and I are here.

"For Plunkett lighted the cigar, — gave me back the paper, — I lighted mine, and threw the rest of the scrap into the grate.

"He made sure of his light, and then said, 'So you burn paper here?'

"'Why, I burnt that,' said I, 'because I had to light the cigars. For a regular fuel I burn Lehigh coal.'

"'Pretty expensive fuel,' said Plunkett, 'to burn paper at two hundred and twenty dollars a ton.'

"I suppose at another time I should have let it go with a laugh. But I felt wretchedly poor, and was not above sixpences, I can tell you. Plunkett, who is a thorough gentleman, would gladly have dropped the subject with his joke; but when I pressed him, he said, earnestly enough, that they had occasion to see the shocking extravagance of the country in their business, that they were at their wits' end to get material for paper, — this was in the war when paper stock was very high; that every man in the country was paying twice as much for his newspaper as he need pay, because every man and every woman was wasting like all the Danaides together; and that that was what had moved him to speak. If I felt sore he would apologize.

"No! I did not feel a bit sore. To tell the truth, even then, I felt a little comforted. And when Plunkett went away, — good fellow, he and his wife are coming to stay with us when the Italians are here, — send Polly round to see her, — I say, when he went away, I got up to examine my stock in trade. And I made this calculation.

"I could stay with Mrs. Thayer, and live just as before, for four dollars and ninety-three cents a day. That is, I could pay my board; I could send home two hundred dollars to my mother; keep up the policy on my life at the old New England Mutual; lay out a hundred and fifty on my summer journey; and have as much for the poor-box, or any poor rascal that had not thriven as well as I. Four dollars and ninety-three cents, with old paper at eleven cents a pound, would be forty-five pounds a day. Thunder! Had not there been days in the past week when I had given away more than that weight of prospectuses? I think poor Dennis would say so, who used to carry them to the post-office! Let me see what I had got on hand.

"1st. Eleven volumes of the Atlantic Monthly, or rather fifty-five numbers. By a curious fatality there were regularly two numbers lost in every year, so I never could bind them. Lucky for me now. For, if they had been books, I might not have thought of them. I took them down, blew off the dust, — and 'hefted' them. Wished I had practised more often on cakes at fairs. Could not guess the weight. So,

"2d. I took down one hundred and eighty-one old Harpers, 'hefted' them.

"3d. Files of the Transcript and Advertiser, not bound for four years. How fortunate that I had had this passion for filing journals. And never once had I unrolled one of the files!

"4th. Play-bills, concert-bills, private theatrical programmes, &c., &c., from a large travelling-trunk, where they had been waiting for me to find the leisure to file them.

"5th. Envelopes for the last eighteen months. I had pitched them all into two empty coal-barrels in my wood-closet for some philanthropist to take off stamps for one of the postage-stamp people who are to be fitted for the University by the dextrine on the back of a million cancelled stamps. Nobody had appeared to claim them; so here was an accumulation of about seven cubic feet of paper, pretty tightly crammed down.

"6th. Reports of charitable societies, copies of the laws, quarterly school reports, and a thousand other pamphlets which I had always kept, I knew not why till now; on the principle of the Chinese, whom I was now learning to respect as a most intelligent nation, never to destroy a piece of paper.

"All these I piled together in a corner of my bedroom, and I gloated over them. I did not know how much they weighed, but I fancied that they weighed a great deal more than they proved to. Not that I deceived myself for an instant. I knew that here were the accumulations of six years. I knew that in sending them to the mill I was but cutting down the ancestral oaks. Still, if by so doing I could be learning how to sell oak timber, and at the same time could plant new acorns for new harvests, and could myself subsist till those new harvests budded, bourgeoned, and fell before the axe, my modest destiny was secure. To this future I addressed myself. I saw I had first to arrange for my sales. Then I had to arrange for packing and transportation; and, essential to the whole, I had to be sure of the sources of supply. But when I thought of the acres of useless paper which were thrust every day across my line of march, I could not but hope that they were thick enough, in all their flimsiness, to weigh on the average forty-five pounds.

"If the thing were to be done, of course it was to be done with system. I remember perfectly the feeling with which I lay in wait for Nolan the teamster, whom we used to employ at the store, and arranged with him to call at my side door early Tuesday morning as he drove down for his day's work. Nolan was fond of me, for I had many a night kept the store open that he might get through his jobs the easier, when I was the youngest apprentice. And I arranged on very cheap terms that he should call early in the morning every Tuesday for my stock, and that on Friday night as he came home after the day's work he should bring me home a crockery crate from Basset's. Cronyn, you know, who is now in the East Indies, arranged about crates for me. I found I could not manage to have them returned to me after they were emptied. Eventually it proved best only to send off one every fortnight. All this detail stands out in my memory now as freshly as if it were yesterday. It was like a boy's examination to enter college. It was really to me the shoving off into a wholly new career.

"But I do not mean to tell you the details, even of that whole year, as I tell you this beginning. Many a begging circular, many a shop advertisement, stuck into my letter-box, many an explanation from Jew oculist about his pebble glasses, and from eclectic physician about the days he would be in Boston and the days he would not, many a notification from Mr. Secretary McCleary that I was to give in my ballot, many a hint from the water commissioner that I must not waste Cochituate, went into my Balaam basket, of which no sign is left beyond what is in my little day-books yonder, and those, I think, will never be edited by living man, or by admiring biographer of mine.

"It is — if you will think of it — a very strange passion we have in our age, this of printing circulars. So far as I know, it works no good under heavens, excepting to rag-men and to printers. No one answers a begging circular, no man goes to the exhibition which is announced by a printed circular, no one remembers even the number in the street on the corn-doctor's card. Yet we print them and send them round as a salve for a wounded conscience. It is as people leave cards when they cannot call. I know I ought to ask John to contribute ten dollars to the Orphan Asylum; I hate to do it, and I therefore excuse myself by printing a hundred circulars, asking a hundred Johns to contribute, and leaving them at a hundred doors. Or, it is as people leave tracts. The Master virtually prohibited sowing seed by the wayside; he said the Devil ate up all such seed, and he most certainly does; he said that if we had any seed to sow, we should sow it in good ground; that we were not to stop to talk by the wayside, and, if we could possibly help it, we were never to waste any seed there. Yet there are even Tract Societies that, for want of good ground, print what they call "Wayside Series," and give them to children in the streets, or people who want shaving-paper, or leave them on the seats of railroad cars. As if Infinite Wisdom had not taken pains to prohibit that very thing.

"These tracts have given me infinite trouble. Because, in forty-five pounds of paper, a good many of them would stray in, and I always had to pick them out and get them back to the offices they started from once a year. I made that distinction between people who wanted to save my soul and people who wanted to line their own pockets. And, while I sent a quack doctor's almanac relentlessly to the mill, I always returned to the office that issued it any short-metre guide to heaven that in its kindness it had sent to me.

"Well here is one of the day-books; you see how methodical I grew. I knew, as I say, that I could not rely on past accumulations. My business was practically to develop such a movement as should bring into those rooms forty-five pounds of paper a day. The receipts varied with the season. After Congress met, the mail supply was always the largest; next to that generally the 'delivery' boys; and least, my own walks. But on election-days, or when there was a circus, I often picked up in the streets as much as the boys brought to my door. There, over here, December 31st, is the footing carried out for that year, you see: —

	lbs.	*oz.*
Mail	13,623	4
Delivery	2,119	3
Pockets	1,863	11

By delivery, I mean things poked under the door or into the box.

"'What are pockets?' O, I had my exercise to keep up, you know, and I had really a good deal to do in so large a business as I soon carried on with the manufacturers. So, after allowing an hour after breakfast to set the batteries running, I walked down town and met all the boys who thrust papers in your face, always was pleasant to them, read what they gave me, and put it in my pocket. If you have leisure for such things, you meet at the reading-rooms and libraries a great many men who would not have thought of you, who ask if you have seen their statement of the method of resuming specie payment, and hand you a copy. As old as you and I are, you are entitled to a good many things by dint of old assessments. You are entitled to a copy of the laws, and the catalogues of a vast number of schools and libraries, to the School Committee's Report, and many other things for which you pay taxes, and it is but fair that you should have back some return. In fact, if you only will take such things, there are a great many people in the world eager to get them out of their offices. Do you not know that the last phase of that precious old humbug, the Smithson, is that they circulate through the world the publications of societies who cannot otherwise get their volumes off their hands? A great central express-office for distributing knowledge in the concrete! But if you want to see the detail, look at any page of my journal."

Accordingly I opened at November 8, 1862.

"State Election to-day: I went to vote. Voted straight ticket. Lots of split tickets. I told them I should not vote them, but they made me take them. Passed the Ward Ten office. They pressed votes on me there. Told them I had voted already. They seemed to want to get rid of the things. Called on

Fergus. He asked me to accept some Reports on Emigration which had been sent him from Belgium. Told him I had no use for them (which was not true). He said they were in his way. Passed ward-room of Ward Eight. More tickets. Told them I had voted. They would crowd them on me. Called on Mrs. Fettyplace. She gave me memoir of her husband's uncle. Stopped at Longmans'. They asked me to notice their reprint of Gulliver. Said they would send it home.

"Home at eleven. Large mail. Clara's wedding cards. What a nice girl she is, and he is a good fellow. Cards thick and heavy. Four of them, too. Two lottery advertisements; a pamphlet about Sozodont; a prospectus of building-lots; circulars of three joint-stock companies; requests to furnish my works for the Adelphic Harmonian Society of Bushrod University, Wisconsin; three requests for autographs; four catalogues of book sales; two more duplicates of the fifth volume of the President's Message of four years ago. They seem behindhand in the printing.

"Walk again before dinner. Election still brisk. They tried to give me more votes, but I would not take them. Four bills of fare; notices of auction sale at Greenville; of new shop opened in Tyler Street; of opposition dentist at No. 111 Fulton Street; and of a new medium in Lowell Street. Dined at club.

"Afternoon. Our majority is immense, they say. Witherspoon, who had been at work all day, trying to run in Ingham to the Legislature on a split ticket, came home to take a cigar. Ingham had but four votes, after all. Witherspoon left here all the tickets he had not distributed. I could not make him take them with him. He seemed cross and out of spirits. Did not stay long. Afternoon mail good. Exhibit of National Steamship Company; three life insurance circulars; memorial for signature against liquor law; another for it. Representation (too late) that Waldo was left off the ticket by a cabal; another (also too late), that he was not. Circular requesting all Republicans to contribute for the expenses of head-quarters. Four other circulars. Full set of documents of Anti-take-hold-of-the-Fork Society, forwarded by Izaaks, good fellow.

"Delivery for the day small; two quack almanacs; notice from city to put out ashes Tuesday morning; notice that grocer has moved to the other corner of the street; that Frye has a new partner, and the firm will be Frye & Co.

"Called on Bertha by appointment, and took her to the Howard. Maggie Mitchell. They have a new style of bills, — a little newspaper. Brought Bertha's home by mistake, but sent it to her afterwards.

		lbs.	*oz.*
"Account for day,	Mail	37	11
	Pockets (3 walks) .	8	9
	Delivery, papers, &c. .	5	2
		51	6

"A good day. Oh! *Si sic omnia!*"

I handed back the book to Haliburton, a little puzzled. I said I did not see how he came to have so many of these things. I had more or less of them, — more than I had ever known what to do with, indeed, more rather than less. But I never had quite forty-five pounds in a day, I thought.

"As to that," said he, "you have had more than you think for. As Plunkett said, a vast deal goes in fuel which you are not aware of. But, I confess, I cultivated my crop. I am, and always was, curious that way. And when I once found that 'lists of respectable names' were considered 'property' in this world, bought and sold by people who distribute circulars, — advertised and bragged of, I saw no objection to my name going in on as many as might be. Thus I wrote one day, in perfectly good faith, for a sort of sun-dial they advertise in New York, — they call it a gilt timekeeper. I got my dial, and forgot it. Now, do you think that letter put my name on 'a list,' and once a month, I suppose, I now receive lottery prospectuses, – schemes for making money out of nothing, proposals to become an agent in this or that rascality, I know not what. There is no way known to me by which to get your name off one of these 'lists,' and so I e'en turn the circulars into white paper as soon as I may.

"I suppose the largest single return I ever got was by starting 'The Unfortunates' Magazine.' I studied the thing with care, and it turned out well. Magazines do not always; but that is because the publishers are over-ambitious. We only printed two hundred and fifty copies of 'The Unfortunates' to begin with. We sent them free to ladies' schools and colleges. We got very few subscribers. We never had two hundred and fifty, and never had to print five hundred copies. We had good large type and cheap paper, so that it was not very burdensome; only forty-eight pages a number, you know. And we had, I can tell you, contributions by the hundred-weight. The rule was to be very generous to new contributors, and we got the reputation in the Sigma Delta Societies, and United Sisters, and all that kind, of introducing many of the younger and newer lights. I think Marie Montrose and Nannie of Nonantum and Olive Oglethorp and Pollie Playfair and Quinsie Quiggle all made their first appearance before the public in 'The Unfortunates' Magazine.' The year we offered our first premiums, fifty dollars for the best story, twenty-five for the second, and twenty for the third, — all manuscripts to be at our disposition, — we had enormous receipts. I think we had four thousand and odd pounds of manuscript. Stock was very high that year, and thirteen or fourteen hundred pounds paid the prizes, so the rest was clear profit."

I suggested that it was hard-earned profit, if Haliburton had to read all the manuscripts. But he explained that it would be entirely improper for the editor himself to make the decision, and that the custom was to select a committee of clergymen of different denominations to read the papers and award the prizes. "We sorted out a dozen or two," said he, "that seemed to be worth saving, but really it was a charity to society to put the rest into the pulp-mill."

"And I do not mean to say," said he, "that I had no conscience about the pulp-mill. If I could have dumped in all the paper that came, without opening envelopes, it would have been another thing. In fact, I only felt at liberty to do so where men were trying to use me to serve their own interest. Then I thought tit for tat was fair. You would be surprised, though, to know how easily a wave would get started. Ingham coaxed me out of twenty dollars for Antioch College one day; I wish it had been twenty thousand. Then my poor twenty was printed in his acknowledgment of contributions. From that hour to this I have received begging circulars for every cause that has a name under heaven, having got my name, I suppose, upon the 'list' of somebody that manages such matters."

The people wanted to clear the dinner-table, and we went into the back-parlor and sat on the veranda. There Haliburton told me the other half of the story.

"I had been in the paper business more than a year," he said, "and I found it was a cash business, needing and giving no credit, and therefore a comfortable one, when one day, as I was coming home, I was poking through Oswego Street, when a pretty little girl in front of me ran suddenly into the middle of the street. I saw in a moment that she was chasing a bit of rag which was blown off the sidewalk. Poor child; she was not quick enough, or she was too eager; she tripped and fell, — struck her head heavily and did not, at the moment, rise again. I ran after the little thing, and found her stunned by the blow. I carried her into the grocer's shop, washed her, and waited till she came to. She was confused for a few minutes, and then said she could go home, — that she knew she could. She asked eagerly for her large bag, which I gave her, — and tried to take it with her.

"But this I would not have. I carried the bag, and led her; or rather she led me, into one of the parallel South Cove streets there. I fairly carried her up three flights of stairs, and there, in attic rooms as sweet and pretty as ever Rigolette's were, we found her sister.

"A charming person, I can tell you. I thought so then, and I have never changed my mind. Broad, sunny forehead, large hazel, wondering eyes, perfectly cut nose, rather large mouth, — all this tells nothing, I know, — head wonderfully poised, voice very sweet, ears — did I say — no bigger than little shells, hair light and dark at the same time, — but what nonsense to talk detail! Some women have an atmosphere, some do not. If they are as beautiful as Juno, it is no good if they have no atmosphere. If they have the atmosphere, I believe their cheeks might be pea-green and it would make no difference. My little girl's sister had more atmosphere than any woman I had ever seen."

Of course, I knew who Haliburton was talking about all this time, — but he had forgotten I knew, — and, as he pleased himself, I let him describe her. He then continued: —

"I told my story, and received her thanks. I saw I must not stay. I could not pretend the doctor was needed. I saw she wanted to put Elsie to bed; so I bowed myself down stairs, and — called the next night to inquire, taking round Miss Leslie's 'Girls' Own Book,' for Elsie. And I called the next night, and I called the next night. But the third night I found Miss Anna was not at home.

"None the less, though Elsie got well obstinately soon, did I call frequently. I made another excuse for calling after Elsie was at school again, in discussing business arrangements. For it seemed that Miss Anna understood enough more of my business than I did. Since her father and mother died, she had supported herself and Walter and Elsie and little Phil by rag-picking, with its professional accompaniments of sorting and packing. I found great help from her experience and suggestions, though it was some time before I told her that I was an humble beginner in her line.

"Of course, if a woman or a man chooses to go about in rags into the dirt, with a long pointed stick, as in the pictures of professional chiffonniers in the magazines and in the exhibitions, either of them may become a very disagreeable being to others or at home. But Miss Anna had no such views for Elsie or the others. Indeed, she said, the profession involved no special hardship, but that of very early hours for the children. She had them up before it was light every blessed day. They had a very merry breakfast, always by lamplight. Then she started them, Walter alone, Elsie and Philip together, with their wagons. These were just such wagons as boys call 'trucks,' with champagne-baskets tied on. The children spent an hour,—much more in summer,—in going to the "out-door places" as they called them. I coaxed them one morning to let me go with them. They knew every back door of every large workshop, where there would be any form of shred swept out by lazy or careless porter. They knew as well what shops were well administered, so that there would be no need even of looking at the gutter. To my surprise they did not stop for paper. Elsie had said to me, when I first knew them, with perfect unconsciousness, that paper was a different business, and that her sister found it did not pay to mix them. The child did not know then why I blushed, nor did I know,—I certainly was not ashamed that I was in that branch of the calling. This hour's out-door work was a good brisk tramp, with the little wagons rattling behind in the still streets. But neither of them was half filled when we came home again,—meeting, almost, at the lower door. I said to myself that there was nothing like forty pounds, there were not five pounds in both baskets. But Walter claimed me this time, — it seemed we were to go to the 'depots' as they called them, — and now I understood matters better.

"It seemed that these nice, well-behaved children, partly, I suppose, by Miss Anna's introduction, and partly from their own good sense, had ingratiated themselves each in eight or ten of the large clothing establishments; not with the chiefs, who probably did not know that there were such children in the world, but with the parties, — younger apprentices, charwomen (the proper spelling would be *chore* women, I believe), or whoever else had the last charge of cleaning up at night for the next day. In many of the work-rooms the small rags — clippings and parings — are the perquisites of these people; all larger pieces belonging, of course, to the establishment. The children had made their own bargains. From five in the afternoon till six or seven, and sometimes till nine, in the evening they were busied in these shops, — sweeping, or running errands, carrying water, doing messages for the sewing-women, according as the bargain might be. And so at each shop, every night, they left the bag of scraps which, on the morning's trip, was to be collected and carried home. They had a reputation, it was clear enough, for neatness, quickness, honesty, and good-nature. They were favorites, I could see, at all these places where they looked in for their store. At one or two Walter supplied the girls with the Herald; that was the contract, he said. At one he carried up a block of ice for the water-pitcher; that was in the contract. Two or three times the night before he only nodded, but there he had done what he had bargained for. It took two trips back to their house to carry home these collections; and when Elsie arrived, a little after us, her stores were quite as large as ours.

"The children washed themselves, told their times, and sat down to rest, while Miss Anna weighed their morning's work. Again it reminded me so of home. She marked it down in their little books, 'Elsie and Phil, twenty-six pounds three ounces. Walter, twenty-four pounds eleven ounces.' The boy doubled up his fist at his sister, but it was clear that he was glad of her success. 'I'll beat you to-morrow,' he said. 'Dear old Morris says they are to take account of stock to-day, and that somehow that is to bring great things into my net.' And so, well pleased with the morning's tramp, they went off to school.

"'Poor things,' said Miss Anna; 'it seems hard they should have it to do. But I had a great deal rather have them with me so, than put her to sewing, or him to carrying parcels in a store. From now till five they will have only to study or to play. Then come from two to four hours of pretty hard work. But it is varied, — and so far they stand it well.'

"'Fifty-one pounds and fourteen ounces would be

a very good average,' said I, more professionally than I meant to do.

"She stared at me a moment with her great eyes, and then said it was higher than her year's average, but that the children grew stronger and better acquainted every year. 'I am laying up for something better for them,' said she; 'and we get on so well that I am quite encouraged. My part begins now that all this trash is to be separated into linen white, cotton white, hemp-cord, cotton-cord, junk, silk, and shoddy.' And after this suggestion of her part, I had to bow myself away.

"'Was that all?' No, it was not all, at all; it was only the beginning of all.

"I got in the habit of calling there every Wednesday evening. Miss Anna would not let me come more than once a week, — I found that out very soon. She would not accept any of my invitations, even for the most modest dissipations. She would not take one of the seats I could offer her at church. She let me take the children to the circus, — but she would not let me join her if I met her walking in the mall, far less would she talk with me. I had dead-head tickets for rehearsals and concerts, because 'The Unfortunates' Magazine' had got on the list of journals in the Directory; yet she would not use them if I sent them, but she would let Walter and Elsie go with them. So I got in the habit of always calling there Wednesday evening, and, unless I met her by good luck in the street, I never saw her at any other time. Walter liked to come up to my room to see my coins and my autographs, and I was always glad to have him, to lend him books, and to help him in his map-drawing.

"Well, we did not always talk shop; but one night I had carried her up Gisquet's Memoirs, with his queer account of the French rag-pickers. She had asked me for this; and this led to my asking her if the children never found things of value in the streets.

"She said they had, two or three times, the more was the pity. She did not want them to get the piratical feeling, but to understand they were in an honorable, above-board business, — earning their living honestly, and serving the country by cheapening paper, as bravely as if they were ramming down cartridges or wiping the brows of sick soldiers. When the children did bring home anything of value, there was the plague of advertising, of watching the advertisements, and all that, — it excited them and did no good to anybody. Then Miss Anna stopped, — began to speak again, — and stopped again. I got confused, and, of course could not think of anything to say; she blushed and laughed, and said, 'I will tell you of our most remarkable prize, — I do not know why I hesitated'; and she took out from her drawer a steel-mounted pocket-book, — a lady's, — which she said Elsie picked up in the fresh snow, in the evening, ten months ago. It had nearly eighty dollars in it, two or three of the owner's cards; and yet Miss Anna had never been able to find her.

"'The name is not in the Directory,' said she. 'I have advertised it at three several times. They have a memorandum of it at the Chief of Police's office; but here it is. Nobody has ever claimed it.

"'The children used to be immensely interested,' she said. 'They liked the handwriting of the cards, and took it for granted that a tin-type there is in it was a portrait of the owner. If it is, she is a very pretty girl. We have made up a great many stories about her. Sometimes we have her an English lady on her travels. Sometimes we have her a distinguished Italian in disguise. Sometimes we have her a hidden agent of Jeff Davis. Indeed,' said she, after another pause, 'the reason I stopped and blushed so absurdly was that I think of her more than you would suppose. It really seems to me sometimes that her destiny was interwoven with mine'; — and she blushed again.

"Now, for myself, I have plenty of such imaginations, and they make me very happy. I once wrote an article for 'The Unfortunates' Magazine' on Castles in the Air, but it got crowded out. But this was the first confession of weakness I had ever heard from this lonely, well-poised, independent girl, who had had to be father, mother, sister, and all, to these children, and who had almost provoked me sometimes by being sweet-tempered, calm, and gentle, when I should have been blazing with rage. I laughed heartily, and cried out: '"The Pocket-Book Recovered; or, The Double Destiny," — or better, "The Lost Destiny, and the Recovered Pocket-Book," — no, let us have it, "The Destined Pocket-Book; or, Two Hearts in One." I foresee a serial for "The Unfortunates' Magazine." Surely this time you will write for me.'

"'No, Mr. Haliburton,' said she; 'and if I did, I would write on tissue paper, in a microscopic hand, so that the article might be placed on a sixpence, like the Declaration of Independence. I am not going to fill up your old crates for you. But why do you not look at the princess?'

"I opened the pocket-book, took out the picture, and recognized it in an instant. 'Why,' said I, 'it is Bertha Traill!'

"'And do you know Bertha Traill?' said Miss Anna, fairly pale this time.

"'I danced with her at Mrs. Gordon's last night, took her down to supper, and afterwards handed her to her carriage,' said I, laughing.

"'You danced with Bertha Traill!' said she; and still she did not get back to her quiet manner, to those average tones, under which it is our general duty to conceal all emotion.

"'Why yes,' said I, 'I know Bertha better than I know almost any one. I have known her since I was in college. She calls our class her class. Witherspoon, her guardian's son, is a great ally of mine. He is as much at home at my mother's as I am, and I am as much at home at his father's. So I have known Bertha since I taught her how to scan; and a very charming person she is too.'

"Miss Anna fairly put down her eternal sewing, and looked me through and through. I tried to keep up the laughing tone I had begun with, or at least the familiar tone of our ordinary conversation. But she was too intent for that. I felt that she had been day-dreaming so much and so long, as she sat there sewing, that she was giving quite too much importance to the accident of my knowing Bertha. And I tried, as quickly as I could and as wisely as I could, to relieve the strain on her mind, and to let her down.

"'Why in the world,' said I, 'did she never see your advertisement? I knew she lost her money. She hated to tell old Mr. Witherspoon; as for the Chief of Police, I thought I went there myself. No, George undertook to. But it was just as they were going to Florida with poor Bessie, — and it was all confusion.'

"Miss Anna had recovered a little, and said she advertised in the Transcript and the Advertiser. That, too, accounted for her failure in part. The old gentleman was as secesh as Bertha was loyal, and would not have either paper in the house. But why had not George seen it? George always was a goose. So I ran on, — trying to give her time.

"And she became wholly herself again in two minutes. Indeed, she almost seemed to avoid the subject. I tried to tell her about Mrs. Gordon's party. I wanted to let her know what a really nice person Bertha is. I thought all that pretty story about the poor child's own mother would please her. But she had got at her sewing again, only said what I made her say, and was more quiet than I ever saw her. But when I got up to go, she took up the pocket-book, and said she wished I would take it to Miss Traill, and say she had done her best that she might have it before.

"'I shall do no such thing,' said I, 'I shall bring Bertha here, and you shall give it to her yourself.'

"She turned as pale as a sheet, as if Bertha belonged underground. 'No! — no! — no! Mr. Haliburton. Do not do that. You must not do that. I — I — I beg you, do not do that.'

"'Why in the world not?' said I. 'Bertha is not the ghoul Amine. She does not eat people's hearts with the end of a bodkin. I know you will like her, and I know she will like you.'

"'Why not?' repeated the poor girl, wistfully, — 'why not, indeed? Why, because I had rather you should not. Do not bring her, Mr. Haliburton. Pray, do not bring her. I ask it as a favor, really.'

"'Of course, I shall not bring her,' said I; and I bowed: the only formal words I ever said to her.

"'Thank you ever so much,' said she, and she tried to smile; still so excited, however. And she gave me the pocket-book, and said, 'Pray, take it to her.'

"I walked home, and I lay awake all night. Anna had asked a favor of me. 'A favor,' — the first time she had said such a word. This lovely girl, — this even-tempered, gentle, kind, true, far-seeing, wise, inspired girl, — this girl who had let me see her and talk with her, and play with her playmates, but had kept me just in my place, no hair's breadth nearer, — had asked a favor of George Haliburton, and George Haliburton had the good luck to be able to grant it.

"What a pity she could not have asked something more!

"But why was the whole thing so dramatic? Why was this pocket-book such a Leyden jar that one could not touch it, inside and outside, without a jump and a quiver? How could it be that Anna and I, — in bed, to myself, I could call her Anna, and, save to Phil and Walter and Elsie, I had never named her name aloud, — how could it be that Anna and I should have been in a gale like that? Were we possibly a little nearer together? Could she perhaps see that there was something in the truth and loyalty and devotion of a poor penniless dog of a rag-picker, which made him, so far, the equal of herself, perfect woman though she was, so nobly planned? No! that was nonsense, and I was a fool. But what made her blush? And what made her turn pale? I was a fool. Somehow or other I had managed to wound acutely the noblest woman in the world, whom I knew I loved with all a man's worship. That was bright in me. Women know women. I had ten minds to tell Bertha the whole story, and ask her why Anna turned pale.

"But of course I did not. I was a fool, but not so bad a fool as that. I took the pocket-book round, gave it to Bertha; and Bertha was amazed indeed. She explained some things which made it not so strange that they had missed the advertisements. But more than her interest in the pocket-book was her interest in Anna. 'Let me go see her,' said she. 'Take me now.'

"I told her that was just what I wanted to do, but that Anna would not let me.

"'Of course not,' said Bertha, turning round in a flash, as is the custom of some sexes, to sustain the opinion which was precisely the reverse of that she had expressed just before, — 'of course not. Do you suppose I should let you bring any girl you chose to call on me, or that I should think much of anybody who let you bring her? I shall call myself on Miss Davenport. I dare say I am the older person, or that I know Boston better than she. Where shall I find her?'

"I felt that I should like to have Bertha know Anna, should like to have her call. But I did not choose to tell her how to find her. Anna had asked as a favor that I should not bring her, and I had promised. I was not going to dodge — or to seem to — by letting her go alone. So I refused to tell. Bertha pressed: I was firm. She persevered: and I.

She scolded: I said nothing. She grew angry: and I. It ended in an up-and-down quarrel, — the first we two ever had. I bowed myself to the door. She would not say good by, and I pensively went home. I had three things to think of now: first, why did Anna turn pale, and then blush, when I told her about Bertha? second, why did she refuse to see Bertha? and, third, why did Bertha want to see her? On these points I meditated much that afternoon, and after I had turned off my gas at night. How little things affect you at such a time! I could tell you now how bad the delivery of that day was; and, of course, I had almost nothing in my pockets, — one or two dentists' cards, and a puzzle Bertha had given me, were all. I know that, all told, that night, there was not fifteen pounds on the balance. Misfortunes never come single.

"And Bertha, as I learned afterwards, as soon as I left the house, put on her hat and shawl, and went to the Quincy School-house. She remembered Walter's name, which I had mentioned; and she guessed rightly that this was his school, down by the South Cove. She asked the head-master which room he was in; then told his teacher that she wanted to find his sister, but had not her address. The teacher gave it, of course; and so, by the time I was well at home at Mrs. Thayer's, Bertha was timidly knocking at Anna Davenport's attic door.

"Anna called, 'Come in,' cheerfully; and Bertha,

eagerly, but frightened to death, went in, to Anna's entire surprise. Bertha saw her, felt the atmosphere, loved her; put out both hands to her, and told her how much obliged she was to her; how her brother Fergus gave her the pocket-book; how she hardly ever carried it; why she took it that particular day; how she went back to look for it; how she cried when she found she had lost it; and then, all wrought up and mixed up with the various successes of the day, — the recovery of Fergus's present, and the outgeneralling me, and the finding Anna so sympathizing and truly lovely, — poor, grand, triumphant Bertha broke down, and had a good cry.

"Which was probably, under her circumstances, the best thing she could do. Anna soothed her; made her sit on the sofa, and put up her feet; brought her cologne, untied her hat, and petted her in general. Then she got her talking about details; and before Bertha knew it, she was telling all about Fergus and his letters from Freyburg, and reading little scraps from them. How women carry such things round in their pockets! And before Anna knew it, she was telling about Walter, and Elsie's smart sayings, and showing Bertha about Elsie's new frock. And so it happened that Bertha stayed there till dark. And Elsie herself came in; and Bertha kissed her, and had a frolic with her, and made her promise to come and see her, and got up to go away. And she and Anna felt as if they had known each other for a thousand years.

" And so it happened that the two next afternoons Bertha called, and took Anna to ride with her, went to church with her Sunday, and insisted on her coming round there to tea Monday night. And that was the way that it happened that, at the theatre that evening, when I caught sight of old Mr. Witherspoon's figure in the balcony, and went round to the other side to see who were the ladies he had with him, I got a very triumphant bow from Miss Bertha, and a very modest, pretty bow from Miss Anna. But I could not get in to speak to them. And I had to go away and guess why Anna would go to the theatre with Bertha, when she would not let me take Bertha to see her.

" She would see Bertha without me. She would not see her with me. Could it be that my personality, my Ego, as Kant would say, was of any kind or sort of consequence to her? Did she think of me enough to care two straws whether I knocked at her door or went and peddled matches in Perth, in West Australia? I thought of her day and night. Had she so little to think of that she ever thought of me, when I was not lecturing there Wednesday evenings? I and Bertha must not go there together. Was there then — could it be possible — was it crazy conceit to suppose that my being mixed up with Bertha was anything of a midge's importance to her, even-balanced, self-sustained, independent Anna? I was an ass to think it. But it was by no means the first time I had been an ass. And thinking it, I was happier than I had been since Wednesday. I knew now, at the least, what I would do on Tuesday morning, or as soon as it was noon. And I did it.

"I walked round to Anna's, and, the hour being wholly unusual, I got in. I told her I loved her, had loved her, and always should love her ; that I was as poor a stick as she thought me, but that I was always true to my friends ; and that I should always be true to her, whatever she chose to say to me ; that I had longed to say this before, but never dared to ; that now she had asked one favor of me, and had broken her guard by doing it, so that I could not help asking another.

"And she — said nothing. And that is the way we came to be here.

"I do not know how long we might have ground on, but for the pocket-book. I do know that she was right when she said her destiny pivoted there, — and mine did as well.

"Bertha was married, you know, that winter, and Anna was a bridesmaid. Anna and I were married in the spring, and Bertha danced at the wedding. And that is the way we came to be here, as I said before."

I intimated that I had not always observed that when two young people married on a limited income, a handsome house on eight lots on Commonwealth

Avenue was the direct or logical consequence. Polly and I had done the same thing, and were well satisfied with our own house three doors from the corner of D Street, as you go south from the Capuchins'. So Haliburton explained.

He took Anna and the children to Mrs. Thayer's. Mrs. Thayer had got tired of keeping lodgers, and went to Sceattle, leaving all the house to them. Anna insisted on it that the children should keep at work till they could do something better. The business on each side reinforced the other, — the union indeed made savings in correspondence and expressage and other expenses. She was a nice accountant as well as a perfect housekeeper, and all ran smoothly. Soon enough, indeed, Anna found her Kelts burning newspapers in kindling the range and furnace fires. "Like the Jew in Thackeray's story, who used Bank-of-England notes to light the candle," said she. This would never do. She made Haliburton send her round a barrel of shavings, and made the women promise, gladly enough, to kindle with them.

Haliburton paid nothing for the shavings. But he had to send down a barrel to the carpenter's and pay fifteen cents for sending it; he had to pay as much more for bringing it back; then he forgot all about it; and so the first morning that the thermometer was eighty-four degrees below zero, he came down stairs to find no fire, and Bridget and Mrs. Flynn triumphantly informed him that this was because the shavings were all gone. Haliburton could not stand that of course. He made the fire without swearing. Good practice that in saving one's soul alive, or learning to possess it in patience, which is the same thing. Then he made the range fire. Meanwhile Anna had boiled some water over the gas, scrambled some eggs on the same furnace, made her dip-toast ditto ditto; and had her coffee done and her milk hot by the time he had washed his hands. They ate their breakfasts shawled and coated. And Haliburton at once proceeded to Nolan's.

He started Nolan's son Stephen that morning with a one-horse express-wagon, paid for the horse and for his keeping for three months. Steve was a bright boy: he is now running a lumber-mill on the North Naguadavick. Every morning he took on his wagon ten barrels of shavings, as soon as fire-lighting began. He carried them from house to house till he got his regular customers. He sold them, not for money, but for newspapers; a barrel of shavings for twenty-five newspapers, after you had paid for the barrel. The profit, of course, was enormous, — too enormous, you would have said, to last; only housekeepers stand everything. The shavings really cost Haliburton almost nothing. They were glad to have their shops regularly cleared. The business grew. One man and cart with a boy could distribute in a winter's day an immense number of barrels, as soon as they got it in system. Haliburton said a steady man, with a bright boy, would distribute in ten hours two hundred barrels when the route was all adjusted. Two hundred barrels, with paper stock at eight cents, brought them in forty dollars a day; and even after they started their own planing-mills, and had to buy their own lumber, half this forty dollars was profit. By this time the business was established. There was not a family in Boston, Chelsea, Dorchester, Cambridge, Brookline, or Roxbury that had not rather kindle with shavings; and when Haliburton had sixty-three carts running regularly, as he had when he told me the story, one thousand two hundred and sixty dollars' profit a day through the winter made a very pretty business. Naturally, at the same time, he got into lumbering and paper-making; he knew the business in its detail, which is always good training for the general, you know; and so it was that he felt able to build his pretty palace in which we were sitting.

He said they had asked him to be President of the Seventy-second National Bank; but he had said, though his fortune was made of rags, he preferred the crude to the manufactured article.

DINNER SPEAKING.

A LETTER TO MY NEPHEW.

So you did not enjoy your first Phi Beta dinner, dear Tom, because you were afraid all the time that the new members would be toasted, and then "the fellows" had said you must reply for them. That is a pity. As, after all, the fellows were not toasted, it is a great pity. I am glad you write to me about it, however, and now it is for me to take care that this never happens to you again.

I will tell you how to be always ready. I will tell you how I do.

My first Phi Beta dinner was, like yours, my first public dinner. It was on the day, which this year everybody remembered who was old enough, when Mr. Emerson delivered his first Phi Beta oration at Cambridge. How proudly he has the right to look back on the generation between, all of which he has seen, so much of which he has been! Well, he is no older this day, to all appearance, than he was then,— and your uncle, my dear boy, though older to appearance, is not older in reality. What is it dear G—— Q—— sings, who sat behind me that early day at Phi Beta?

"When we 've been there ten million years,
Bright shining as the sun,
We 'll *have more days*
To sing God's praise,
Than when we first begun!"

Remember that, my dear oldest nephew, as the ten million years go by, — and, remembering it, keep young or grow young.

Mr. Emerson was young, I say, — and I. We were all young.

Mr. Edward Everett was young. He was then Governor, — and, I think, presided, certainly spoke, at that Phi Beta dinner. By the almanac he must have been that year forty-five years old, — just as old, dear Tom, as some other people are this year by the almanac. He had been pretty much everything, had gone most everywhere, had seen almost all the people that were worth seeing, and remembered more than all the rest of us had forgotten. And he was very young. To those who knew him he always was. The day he died he was about the youngest man in most things that I knew.

And so it happened that he made the first dinner speech that I remember. We were all in the South Commons Hall of University, now used as somebody's lecture-room, say, at a guess, Professor Lovering's. And he gave some charming reminiscences of Edward Emerson, brother of the philosopher, too early lost, and everywhere loved, — and then, speaking of the oration of the day, and of the new philosophy to which it belonged, and of which the orator was, is, and will be the prophet, he said, in his gracious, funny, courtly, and hearty way, that he always thought of its thunders as he did of the bolts of Jupiter himself! Could one have complimented an orator more than to compare him to Jupiter? And then he went on to verify the comparison by quoting the description, —

> "Tres imbris torti radios, tres nubis aquosæ
> Addiderant, rutili tres ignis, et alitis Austri," —

and translated the words for his purpose, —

> "Three parts were raging fire, and three were whelming waves!
> But three were *thirsty cloud,* and three were *empty wind!*"

Ah well, my boy! You do not remember what all the world, except a few of the elect, then said of "Transcendentalism." So you cannot imagine the scream of fun and applause which saluted this good-natured analysis of its thunder.

And I, — I was delighted at this aptness of quotation. Should I ever bring my capping lines to such a market? Here was a hit as good as the famous parliamentary retorts, which were so precious to us in the I. O. H. and in the Harvard Union. Should I ever live to see the happy day when I should find that it was wise, witty, and just the thing to say,

> "Tu quoque litoribus nostris, Æneia nutrix"?

or,

> "Tityre dum redeo, brevis est via, pasce capellas,"

or any other of the T's? Or,

> "Æsopus auctor quam materiam reperit,"

or,

> "Æacus ingemuit, tristique ita voce locutus,"

or any other of the Æ diphthongs? It did not seem possible, but we would see.

Now it happened that, in the vacation following, a French steamer, I think the Geryon, came to Boston. And there was, perhaps a civic dinner, certainly an excursion down the harbor, to persuade her officers, and through them Louis Philippe, for this was in the early age of stone, that Boston Harbor was the best point for the projected line of French packets to stop at, — and somebody invited me to go. And it turned out that few of the Frenchmen spoke English, and few of the Common Councilmen spoke French, so that poor little I came to some miserable use as a half-interpreter. I remember telling a Lieutenant de Vaisseau that the "Centurion" rock was called so because the 74 Centurion was lost there; and that an indignant civic authority, guessing out my speech, told me they did not want the Frenchmen to know anything was ever lost in Boston Harbor! Perhaps that was the reason the French packets never came. Well, by and by there was the inevitable collation in the cabin. (A collation, dear boy, is a dinner where you have nothing to eat.) And we went down stairs to collate. I began to think of the speeches. Suppose they should call on the youngest of the interpreters, what could he say? What Latin quotation that would answer?

Not Tityrus certainly! No. Nor Æneas's nurse certainly, for she went overboard, — bad luck to her! — or was she buried decently? Bad omen that! But — yes! certainly — what better than the thunderbolts of Jove? Steam-navigation forever, — Robert Fulton, Marquis of Worcester, madman in the French bedlam, — bolts of heaven secured for service of earth, — Franklin, — the great alliance, — steam-navigation uniting the world! Was not the whole prefigured, *messieurs, quand le grand poète* forged the very thunderbolts of the *Dieu des Cieux?*

> " Tres imbris torti radios, tres nubis aquosæ
> Addiderant, rutili tres ignis, et alitis Austri."

What better description of the power which at that moment was driving us along, —

> " Three rays of writhen rain, of fire three more,
> Of winged southern winds, and cloudy store,
> As many parts the dreadful mixture frame " ?

Could anything have been more happy? And fortunately no member of Phi Beta was present but myself. But, unfortunately, there was no speaking, and for the moment I lost my opportunity.

But not my preparation, dear Tom. And for this purpose have I written this long story, to show you how, in thirty happy years since, when I have had nothing else to say, " Tres imbris torti radios " has always stood me in stead. One good quotation makes an after-dinner speaker the match of the whole world.

And if you have it in Latin, the people who understand that language enjoy it especially, and those who do not always appear to enjoy it more especially. Perhaps they do. There is also the advantage of slight variations in the translation. Note the difference between Mr. Everett's above, and John Dryden's.

Imagine yourself, for instance, an invited guest at a Cincinnati dinner in Wisconsin. Unfortunately, my dear boy, none of your ancestors rose even to the rank of drummer in the army of the Revolution. Your great-grandfather's brother had Chastellux to dinner one day. If you can, make your speech out of that. But I do not think you can. Still, you are called up to speak: "Our friend from New England," — "Connecticut, — Israel Putnam, — Bunker Hill, — Groton, — Wooster," &c., &c. What will you do, my boy? You must do something, and you must not disgrace old Wooster. Do? You have your thunderbolts.

"This army," — "gathered from North and South and East and West," — "like another army," — "whose brave officers still linger among us, — cheer us," &c., &c., — "this army," — "combining such various elements of power, endurance, and wisdom, — this army, always when I think of it, — more than ever to-day, sir, when I see these who represent it in another generation, — when I think of Manly coming from the yeasty waves of the outstretched Cape, — of Ethan Allen descending from the cloudy tops of the Green Mountains, — of Knox, sweaty and black from the hot furnace work of Salisbury, where

> 'He created all the stores of war,'—

all meeting at the same moment with the Morgans, and Marions, and the one Washington from the distant South, — this army always seems to me to be the prefigured thunderbolt which the Cyclops forged for Jupiter.

> 'Tres imbris torti radios, tres nubis aquosæ
> Addiderant, rutili tres ignis, et alitis Austri.'

> 'Three from the sultry South, three from the storm-beat shore,
> Three parts from distant mountains' cloudy store,
> While raging heat fused all with three parts more!'"

You see, dear Tom, these audiences are always good-natured, and by no means critical of your version.

Why, at the only time I was ever at a regimental dinner on the Plains, long before the war, you know, when to the untaught mind it did seem as if there was no reason why we were there, and no pretence for mutual congratulation, I remember when poor Pendergrast called me up to represent science (I was at that time in the telegraph business), the dear old quotation came to my relief like an inspiration. I got round to the Flag. Do you remember how safe General Halleck always found it to allude to the Flag?

10

"The flag, gentlemen," — "colors," — "rainbow of our liberties," — "Liberty everywhere." "Blue, white, and red of Low Countries," — "Red, white, and blue of France," — "English Constitution," — "Puritan fathers, Cavaliers," &c., &c.

"Does it seem too much to say, gentlemen, that, with the divine instinct of poetry, the unequalled bard of the court of Augustus, looking down the ages beyond the sickly purple of the palace, to the days when armies should be the armies of freemen, and not the Prætorian guards of a tyrant, — that he veiled the glad prophecy of the future in the words in which he describes even the thunderbolt itself? The white crest of the foam, the blue of the sky, the red of the fiery furnace, are all tossed together, and play together, and rejoice together there, in the smiles or in the rage of the very breeze of Heaven.

'Tres imbris torti radios, tres nubis aquosæ
Addiderant, rutili tres ignis, et alitis Austri.'

'Three parts of white the crested billows lent,
Three parts of blue the heavens themselves had sent,
Three parts of fiery red with these were blent,
And on the free-born wind across the world they went.'"

You are not old enough, my dear nephew, to remember the great consistory which the Pope held at Somerville, when for a moment he thought that the churches of the world had recognized that Union which in fact does make them one, and were willing to offer one front to the Devil, instead of fighting, as they always had done, on ten thousand hooks of their own. You understand, it was not this Pope, Pius IX. It was the pope who came after Gregory XVI. and before Pius IX. Well, at that immense dinner-table, which had been built on the plan of John O'Groat's, so that each of the eleven thousand six hundred and thirty folks present might sit at the head, — I was fortunate enough to be appointed to represent the Sandemanian clergy, — the only body, as I will venture to say to you, which really preserves the simplicity of Gospel institutions, or in the least carries into our own time the spirit and life of fundamental Christianity. Now you may imagine the difficulty of speaking on such an occasion. I had thought it proper to speak in Latin. The difficulty was not so much in the language as in what to say, that one might be at once brave as a Sandemanian, and at the same time tolerant, and catholic as a Christian. Now it is not for me to say how well I acquitted myself. If you want to see my speech, you had better look in the *Annales de Foi;* and, if it is there, you will certainly find it. I did not think it amiss, certainly, that I was able to close by comparing the great agencies which the United Church would be able to employ to the thunderbolt itself. We had there present bishops from England of perpetual rain, from Sitka of perpetual cloud, from the eternal fires of the torrid zone, and from the farthest south of Patagonia. When we selected our sacred twelve, it was easy for us to take them, as if we were forging thunders.

> "Tres imbris torti radios, tres nubis aquosæ
> Addiderant, rutili tres ignis, et alitis Austri."

Now, my dear Tom, I am sure my lesson needs no moral. Of course I do not think you had better start in life with my quotation. To tell you the truth, I am still young. I am a life-member of many societies, and, as they outlive other usefulness, the more frequently do they dine together. I may therefore have some other occasion when I may be reminded of the Cyclops. But if, at your dinner, I had happened to be called upon, I think, — I do not know, but I think that, seeing such men as you describe, I should have been irresistibly led to consider the varied gifts which the University every year scatters over the land, and the exquisite harmony by which, from such different callings, different homes, and different destinies, they unite in the merriment or in the wisdom of her festivities. The men of practice who have been taming the waterfall, and made it subservient; the men of the gentle ministries of peace, whose blessings distil upon us like the very dews of heaven; and the men of the spoken word, — of the spirit of truth, of which, like the wind itself, no man knoweth whence it cometh or whither it goeth, — these, and the men of war who have passed through its fires to give us the free America of to-day, all were around you.

Surely in such a union I should have been reminded of the divine harmony by which elements the most diverse were welded into the bolts of Jove.

> "Tres imbris torti radios, tres nubis aquosæ
> Addiderant, rutili tres ignis, et alitis Austri."

> "Three parts like dews from heaven, three from the wave-beat shore,
> Three from the soft-winged breeze, and three from blood-red war."

Always, dear Tom, your affectionate uncle,

FREDERIC INGHAM.

SUBSEQUENT POSTSCRIPT BY MR. INGHAM.

The subject, perhaps, needs no further illustration; but I am tempted to add, — as I file this printed copy of the letter away, — that my friend, George Hussey, hearing, the week after it was printed, that we had no good cherry-brandy at our house, sent me round some, which has proved excellent in a year's medical practice, with the following formula for its manufacture: —

> "Tres imbris torti radios, tres nubis aquosæ
> Addiderant, rutili tres ignis, et alitis Austri."

> "Three parts from fruits wet from the dews of Heaven,
> Three by stiff southern gales brought from Jamaica's shore;
> Three rays of torrid heat in tropic cave inwoven,
> And three of pelting rain from Nature's aqueous store."

Nor was it long after, that I found myself called on for a few after-dinner remarks at the Beta Phi.

It was just after Edward Rice had delivered his admirable poem of "Andromeda," "The old world set free," in which were brilliant passages on our late war, and the various European revolutions. What more inevitable than that I should be reminded — as I saw the thunderbolt which had been thus in forge for the overthrow of tyrants — of

"Tres imbris torti radios,"

which for the purpose I rendered as follows :—

"Three tempest blasts of Prussia's wrath divine,
Forged in three twisted rays of Western sunset shine,
Fanned by three blasts of stormy Apennine,
And three, — O wild Euroclydon of Crete ! — were thine."

F. I.

GOOD SOCIETY.

[First published in the New York Ledger of October 31, 1868.]

I.

WE were very fond of Maria. She was a thoroughly good girl, and at heart thoroughly sensible; and I, who told her her faults when it was best for her, which was not often, for it is not best to talk much of faults to any one, — I never scolded her for anything but taking dark views instead of bright of a world which a good God had made, and in which he had chosen that she should live.

One day she said, in reply to me, that this was all very well for me, because I lived in a pleasant town among pleasant people. I lived then in Worcester, Massachusetts. But, she said, if I had to live where she did, I should sing to a different tune. She had no difficulty, whatever, in taking bright views of things in Worcester. She always did when she made a visit there. But if I would come and make them a visit in that smoky, snuffy, musty, fusty old forlorn New-Altona, that they lived in, I should not take any brighter view of life than she.

I have looked in the Gazetteer, dear reader, to make sure that there is no such town as New-Altona.

Really, Maria, whose real name is not Maria, lived in a driving manufacturing town, which was not old, though she called it so. I call it New-Altona for fear of hurting the people's feelings there, when they open the *Ledger;* because this is a true story we are engaged on — in the substance. You can call the town anything you choose, — call it Paterson or New Brunswick, or Germantown or Newark. Newark is a good name, only it is not the right one.

"Well," said I, "what is the matter with New-Altona? Emily has a very good sewing-bird that was made there."

"Suppose she has. Do you suppose I want to eat and drink sewing-birds, — and to have sewing-birds for tea, cooked with French sauce, — to give an evening party and have nothing but sewing-birds come to it? That is just it, — there is no society in New-Altona." So groaned poor Maria, half crying, half laughing.

"There must be society," said I, "because there are forty thousand people there. And you must have social intercourse with them, for I know you bought your pretty hat there, which so astonished our natives. You did not pick it off a tree as they do in the Swiss Family Robinson!" (Foul Play was not then written.)

"No," said Maria, rather seriously this time. "You have just hit it. I can buy a bonnet there, or a mutton-chop. I can tell Mr. Doak what pear-trees I want to set out in the spring. And I can call on Madam Chenavard, and have her tell me how the Chenavards are an old Huguenot family (as they are not), whose name ought to be spelt something else, which is all a mistake of hers. But this is all the same, one day as another. And it is horribly tedious. You say it is society. Suppose it is. It is not good society."

"And you must own," said Polly Ingham, who had come up at that moment, a very bright person she, who is wholly at home in our house, — "you must own that good society means something."

"Of course it does," interrupted Maria, "it means such society as I have in this house." We all bowed double. "You shall not laugh me out of it; it means society where people know something, where they talk about nice things, — about books, and pictures, and music, and political economy, and flowers, and people, and history, and religion, and talk easily, not because they want to teach you nor because they want to learn, but because they are nice themselves, and because the others are nice. That is what I mean by good society. Such society as you read about in books. Such society as Mr. Warrington lived in sometimes. Well, such society as they have in Europe."

"Yes," said Polly, dreamily, "do you remember those charming three months we spent with the Steins, — the Von Steins, when Fred was laying the wire in Siberia? That was really good society."

I saw what Polly meant, and I confessed that it was. So Maria begged me not to scold her any more, but tell all about it, and I sent for the photograph portfolio, and showed her Baron Von Stein's house, before and behind, and the lovely bow-window, and the interior, with the old Baroness knitting, and the family pictures, and then told her of the pleasant time we spent there. I was not there three months, nor anything like it. But I believe the ladies were, and I was there long enough to see and enjoy.

It was one of those immense Silesian estates, as big as a reasonable county, and the life was indeed thorough domestic life. There were guests distinguished, and guests not distinguished. Most of us met at breakfast, all of us at dinner, — and after dinner we generally were all together, on the lawn, or in the great library, or in the music-room. Billiards, if you wanted billiards; books, if you wanted books; cards, if you wanted cards; and music, if you wanted music. But really the talk was so good, that, for my part, I liked that better than all the rest, and so did most of the company; and so we fell to telling Maria about the company, about Von Stein himself, how well he bore his almost total blindness, how little he complained of his sufferings, what a marvellous man he was, in his remembrances and in his accomplishments. A nobleman of the bluest blood, with sixteen times sixteen quarterings; one of his ancestors, whose autograph and sword and boots he showed us, was a nobleman in Luther's time, and distinguished in that Protestant history; and Von Stein himself had inherited all that Protestantism. He was the most radical of noblemen. His house was even then full of exiles. "A perfect State Prison for State offenders," he used to call it. There was Rivoli from Genoa, the popular preacher of yesterday; there was young Rodinoff and his pretty German wife. His father was in Siberia, and it had been intimated to him that he had better travel outside of Russia. There was Van der Donck, who had lived so long in the Levant; and those charming Lavater girls, whose poor father — "O, there were too many, too many for to name." But we told Maria enough about them to interest her, and I sent Nelly to bring the Christmas album which Von Stein printed in memory of our visit.

It had exquisite etchings and lithographs of the drawings the ladies and Van der Donck had made. It had two little waltzes which Friesland had written for Clara Lavater. It had a long letter which I had written them from Bellinzona, after I left them. It had a sermon which Rivoli preached to us one Sunday on the terrace, — which had been privily taken down in short-hand by Emert Von Stein. It had a ballad by Count George, and a story by Fanny. Polly said there was nothing of hers but a crochet pattern, which she had given the Baroness. There was something from everybody, and Von Stein had had forty copies elegantly printed that autumn, and had sent one to each of us with his Christmas wishes for many happy returns of our visit.

I said Von Stein was certainly one of the most accomplished men I ever knew. Such a master of languages, — for his English was as grammatical as mine, — and he seemed to speak six other languages as well; he drew so well, he played on the violin and piano so well, he rode so well, he danced so well, and he talked so well. Then, best accomplishment of all, — for it did not come of nature, but by grace to Von Stein, — he was so lovely to every one, — kept his hot temper under so completely, and was so perfectly unselfish.

Polly laughed at my enthusiasm, and said, —

"The Baron always was your hero; but, for my part, I liked our dear George the best of all that brilliant company."

"There is no need of telling me that," said I.

And my wife laughed, and Polly blushed.

"I don't care," said she, "you may laugh as much as you choose, but I like him, and I like his wife, too. There 's a nice letter I had from Gertrude only yesterday. If you could see him with the children as much as I have, if you knew how he brought everything into play for them, and for everybody; if Wilhelm was tired in the train, he would take out his scissors and cut out stags and boars and knights out of the newspaper. If little Minnie was sleepy, he would tell such ravishing fairy stories. I had rather a man should do that than compose sixty sonatas."

"Especially," said I, "if he be a real count, and be named on the great book at Vienna."

And we all laughed, and went out to dinner.

II.

After I had helped every one to boiled mutton, and had given red gravy to all who would, Maria began again.

"Now, cousin," said she, "you will own that there is such a thing as good society, and that such people as the Baron and Mrs. Ingham's Count give you good society when you meet them, and that that is better society than a tea-party at Madam Chenavard's, or a sewing-society with the Dorcases."

"Well, Maria," said I, "I never met the Dorcases, and I do not know Madam Chenavard; but I dare say what you say is true, and that Polly's Count George and my Baron Von Stein received me into better society than either."

Maria thanked me, and said I was not cross a bit, and was a real reasonable cousin. And Polly's eyes twinkled, for the whole conversation had been her plan. "And how, do you think," said she, "that we got received into this good society?"

Maria said she had meant to ask.

"I will tell you," said I. "I saw the Baron first on the stoop here. I was sitting just where you were when the dinner-bell rang. He came up Hammond Street, from Main Street, looking very dusty and very tired. He was very shabby, too. He had a little bundle made of a red cotton handkerchief, and a walking-stick. I asked him to sit down, and said he looked tired, and sent for a glass of water. Then I found he had had no dinner, and I ordered cold mutton here, and bread and cheese. And we came in, and he sat just where you are sitting now, and he ate and talked, and I sat here and questioned. After he had eaten his mutton, he had a pear, as I hope you will when you have eaten yours. Then we crossed the entry and came into the study, and we had a long talk together. At last we got more at ease, and I said to him that I thought he was about my size, and that I had an old coat which I thought would about fit him, and would he like to try it on. He said he would, and I went up stairs and got it; and that was my first acquaintance with the Baron Von Stein, and that was the way that afterward he came to ask us to stay with him in Silesia."

"O cousin," said Maria, "you are joking!"

"Not in the least, my dear child. The poor fellow had been exiled after '49, and had come over here. Here, it was the old story of exile. He very soon ran through his ready money. What could he do here? Why, he could write, he could translate. And he did; wrote his twelve hours a day, and I do not know how many a night. Ruined his eyesight by his night proof-reading. He must do it, or starve, you know. Then he was blind for months. Then he got a little sight, — just enough to go from door to door. What could he do? What but what he did? He went bravely from town to town, looking for pupils. But who wanted a teacher that could not see the book nor read the exercises? Ah, Maria, you do not know exile yet, nor how soon such a man's coat comes out at elbows."

"But for all that, he was as accomplished a man when he ate his cold mutton here as he was in his own palace. And I remember I enjoyed our talk about Ulric Von Hutten as much, that afternoon, as I ever did any talk with him or with any man. I felt that we had been in very good society that day. As it happened, you see, he was the first baron I had ever shaken hands with."

"And I," said Polly, — who, as I said, had led this whole talk, almost unknown to me, and wholly to Maria, — "I came into the society of the high nobility of the old families in this way. I was spending the summer and autumn in Cincinnati. Fred was supplying the pulpit there. There came down a note from Governor Vance, to say that he had heard nothing from a German artist, named George Lichtenstein, who had promised to write to him. Would Fred or I call and see if they were all well? I went to the place, and found the furniture had been sold at auction the week before. This looked odd; and on inquiry it proved that it had all been pledged for the rent and seized by the landlord. Then where were Mr. George and his wife and little girls? A pretty hunt they gave me. But what with the police and the schoolmistress, and some children in the street, after three or four days, I found them in a tenement room, three stories high, perhaps twelve feet square. The Count George was on his knees scrubbing up the floor, and his three daughters were sitting on a trunk, because there was nothing else to sit on, eating three doughnuts, with nothing else to eat. That was the way Fred and I came to be invited afterwards to visit them in Wirtemburg, and then went with them to Von Stein's. He and Von Stein had been at Halle together when they were young men."

"I do not say, Maria," said I, "that my luck with tramps was always as good as this. They are often sad sticks, — almost always."

"And I do not say," said Polly, "that in up-stairs ten-foot tenements, where are people who have run away from their landlords, I have always found lovely German girls or Counts of the Empire."

"But I do say," said I, "that the first requisite of good society is, that you shall find some one who knows what you do not, and has some notions to exchange against yours, and that the wider the range of my acquaintance the more good society have I found."

"And I say," said Polly, "that, though I never made any effort about good society, it has happened that I have found it as often among the people who were not trained in my way, at my schools, in my set, or among my relatives, as anywhere."

"And I have found," said I, "that by entertaining strangers, I have sometimes entertained angels unawares."

DAILY BREAD.

A CHRISTMAS STORY.

[First published in the Boston Daily Advertiser of Dec. 25, 1868.]

I.

A QUESTION OF NOURISHMENT.

"AND how is he?" said Robert, as he came in from his day's work, in every moment of which he had thought of his child. He spoke in a whisper to his wife, who met him in the narrow entry at the head of the stairs. And in a whisper she replied.

"He is certainly no worse," said Mary; "the doctor says, maybe a shade better. At least," she said, sitting on the lower step, and holding her husband's hand, and still whispering, — "at least he said that the breathing seemed to him a shade easier, one lung seemed to him a little more free, and that it is now a question of time and nourishment."

"Nourishment?"

"Yes, nourishment, — and I own my heart sunk as he said so. Poor little thing, he loathes the slops, and I told the doctor so. I told him the struggle and fight to get them down his poor little throat gave him more flush and fever than anything. And then he begged me not to try that again, asked if there were really nothing that the child would take, and suggested everything so kindly. But the poor little thing, weak as he is, seems to rise up with supernatural strength against them all. I am not sure, though, but perhaps we may do something with the old milk and water; that is really my only hope now, and that is the reason I spoke to you so cheerfully."

Then poor Mary explained more at length that Emily had brought in Dr. Cummings's Manual about the use of milk with children, and that they had sent round to the Corlisses', who always had good milk, and had set a pint according to the direction, and had watered it thus and so according to the formula; and that though dear little Jamie had refused the groats and the barley, and I know not what else, that at six he had gladly taken all the watered milk they dared to give him, and that it now had rested on his stomach half an hour, so that she could not but hope that the tide had turned, only she hoped with trembling, because he had so steadily refused cow's milk only the week before.

This rapid review in her entry, of the bulletins of a day, is really the beginning of this Christmas story. No matter which day it was, — it was a little before Christmas, and one of the shortest days, but I have forgotten which. Enough that the baby, for he was a baby still, just entering his thirteenth month, — enough that he did relish the milk, so carefully measured and prepared, and hour by hour took his little dole of it as if it had come from his mother's breast. Enough that three or four days went by so, the little thing lying so still on his back in his crib, his lips still so blue, and his skin of such deadly color against the white of his pillow; and that, twice a day, as Dr. Morton came in and felt his pulse, and listened to the panting, he smiled and looked pleased, and said, "We are getting on better than I dared expect." Only every time he said, "Does he still relish the milk?" and every time was so pleased to know that he took to it still, and every day he added a teaspoonful or two to the hourly dole; and so poor Mary's heart was lifted day by day.

This lasted till St. Victoria's day. Do you know which day that is? It is the second day before Christmas, and here, properly speaking, the story begins.

II.

ST. VICTORIA'S DAY.

St. Victoria's day the doctor was full two hours late. Mary was not anxious about this. She was beginning to feel bravely about the boy, and no longer counted the minutes till she could hear the door-bell ring. When he came he loitered in the entry below, — or she thought he did. He was long coming up stairs. And, when he came in, she saw that he was excited by something, — was really even then panting for breath.

"I am here at last," he said. "Did you think I should fail you?"

Why no, poor innocent Mary had not thought of any such thing. She had known he would come; and baby was so well that she had not minded his delay.

Morton looked up at the close-drawn shades, which shut out the light, and said, "You did not think of the storm?"

"Storm? no!" said poor Mary. She had noticed, when Robert went to the door at seven and she closed it after him, that some snow was falling. But she had not thought of it again. She had kissed him, told him to keep up good heart, and had come back to her baby.

Then the doctor told her that the storm which had begun before daybreak had been gathering more and more severely; that the drifts were already heavier than he remembered them in all his Boston life; that after half an hour's trial in his sleigh he had been glad to get back to the stable with his horse, and that all he had done since he had done on foot, with difficulty she could not conceive of. He had been so long down stairs while he brushed the snow off, that he might be fit to come near the child.

"And really, Mrs. Walter, we are doing so well here," he said cheerfully, "that I will not try to come round this afternoon, unless you see a change. If you do, your husband must come up for me, you know. But you will not need me, I am sure."

Mary felt quite brave to think that they should not need him really for twenty-four hours, and said so; and added, with the first smile he had seen for a fortnight: "I do not know anybody to whom it is of less account than to me, whether the streets are blocked or open. Only I am sorry for you."

Poor Mary, how often she thought of that speech, before Christmas day went by! But she did not think of it all through St. Victoria's day. Her husband did not come home to dinner. She did not expect him. The children came from school at two, rejoicing in the long morning session and the half-holiday of the afternoon which had been earned by it. They had some story of their frolic in the snow, and after dinner went quietly away to their little play-room in the attic. And Mary sat with her baby all the afternoon, nor wanted other company. She could count his breathing now, and knew how to time it by the watch, and she knew that it was steadier and slower than it was the day before. And really he almost showed an appetite for the hourly dole. Her husband was not late. He had taken care of that, and had left the shop an hour early. And as he came in and looked at the child from the other side of the crib, and smiled so cheerfully on her, Mary felt that she could not enough thank God for his mercy.

III.

ST. VICTORIA'S DAY IN THE COUNTRY.

Five-and-twenty miles away was another mother, with a baby born the same day as Jamie. Mary had never heard of her and never has heard of her, and, unless she reads this story, never will hear of her till they meet together in the other home, look each other in the face, and know as they are known. Yet their two lives, as you shall see, are twisted together, as indeed are all lives, only they do not know it, — as how should they ?

A great day for Huldah Stevens was this St. Victoria's day. Not that she knew its name more than Mary did. Indeed, it was only of late years that Huldah Stevens had cared much for keeping Christmas day. But of late years they had all thought of it more ; and, this year, on Thanksgiving day, at old Mr. Stevens's, after great joking about the young people's housekeeping, it had been determined, with some banter, that the same party should meet with John and Huldah on Christmas eve, with all Huldah's side of the house besides, to a late dinner or early supper, as the guests might please to call it. Little difference between the meals, indeed, was there ever in the profusion of these country homes. The men folks were seldom at home at the noonday meal, call it what you will ; for they were all in the milk business, as you will see. And, what with collecting the milk from the hill-farms, on the one hand, and then carrying it for delivery at the three-o'clock morning milk-train, on the other hand, any hours which you, dear reader, might consider systematic, or of course in country life, were certainly always set aside. But, after much conference, as I have said, it had been determined at the Thanksgiving party that all hands of both families should meet at John and Huldah's as near three o'clock as they could the day before Christmas; and then and there Huldah was to show her powers in entertaining, at her first state family party.

So this St. Victoria's day was a great day of preparation for Huldah, if she had only known its name, as she did not. For she was of the kind which prepares in time, not of the kind that is caught out when the company come, with the work half done. And as John started on his collection beat that morning at about the hour Robert, in town, kissed Mary good by, Huldah stood on the step with him, and looked with satisfaction on the gathering snow, because it would make better sleighing the next day for her father and mother to come over. She charged him not to forget her box of raisins when he came back, and to ask at the express if anything came up from town, bade him good by, and turned back into the house, not wholly dissatisfied to be almost alone. She washed her baby, gave her her first lunch, and put her to bed. Then, with the coast fairly clear, — what woman does not enjoy a clear coast, if it only be early enough in the morning? — she dipped boldly and wisely into her flour-barrel, stripped her plump round arms to their work, and began on the pie-crust which was to appear to-morrow in the fivefold forms of apple, cranberry, Marlborough, mince, and squash, careful and discriminating in the nice chemistry of her mixtures and the nice manipulations of her handicraft, but in no wise dreading the issue. A long, active, lively morning she had of it. Not dissatisfied with the stages of her work, step by step she advanced, stage by stage she attained of the elaborate plan which was well laid out in her head, but of course, had never been intrusted to words, far less to telltale paper. From the oven at last came the pies, — and she was satisfied with the color; from the other oven came the turkey, which she proposed to have cold, as a relay, or *piéce de resistance*, for any who might not be at hand at the right moment for dinner. Into the empty oven went the clove-blossoming ham, which, as it boiled, had given the least appetizing odor to the kitchen. In the pretty moulds in the wood-shed stood the translucent cranberry hardening to its fixed consistency. In other moulds the obedient calf's-foot already announced its willingness and intention to "gell" as she directed. Huldah's decks were cleared again, her kitchen table fit to cut out "work" upon, — all the pans and plates were put away, which accumulate so mysteriously where cooking is going forward; on its nail hung the weary jigger, on its hook the spicy grater, on the roller a fresh towel. Everything gave sign of victory, — the whole kitchen looking only a little nicer than usual. Huldah herself was dressed for the afternoon, and so was the baby; and nobody but as acute observers as you and I would have known that she had been in action all along the line, and had won the battle at every point, when two o'clock came, the earliest moment at which her husband ever returned.

Then, for the first time, it occurred to Huldah to look out doors and see how fast the snow was gathering. She knew it was still falling. But the storm was a quiet one, and she had had too much to do to be gaping out of the windows. She went to the shed door, and, to her amazement, saw that the north woodpile was wholly drifted in! Nor could she, as she stood, see the fences of the roadway!

Huldah ran back into the house, opened the parlor door and drew up the curtain, to see that there were indeed no fences on the front of the house to be seen. On the northwest, where the wind had full sweep, between her and the barn, the ground was bare. But all that snow, and who should say how much more, was piled up in front of her; so that unless Huldah had known every landmark, she would not have suspected that any road was ever there. She looked uneasily out at the northwest windows, but she could not see an inch to windward; dogged snow, snow, snow, as if it would never be done.

Huldah knew very well then that there was no husband for her in the next hour, nor most like in the next or the next. She knew very well, too, what she had to do, — and, knowing it, she did it. She tied on her hood, and buttoned tight around her her rough sack, passed through the shed and crossed that bare strip to the barn, opened the door with some difficulty, because snow was already drifting into the doorway, and entered. She gave the cows and oxen their water, and the two night horses theirs; went up into the loft and pitched down hay enough for all; went down stairs to the pigs and cared for them; took one of the barn shovels and cleared a path where she had had to plunge into the snow at the doorway; took the shovel back, and then crossed home again to her baby. She thought she saw the Empsons' chimney smoking as she went home, and that seemed companionable. She took off her over-shoes, sack, and hood, said aloud, "This will be a good stay-at-home day," brought round her desk to the kitchen table, and began on a nice long letter to her brother Cephas in Sceattle.

That letter was finished, eight good quarto pages written, and a long-delayed letter to Emily Tabor, whom Huldah had not seen since she was married; and a long pull at her milk accounts had brought them up to date, — and still no John. Huldah had the table all set, you may be sure of that; but for herself, she had had no heart to go through the formalities of lunch or dinner. A cup of tea and something to eat with it as she wrote did better, she thought, for her; and she could eat when the men came. It is a way women have. Not till it became quite dark, and she set her kerosene lamp in the window that he might have a chance to see it when he turned the Locust Grove corner, did Huldah once feel herself lonely, or permit herself to wish that she did not live in a place where she could be cut off from all her race. "If John had gone into partnership with Jo Winter, and we had lived in Boston!" This was the thought that crossed her mind. Dear Huldah, from the end of one summer to the beginning of the next, Jo Winter does not go home to his dinner; and what you experience to-day, so far as absence from your husband goes, is what his wife experiences in Boston ten months, save Sundays, in every year.

I do not mean that Huldah winced or whined. Not she. Only she did think "if." Then she sat in front of the stove and watched the coals, and for a little while continued to think "if." Not long. Very soon she was engaged in planning how she would arrange the table to-morrow, — whether mother Stevens should cut the chicken-pie, or whether she would have that in front of her own mother. Then she fell to planning what she would make for Cynthia's baby; and then to wondering whether Cephas was in earnest in that half-nonsense he wrote about Sibyl Dyer; and then the clock struck six!

No bells yet, no husband, no anybody. Lantern out and lighted. Rubber boots on, hood and sack. Shed-shovel in one hand, lantern in the other. Roadway still bare, but a drift as high as Huldah's shoulders at the barn door. Lantern on the ground; snow-shovel in both hands now. One, two, three! — one cubic foot out. One, two, three! — another cubic foot out. And so on, and so on, and so on, till the doorway is clear again. Lantern in one hand, snow-shovel in the other, we enter the barn, draw the water for cows and oxen; we shake down more hay, and see to the pigs again. This time we make beds of straw for the horses and the cattle. Nay, we linger a minute or two, for there is something companionable there. Then we shut them in the dark, and cross the well-cleared roadway to the shed, and so home again. Certainly Mrs. Empson's kerosene lamp is in her window. That must be her light which gives a little halo in that direction in the falling snow. That looks like society.

And this time Huldah undresses the baby, puts on her yellow flannel nightgown, — makes the whole as long as it may be, — and then, still making believe be jolly, lights another lamp, eats her own supper, clears it away, and cuts into the new Harper which John had brought up to her the day before.

But the Harper is dull reading to her, though generally so attractive. And when her Plymouth Hollow clock consents to strike eight at last, Huldah, who has stented herself to read till eight, gladly puts down the "Travels in Arizona," which seem to her as much like the "Travels in Peru," of the month before, as those had seemed like the "Travels in Chinchilla." Rubber boots again, lantern again, sack and hood again. The men will be in no case for milking when they come. So Huldah brings together their pails, takes her shovel once more and her lantern, digs out the barn drift again, and goes over to milk little Carry and big Fanchon. For, though the milk of a hundred cows passes under those roofs and out again every day, Huldah is far too conservative to abandon the custom which she inherits from some Thorfinn or some Elfrida; and her husband is well pleased to humor her, in keeping in that barn always at least two of the choicest three-quarter blood cows that he can choose for the family supply. Only, in general, he or Reuben milks them; as duties are divided there, this is not Huldah's share. But on this eve of St. Spiridon the gentle creatures were glad when she came in; and in two journeys back and forth Huldah had carried her well-filled pails into her dairy. This helped along the hour, and just after nine o'clock struck she could hear the cheers of the men at last. She ran out again with the ready lighted lantern to the shed door, — in an instant had on her boots and sack and hood, — had crossed to the barn, and slid open the great barn door, — and stood there with her light, — another Hero for another Leander to buffet towards, through the snow. A sight to see were the two men, to be sure! And a story indeed they had to tell! On their different beats they had fought snow all day; had been breaking roads with the help of the farmers where they could; had had to give up more than halt of the outlying farms, sending such messages as they might, that the outlying farmers might bring down to-morrow's milk to such stations as they could arrange; and, at last, by good luck, had both met at the depot in the hollow, where each had gone to learn at what hour the milk-train might be expected in the morning. Little reason was there indeed to expect it at all. Nothing had passed the station-master since the morning express, called lightning by satire, had slowly pushed up with three or four engines five hours behind its time, and just now had come down a messenger from them that he should telegraph to Boston that they were all blocked up at Tyler's Summit, — the snow drifting beneath their wheels faster than they could clear it. Above, the station-master said, nothing whatever had yet passed Winchendon. Five engines had gone out from Fitchburg eastward, but in the whole day they had not come as far as Leominster. It was very clear that no milk-train nor any other train would be on time the next morning.

Such was, in brief, John's report to Huldah, when they had got to that state of things in which a man can make a report; that is, after they had rubbed dry the horses, had locked up the barn, after the men had rubbed themselves dry and had put on dry clothing, and after each of them, sitting on the fire side of the table, had drunk his first cup of tea and eaten his first square cubit of dip-toast. After the dip-toast, they were going to begin on Huldah's fried potatoes and sausages.

Huldah heard their stories with all their infinite little details; knew every corner and turn by which they had husbanded strength and life; was grateful to the Corbetts and Varnums and Prescotts and the rest, who, with their oxen and their red right-hands had given such loyal help for the common good; and she heaved a deep sigh when the story ended with the verdict of the failure of the whole, — "No trains on time to-morrow."

"Bad for the Boston babies," said Reuben bluntly, giving words to what the others were feeling. "Poor little things!" said Huldah, "Alice has been so pretty all day." And she gulped down just one more sigh, disgusted with herself as she remembered that "if" of the afternoon, "If John had only gone into partnership with Jo Winter."

IV.

HOW THEY BROKE THE BLOCKADE.

Three o'clock in the morning saw Huldah's fire burning in the stove, her water boiling in the kettle, her slices of ham broiling on the gridiron, and quarter past three saw the men come across from the barn, where they had been shaking down hay for the cows and horses, and yoking the oxen for the terrible onset of the day. It was bright starlight above, — thank Heaven for that. This strip of three hundred thousand square miles of snow cloud, which had been drifting steadily east over a continent, was, it seemed, only twenty hours wide, — say two hundred miles, more or less, — and at about midnight its last flecks had fallen, and all the heaven was washed black and clear. The men were well rested by those five hours of hard sleep. They were fitly dressed for their great encounter, and started cheerily upon it, as men who meant to do their duty, and to both of whom, indeed, the thought had come that life and death might be trembling in their hands. They did not take out the pungs to-day, nor, of course, the horses. Such milk as they had collected on St. Victoria's day they had stored already at the station and at Stacy's, and the best they could do to-day would be to break open the road from the Four Corners to the station, that they might place as many cans as possible there before the down train came. From the house, then, they had only to drive down their oxen that they might work with the other teams from the Four Corners; and it was only by begging him that Huldah persuaded Reuben to take one lunch can for them both. Then, as Reuben left the door, leaving John to kiss her good by, and to tell her not to be alarmed if they did not come home at night,

— she gave to John the full milk-can into which she had poured every drop of Carry's milk, and said, "It will be one more, and God knows what child may be crying for it now."

So they parted for eight-and-twenty hours; and in place of Huldah's first state party of both families, she and Alice reigned solitary that day, and held their little court with never a suitor. And when her lunch-time came, Huldah looked half mournfully, half merrily, on her array of dainties prepared for the feast, and she would not touch one of them. She toasted some bread before the fire, made a cup of tea, boiled an egg, and would not so much as set the table. As has been before stated, this is the way with women.

And of the men, who shall tell the story of the pluck and endurance, of the unfailing good-will, of the resource in strange emergency, of the mutual help and common courage, with which they all worked that day on that wellnigh hopeless task, of breaking open the highway from the Corners to the station? Wellnigh hopeless, indeed; for although at first, with fresh cattle and united effort, they made in the hours, which passed so quickly up to ten o'clock, near two miles' headway, and had brought yesterday's milk thus far, — more than half-way to their point of delivery, — at ten o'clock it was quite evident that this sharp north-west wind, which told so heavily on the oxen and even on the men, was filling in the very roadway they had opened, and so was cutting them off from their base, and, by its new drifts, was leaving the roadway for to-day's milk even worse than it was when they began. In one of those extemporized councils, then, — such as fought the battle of Bunker Hill, and threw the tea into Boston Harbor, — it was determined, at ten o'clock, to divide the working parties. The larger body should work back to the Four Corners, and by proper relays keep that trunk line of road open, if they could; while six yoke, with their owners, still pressing forward to the station, should make a new base at Lovejoy's, where, when these oxen gave out, they could be put up at his barn. It was quite clear, indeed, to the experts, that that time was not far distant.

And so indeed it proved. By three in the afternoon, John and Reuben, and the other leaders of the advance party, namely, the whole of it, for such is the custom of New England, gathered around the fire at Lovejoy's, conscious that after twelve hours of such battle as Pavia never saw, nor Roncesvalles, they were defeated at every point but one. Before them the mile of road, which they had made in the steady work of hours, was drifted in again as smooth as the surrounding pastures, only, if possible, a little more treacherous for the labor which they had thrown away upon it. The oxen which had worked kindly and patiently, well handled by good-tempered men, yet all confused and half dead with exposure, could do no more. Well, indeed, if those that had been stalled fast, and had had to stand in that biting wind after gigantic effort, escaped with their lives from such exposure. All that the men had gained was, that they had advanced their first depot of milk, — two hundred and thirty-nine cans — as far as Lovejoy's. What supply might have worked down to the Four Corners behind them, they did not know and hardly cared, their communications that way being wellnigh cut off again. What they thought of and planned for was simply how these cans at Lovejoy's could be put on any downward-train. For, by this time, they knew that all trains would have lost their grades and their names, and that this milk would go into Boston by the first engine that went there, though it rode on the velvet of a "palace car."

What train this might be they did not know. From the hill above Lovejoy's they could see poor old Dix, the station-master, with his wife and boys, doing his best to make an appearance of shovelling in front of his little station. But Dix's best was but little, for he had but one arm, having lost the other in a collision; and so, as a sort of pension, the company had placed him at this little flag-station, where was a roof over his head, a few tickets to sell, and generally very little else to do. It was clear enough that no working parties on the railroad had worked up to Dix, or had worked down, nor was it very likely that any would before night, unless the railroad people had better luck with their drifts than our friends had found. But as to this, who should say? Snow-drifts are "mighty onsartain." The line of that road is in general north-west, and to-day's wind might have cleaned out its gorges as persistently as it had filled up our cross-cuts. From Lovejoy's barn they could see that the track was now perfectly clear for the half-mile where it crossed the Prescott meadows.

I am sorry to have been so long in describing thus the aspect of the field after the first engagement. But it was on this condition of affairs that, after full conference, the enterprises of the night were determined. Whatever was to be done was to be done by men. And after thorough regale on Mrs. Lovejoy's green tea, and continual return to her constant relays of thin bacon gilded by unnumbered eggs; after cutting and coming again upon unnumbered mince-pies, which, I am sorry to say, did not in any point compare well with Huldah's, — each man thrust many doughnuts into his outside pockets, drew on the long boots again, and his buckskin gloves and mittens, and, unencumbered now by the care of animals, started on the work of the evening. The sun was just taking his last look at them from the western hills, where Reuben and John could see Huldah's chimney smoking. The plan was, by taking a double hand-sled of Lovejoy's, and by knocking together two or three more, jumper-fashion, to work their way across the meadow to the railroad causeway, and establish a milk depot there, where the line was not half a mile from Lovejoy's. By going and coming often, following certain tracks well known to Lovejoy on the windward side of walls and fences, these eight men felt quite sure that, by midnight, they could place all their milk at the spot where the old farm crossing strikes the railroad. Meanwhile Silas Lovejoy, a boy of fourteen, was to put on a pair of snow-shoes, go down to the station, state the case to old Dix, and get from him a red lantern and permission to stop the first train where it swept out from the Pitman cut upon the causeway. Old Dix had no more right to give this permission than had the humblest street-sweeper in Ispahan, and this they all knew. But the fact that Silas had asked for it would show a willingness on their part to submit to authority, if authority there had been. This satisfied the New England love of law on the one hand. On the other hand, the train would be stopped, and this satisfied the New England determination to get the thing done any way. To give additional force to Silas, John provided him with a note to Dix, and it was generally agreed that, if Dix was n't ugly, he would give the red lantern and the permission. Silas was then to work up the road and station himself as far beyond the curve as he could, and stop the first down train. He was to tell the conductor where the men were waiting with the milk, was to come down to them on the train, and his duty would be done. Lest Dix should be ugly, Silas was provided with Lovejoy's only lantern, but he was directed not to show this at the station until his interview was finished. Silas started cheerfully on his snow-shoes; John and Lovejoy, at the same time, starting with the first hand-sled of the cans. First of all into the sled John put Huldah's well-known can, a little shorter than the others, and with a different handle. "Whatever else went to Boston," he said, "that can was bound to go through."

They established the basis of their pyramid, and met the three new jumpers with their makers as they went back for more. This party enlarged the base of the pyramid, and, as they worked, Silas passed them cheerfully with his red lantern. Old Dix had not been ugly, had given the lantern and all the permission he had to give, and had communicated some intelligence also. The intelligence was, that an accumulated force of seven engines, with a large working party, had left Groton Junction downward at three. Nothing had arrived upward at Groton Junction, and, from Boston, Dix learned that nothing more would leave there till early morning. No trains had arrived in Boston from any quarter for twenty-four hours. So long the blockade had lasted already.

On this intelligence it was clear that, with good luck, the down train might reach them at any moment. Still the men resolved to leave their milk, while they went back for more, relying on Silas and the "large working party" to put it on the cars, if the train chanced to pass before any of them returned. So back they fared to Lovejoy's for their next relay, and met John and Reuben working in successfully with their second. But no one need have hurried; for, as, trip after trip, they built their pyramid of cans higher and higher, no welcome whistle broke the stillness of the night, and by ten o'clock, when all these cans were in place by the rail, the train had not yet come.

John and Reuben then proposed to go up into the cut, and to relieve poor Silas, who had not been heard from since he swung along so cheerfully like an "Excelsior" boy on his way up the Alps. But they had hardly started, when a horn from the meadow recalled them, and, retracing their way, they met a messenger who had come in to say that a fresh team from the Four Corners had been reported at Lovejoy's, with a dozen or more men, who had succeeded in bringing down nearly as far as Lovejoy's mowing-lot near a hundred more cans; that it was quite possible in two or three hours more to bring these over also; and, although the first train was probably now close at hand, it was clearly worth while to place this relief in readiness for a second. So poor Silas was left for the moment to his loneliness, and Reuben and John returned again upon their steps. They passed the house, where they found Mrs. Lovejoy and Mrs. Stacy at work in the shed, finishing off two more jumpers, and claiming congratulation for their skill; and after a cup of tea again, — for no man touched spirit that day nor that night, — they reported at the new station by the Mowing-Lot.

And Silas Lovejoy, — who had turned the corner into the Pitman Cut, and so shut himself out from sight of the station light, or his father's windows, or the lanterns of the party at the Pyramid of Cans, — Silas Lovejoy held his watch there hour by hour, with such courage as the sense of the advance gives boy or man. He had not neglected to take the indispensable shovel as he came. In going over the causeway he had slipped off the snow-shoes and hung them on his back. Then there was heavy wading as he turned into the Pitman Cut, knee deep, middle deep, and he laid his snow-shoes on the snow, and set the red lantern on them, as he reconnoitred. Middle deep, neck deep, and he fell forward on his face into the yielding mass. "This will not do; I must not fall like that often," said Silas to himself, as he gained his balance and threw himself backward against the snow. Slowly he turned round, worked back to the lantern, worked out to the causeway, and fastened on the shoes again. With their safer help he easily skimmed up to Pitman's bridge, which he had determined on for his station. He knew that thence his lantern could be seen for a mile, and that yet there the train might safely be stopped, so near was the open causeway which he had just traversed. He had no fear of an up train behind him.

So Silas walked back and forth, and sang, and spouted "pieces," and mused on the future of his life, and spouted "pieces" again, and sang in the loneliness. How the time passed he did not know. No sound of clock, no baying of dog, no plash of waterfall, broke that utter stillness. The wind, thank God, had at last died away, and Silas paced his beat in a long oval he made for himself, under and beyond the bridge, with no sound but his own voice when he chose to raise it. He expected, as they all did, that every moment the whistle of the train, as it swept into sight a mile or more away, would break the silence ; so he paced, and shouted, and sang.

"This is a man's duty," he said to himself; "they would not let me go with the Fifth Regiment, not as a drummer-boy ; but this is duty such as no drummer-boy of them all is doing. Company, march!" and he "stepped forward smartly" with his left foot. "Really I am placed on guard here quite as much as if I were on picket in Virginia." "Who goes there? Advance, friend, and give the countersign." Not that any one did go there, or could go there ; but the boy's fancy was ready, and so he amused himself during the first hours. Then he began to wonder whether they were hours, as they seemed, or whether this was all a wretched illusion, — whether the time passed slowly to him because he was nothing but a boy, and did not know how to occupy his mind. So he resolutely said the multiplication-table from the beginning to the end, and from the end to the beginning, — first to himself, and again aloud, to make it slower. Then he tried the ten commandments. "Thou shalt have none other gods before me"; easy to say that beneath those stars; and he said them again. "No, it is no illusion. I must have been here hours long!" Then he began on Milton's hymn: —

> "It was the winter wild
> While the heaven-born child
> All meanly wrapt, in the rude manger lies."

"Winter wild indeed," said Silas aloud; and if he had only known it, at that moment the sun beneath his feet was crossing the meridian, midnight had passed already, and Christmas day was born!

> "Only with speeches fair
> She wooes the gentle air
> To hide her guilty front with innocent snow."

"Innocent, indeed," said poor Silas, still aloud; "much did he know of innocent snow"; and vainly did he try to recall the other stanzas as he paced back and forth, round and round, and began now to wonder where his father and the others were, and if they could have come to any misfortune. Surely, they could not have forgotten that he was here. Would that train never come?

If he were not afraid of its coming at once, he would have run back to the causeway to look for their lights, — and perhaps they had a fire. Why had he not brought an axe for a fire? "That rail-fence above would have served perfectly, nay, it is not five rods to a load of hickory we left the day before Thanksgiving. Surely one of them might come up to me with an axe. But maybe there is trouble below. They might have come with an axe, — with an axe, — with an axe, — with an —— axe ——" "I am going to sleep," cried Silas, — aloud again this time, — as his head dropped heavily on the handle of the shovel he was resting on there in the lee of the stone-wall. "I am going to sleep, — that will never do. Sentinel asleep at his post. Order out the relief. Blind his eyes. Kneel, sir. Make ready. Fire. That, sir, for sentinels asleep." And so Silas laughed grimly and began his march again. Then he took his shovel and began a great pit where he supposed the track might be beneath him. "Anything to keep warm and to keep awake. But why did they not send up to him? Why was he here? Why was he all alone? He who had never been alone before. Was he alone? Was there companionship in the stars, — or in the good God who held the stars? Did the good God put me here? If He put me here, will He keep me here? Or did He put me here to die! To die in this cold? It is cold; it is very cold! Is there any good in my dying? The train will run down, and they will see a dead body lying under the bridge, — black on the snow, with a red lantern by it. Then they will stop. Shall I — I will — just go back to see if the lights are at the bend. I will leave the lantern here on the edge of this wall!" And so Silas turned, half benumbed, worked his way nearly out of the gorge, and started as he heard, or thought he heard, a baby's scream. "A thousand babies are starving, and I am afraid to stay here to give them their life," he said. "There is a boy fit for a soldier! Order out the relief! Drum-head court-martial! Prisoner, hear your sentence! Deserter to be shot! Blindfold, — kneel, sir! Fire! Good enough for deserters!" And so poor Silas worked back again to the lantern.

And now he saw and felt sure that Orion was bending downward, and he knew that the night must be broken; and, with some new hope, throwing down the shovel with which he had been working, he began his soldier tramp once more, — as far as soldier tramp was possible with those trailing snow-shoes, — tried again on "No war nor battle sound," — broke down on "Cynthia's seat" and the music of the spheres, — but at last, — working on "beams," "long beams," and "that with long beams," — he caught the stanzas he was feeling for, and broke out exulting with,

"At last surrounds their sight,
A globe of circular light,
That with long beams the shame-faced night arrayed;
The helmed cherubim
And sworded seraphim
Are seen in glittering ranks — "

"Globe of circular light, — am I dreaming, or have they come?"

Come they had! The globe of circular light swept full over the valley, and the scream of the engine was welcomed by the freezing boy as if it had been an angel's whisper to him. Not unprepared did it find him. The red lantern swung to and fro in a well-practised hand, and he was in waiting on his firmest spot as the train *slowed* and the engine passed him.

"Do not stop for me," he cried, as he threw his weight heavily on the tender side, and the workmen dragged him in. "Only run slow till you are out of the ledge; we have made a milk station at the cross-road."

"Good for you," said the wondering fireman, who in a moment understood the exigency. The heavy plough threw out the snow steadily still. In ten seconds they were clear of the ledge, and saw the fire-light shimmering on the great pyramids of milk-cans. Slower and slower ran the train, and by the blazing fire stopped, for once because its masters chose to stop. And the working party on the train cheered lustily as they tumbled out of the cars, as they apprehended the situation, and were cheered by the working party from the village.

Two or three cans of milk stood on the embers of the fire, that they might be ready for the men on the train with something that was at least warm. An empty passenger car was opened, and the pyramids of milk-cans were hurried into it, forty men now assisting.

"You will find Jo Winter at the Boston station," said John Stevens to the "gentlemanly conductor" of the express, whose lightning train had thus become a milk convoy. "Tell Winter to distribute this among all the carts, that everybody may have some. Good luck to you. Good by!" And the engines snorted again, and John Stevens turned back, not so much as thinking that he had made his Christmas present to a starving town.

V.

CHRISTMAS MORNING.

The children were around Robert Walter's knees, and each of the two spelled out a verse of the second chapter of Luke, on Christmas morning. And Robert and Mary kneeled with them, and they said together, "Our Father who art in heaven." Mary's voice broke a little when they came to "daily bread," but with the two, and her husband, she continued to the end, and could say "Thine is the power," and believe it too.

"Mamma," whispered little Fanny, as she kissed her mother after the prayer, "when I said my prayers up stairs last night, I said 'our daily milk,' and so did Robert." This was more than poor Mary could bear. She kissed the child, and she hurried away.

For last night at six o'clock it was clear that the milk was sour, and little Jamie had detected it first of all. Then, with every one of the old wiles, they had gone back over the old slops, but the child, with that old weird strength, had pushed them all away.

Christmas morning broke, and poor Robert, as soon as light would serve, had gone to the neighbors all, — their nearest intimates they had tried the night before, — and from all had brought back the same reply ; one friend had sent a wretched sample, but the boy detected the taint and pushed it, untasted, away. Dr. Morton had taken the alarm the day before. He was at the house earlier than usual with some condensed milk, which his wife's stores had furnished ; but that would not answer. Poor Jamie pushed this by. There was some smoke or something, — who should say what ? — it would not do. The doctor could see in an instant how his patient had fallen back in the night. That weird, anxious, entreating look, as his head lay back on the little pillow, had all come back again. Robert and Robert's friends, Gaisford and Warren, then went down to the Old Colony, to the Worcester, and to the Hartford stations. Perhaps their trains were doing better. The door-bell rang yet again. " Mrs. Appleton's love to Mrs. Walter, and perhaps her child will try some fresh beef-tea." As if poor Jamie did not hate beef-tea ; still Morton resolutely forced three spoonfuls down. Half an hour more and Mrs. Dudley's compliments. " Mrs. Dudley heard that Mrs. Walter was out of milk, and took the liberty to send round some very particularly nice Scotch groats, which her brother had just brought from Edinburgh." " Do your best with it, Fanny," said poor Mary ; but she knew that if Jamie took those

Scotch groats, it was only because they were a Christmas present. Half an hour more! Three more spoonfuls of beef-tea after a fight. Door-bell again. Carriage at the door. "Would Mrs. Walter come down and see Mrs. Fitch? It was really very particular." Mary was half dazed, and went down, she did not know why.

"Dear Mrs. Walter, you do not remember me," said this eager girl, crossing the room and taking her by both hands.

"Why no, — yes, — do I?" said Mary, crying and laughing together.

"Yes, you will remember, it was at church, at the baptism. My Jennie and your Jamie were christened the same day. And now I hear, — we all know how low he is, — and perhaps he will share my Jennie's breakfast. Dear Mrs. Walter, do let me try."

Then Mary saw that the little woman's cloak and hat were already thrown off, — which had not seemed strange to her before, — and the two passed quietly up stairs together; and Julia Fitch bent gently over him, and cooed to him, and smiled to him, but could not make the poor child smile. And they lifted him so gently on the pillow, — but only to hear him scream. And she brought his head gently to her heart, and drew back the little curtain that was left, and offered to him her life; but he was frightened, and did not know her, and had forgotten what it was she gave him, and screamed again; and so they had to lay him back gently upon the pillow. And then, — as Julia was saying she would stay, — and how they could try again, — and could do this and that, — then the door-bell rang again, and Mrs. Coleman had herself come round with a little white pitcher, and herself run up stairs with it, and herself knocked at the door!

The blockade was broken, and
The milk had come!

Mary never knew that it was from Huldah Stevens's milk-can that her boy drank in the first drops of his new life. Nor did Huldah know it. Nor did John know it, nor the paladins who fought that day at his side. Nor did Silas Lovejoy know it.

But the good God and all good angels knew it. Why ask for more?

And you and I, dear reader, if we ever forget that always our daily bread comes to us, because a thousand brave men and a thousand brave women are at work in the world, praying to God and trying to serve him, we will not forget it as we meet at breakfast on this blessed Christmas day!

THE END.

Cambridge: Stereotyped and Printed by Welch, Bigelow, & Co.